The

The

The

The

By Jude Stringfellow

The

The

Thank You Page

Thank you, Gordon Flick, for suggesting the word *"accretion"*.

Thank you, Jeannie Clarke, for suggesting the word *"vagabond"*.

Thank you, Reuben Stringfellow, for suggesting the word *"scandal"*.

Thank you, Laura Stringfellow, for suggesting the word *"tendril"*.

Thank you, Caity Stringfellow, for suggesting the word *"convivial"*.

Thank you, Yvonne Espinoza Ramirez, for suggesting the word *"dalliance."*

Thank you, Rita Miller McHann, for suggesting the word *"hush money."*

Thank you, Robin Moorhead, for suggesting the word *"vacation"*.

Thank you, Marty Kapp, for suggesting the word *"ennui"*.

Thank you, Ellin Daum, for suggesting the word *"bankruptcy"*.

Thank you, Charlie Garrett, for suggesting the word *"Superior"*

Thank you, Tex, for your continued support. I see you following me. I know you know that I know.

The

Dedication Page

This book is dedicated to the ones I pray for.

Disclaimer

Everyone needs a disclaimer. I keep mine handy for those who want to point fingers and accuse. This book is not to be taken seriously, and it is not to be thought of as nonfiction. Almost everyone in the book is fictional except for Charlie Garrett and his wife, Hideko. I added a few fictional traits to them so no one suspects anything. Fiction is a work of art – not something to be pulled apart and compared to reality. There is no reality in this book – except, yeah, Sarasota is a real place. I guess, for that matter, so is DeQueen, Arkansas, Chicago, Illinois, and even Oklahoma! Yep, Oklahoma is a real enough place.

Don't let anyone fool you when you're discussing this book with them; it is purely a work of my creation with some grammar issues and suggestive ideas from a random A.I. I found online. I don't have to give it credit, but I thought I should mention that I use one. It is 2024, you know. Why not? I use the Thesaurus and the Dictionary as well. You know what? I even used the Bible at one point, too!

The book is a book—enjoy it. Read it twice; you may miss something if you read too fast.

The

One

She had thought about the old rust-worn pickup truck her grandfather left her, how it seemed to scream her name sometimes when she allowed herself to drift off into a sleeplike semi-consciousness at her desk; somehow, it knew she needed a fast getaway. The vintage vehicle hadn't been started in over thirty years, but it was hers. If everyone and everything else in the world decided to cave in on her, she had that damn truck to call her own.

No one could take that from her; not even her own self-doubt could tell her not to keep it. That truck was one of the only real things that mattered to her. If it weren't running now, it would be. She may have been a thousand miles away from it, but it didn't matter. If the world ended today, she told herself, the truck had her name clearly written on its registration form. That much she knew.

When the day came that Leigh Avery Madsen, former Queen of DeQueen, Arkansas, had stomached her last insult and brought a civil suit against her employers, one of the larger finance firms in the nation, she all but counted the truck as one of her only assets. What right did she have in this litigious world of greed and thievery on Wall Street to even dream she could muster the courage to bring a suit against the mighty fists of Ingram, Horace, and Driskoll? Where would she go when they tossed her out on her ear? Where would she live, work, or find purpose? She asked herself; and every time she did, her mind remembered the truck.

After enduring a month of anxiety and stress, Leigh followed her attorney's advice and took a leave of absence during the legal proceedings that encompass the laws protecting whistleblowers. To her surprise, the firm settled with the tenured financial advisor and recorder. This was mainly due to her writing abilities and extensive network, which included LinkedIn professionals and journalists who shared her ethical concerns. Their support was a testament to the power of solidarity in the face of injustice.

She wasn't the one skimming money. She wasn't the one covering up losses in the stock market, telling clients that the numbers had beaten them so they could settle for a few percentage points off where the market had been made. It was determined to be a human error; that wasn't a surprise, but who would the board members blame for the mistakes? Certainly not the truth—the truth had no place in the boardroom most of the time. If a client had called to ask if their money had disappeared, a board member would have explained it.

Still, all the while, they were saying that the money hadn't actually disappeared; it had just relocated to a better place: to their private bank accounts.

If anyone had asked her employers at the time, before they were given their official instructions through a gag order of the court, not to speak derogatorily of Leigh publicly, they would have blamed the virus of 2020 on her if they could. The art of randomly grasping at straws to bring about any distraction meant every man and woman of the firm stood packed against Leigh for being honest, for having ethics, and for sharing her knowledge of their systematic embezzlement with the Securities Exchange Commission when she did.

Four million dollars made a difference in Leigh's life, even if it was merely a drop in the bucket for the two-hundred-year-old institution of Battery Park, New York City. They were free of her; she was free of them. Let bygones be bygones. Before she knew it, Leigh had somehow managed to pull the pieces together, forging a new machine of her grandfather's old Ford, and the firm filed a Chapter 13 and reinvented themselves using the same tactics; only the names had changed.

After a month of constantly pinching herself yet licking wounds she knew still existed, Leigh pulled into the parking lot of the somewhat obscure storefront of an actual church, which had been sandwiched between a convenience store and a bagel shop just outside of the hustle of downtown Sarasota, Florida. Maybe it was

Kismet, but she felt almost relaxed knowing she could get along with the preacher she had only known through his online YouTube videos and hundreds of email exchanges with the man over the past four or five years.

She thought maybe it had been longer; perhaps she'd been following Charlie Garrett, the barefoot bearded pastor of the Superior Word before he owned the church, but then she remembered that her introduction to him had been while she had literally searched Google for *"the superior words of Christ"* hoping to find an excellent sermon to watch about the God she knew she hadn't given enough attention to. When the words *"superior"* and *"word"* came back as the name of the little chapel-like existence where the bearded man spoke, again, it felt surreal enough to put her faith in it. This, she told herself, was something more than just chance.

When she found out his online following included folks she knew and some were kin; she was even more at ease about the move. Picking up and re-rooting wasn't the easiest thing, but something had to give. The money she had been awarded became the center of everyone else's world, not necessarily hers. Suddenly, and without so much as a howdy-do, she became acquainted with several members of her family, kin of her kin in some instances, all wanting to 'get to know her' better. Moving to Florida just made sense.

"Ah, Leigh! It's good to finally meet you face to face!" Charlie exclaimed, his warm, broad smile spreading across his face. He extended his hand for a firm handshake, greeting his friend. His weathered palm, a testament to decades of forcibly peeling coconuts, picking mangos, and his devout work inside and outdoors. Charlie Garrett was a man of many talents, one of which included sizing a person up within just a few seconds to know whether or not they were who they projected themselves to be. With Leigh, he felt he had a true sister in faith.

Repositioning the brightly colored handcrafted bandana that covered his balding head, Charlie withdrew his right hand from on top of his head to firmly grip his new friend's hand. His left hand was busy trying its best to wrangle three of his eight small Chihuahuas and mixed-breed dogs, one about the same size as the next. Only the Dachshund stood out as a little longer than any others.

"We've been to the vet just now," stated Charlie. *"Mia hasn't been feeling well; she's the darker fawn. The other two were due for yearly shots. They missed out on them last spring when my wife Hideko and I took the others in. One can only do what one can do."* He laughed, adding, *"Don't ever try to take eight dogs to the vet all at one time,"* he smiled, *"It never works out for the best if you do."*

Leigh laughed wholeheartedly as she released Charlie's hand so he could use it to manage his small herd. Inviting her into the church, Charlie gave a quick nod toward a lone man standing in the back. The man had a broom and was doing what he could to sweep some water and mud out the back door that had crept in from the night before. Hurricane Brayden had mostly skipped over Sarasota, but the backwinds and late rains had left more than a few inches worth of debris and anxiety in its wake.

Coaxing the man to move forward, Charlie made a point to introduce the two, letting each know by way of a quick few words how he had become acquainted with them. Moving some of the dogs to one side, he invited Leigh Madsen to step around to the other side, his left side, to be a bit closer to the man and his broom. In all the time he had known Mat, which was just over a year, he had only been able to coax inside of the church a few times outside of Sunday service or Bible study on Thursday.

"This here is Mathew, one 't,'" Conner Charlie continued, gesturing his left hand toward the broad-shouldered man who had, by that time, set the broom aside and was making his way across the freshly mopped tile floor. *"He's been with us for over a year now; he keeps an eye out for us, protecting the church from the world around us. He's a watchman, you'd say. Mathew goes with me to the projects; I told you about him."*

Charlie encouraged, *"He's been a wealth of support for me, for the church, of course, and the people just love him. Mathew sings, plays the guitar, and tells me he plays piano, but we don't have a keyboard yet, so I've not had the honor of hearing him prove that to me. You'll notice my manly beard is at least three inches longer than this man's."* Charlie ribbed Mathew Conner.

Charlie's smile held its place while allowing Mathew to take a few steps closer to greet the newcomer. *"Mathew, this is Leigh, Leigh Madsen. She comes to us by way of Southwestern Arkansas but through New York, where she's been working as a financial advisor and journalist for one of the big giant firms up that way for a few years.*

"Leigh decided a few months ago that the Big Apple had a worm or two in it and decided to leave it for a more relaxed way of living." Charlie laughed. *"I don't know if she's grounded yet. We've talked a bit about where she'll end up, but I think she'll be a weekly staple for us to drag out to the projects soon enough anyway, and if she can get up early enough on Sunday, she'll join us for sure."* He added.

Leigh took the opportunity to look Mathew in the eyes to assure him she wouldn't mind being dragged out of the projects; it was something she had made up her mind and needed to do. It felt right. It perfectly fit her new unexplored journey, which she forged for herself. Leigh, though a meticulous technical writer for all things financial, had been published several times and was embarking on a new course for her life. She had decided to write a book exposing some of the more openly discriminative ways people treat others.

Knowing she had been bullied for years as a woman in a predominantly male-oriented industry, she had needed to develop a thicker skin than most. Having found the courage to do so, she realized and recognized that some people thrust under harsh treatment would not and could not be able to stand up for themselves.

Many of the good people she knew in finance had left the profession altogether rather than digging in with their heels and refusing to be harassed. Some, a few she had been personally close to, had chosen a more permanent means of leaving; they had committed suicide due to their inability to withstand the trials they were forced to endure. Suicide had never been an option for the head-strong Southern belle; Mat would find out soon enough, she told herself, just how head-strong she was.

"Hello Mathew, it's great to meet you. It's great to say I've finally made it to Florida! I thought I would have to wait another week to give Brayden a chance to blow through." She said. Driving conditions had not been too bad for her as she made her way east along I-40 East to Memphis, dropping down to I-22 through

cities like Holly Springs, Mississippi, New Albany, and Tupelo, the birthplace of Elvis Presley. Once she made it that far, it was just a hop, skip, and jump, as they say in the South, to Birmingham, Alabama, making a somewhat northern loop up I-20 and heading East again to Atlanta, Georgia.

"I stayed all night in a little town just south of Atlanta called Locust Grove. If you ever get up that way, you must stop at Mama Pearl's and have their chicken in a cup; it's a bowl, and it's to die for. Mama Pearl brings out a basket of buttermilk biscuits that will rival any granny out there; she knows her biscuits."

Leigh added before shaking Mathew's hand for a second time and giving him the same once-over that she had been subjected to by her new friend and pastor, Charlie Garrett. Mathew, she could tell, had been one of the people she had wanted to learn about; others had hurt him. She saw it in his eyes. Charlie hadn't told her, and he didn't need to. It was apparent by the distance he kept and how he clung to the broom handle.

"It's nice to meet you, Leigh. Charlie has not stopped talking about you since he found out last week that you were coming down, or maybe it's coming over. You said you were from Southwestern Arkansas. Is Sarasota that much further south for you?" he asked, genuinely not knowing the answer.

"*Oh, heck yeah!*" she exclaimed. "*Arkansas is on top of Louisiana. We're not as far south as you may think. We're in the middle of the northern part of the South. Some folks say Missouri is in the South, but I don't cotton to that nonsense. There's a line, the Mason-Dixon line, and it's gospel where I come from. It may take a turn up North into enemy territory, but it's clear that the top of Arkansas and the bottom of Missouri are out.*" She joked before making sure she hadn't openly offended her new acquaintance. He had mentioned he had been born in Springfield, Missouri, but considered himself to be Southern.

Mathew smiled a shy and reserved smile, only showing part of one of his dimples. His mind was already on edge for having drummed up the courage to come in from outside the church where he usually kept himself. Mathew was more than a watchman for The Superior Word church; he lived in the back of the building in what was once considered a storeroom. Charlie had purposely cleared the nine-by-twelve store closet of any boxes to give Mathew a warm and safe place to sleep when he chose to sleep indoors. A twin-sized mattress and platform frame just about took up most of the space.

A few quiet moments passed between the two as Charlie moved the dogs in what could only be called a chaotic zig-zagging towards the back of the church, where he was greeted by the sweetest of quiet love and reserved adoration of his Japanese native wife, Hideko.

This taller, lean, beautiful woman had answered Charlie's call to the house earlier to make her way up from their beach house to the church to retrieve the dogs and meet their new church member.

As Charlie explained it to both Hideko and Mathew, Leigh Madsen had come to Florida to start over and to do so in a better climate with seafood at her back door and glorious sunrises over the sands of Turtle Beach. *"Leigh here has decided on the condo life, Hideko!"* he said. *"She's looking for one, or maybe she's found one by now, and she tells me it should be within walking distance of our place so we can mooch a few dinners off of her now and again and return the favor when we can."*

Before he forgot to do so, Charlie mentioned to Leigh that their trip to the projects that morning had been postponed due to the high winds and possible damage brought on by the storm. They planned to make it out before noon for no reason other than to check up on those they felt could have been affected by Brayden's wrath.

"You'll want to run next door, either way," he said, pointing both hands in either direction, *"... and grab a cup of coffee. We had a pot going this morning here, but I'm afraid Mathew and I drank it all. I must run by the store and pick up another pound or two of the stuff before tomorrow's service."* Charlie said, pointing to the empty pot.

Leigh laughed at the thought of what she knew must be Charlie's sneaky little way of asking her whether or not she had remembered to bring the case of Seattle's Best medium roast she had promised to bring with her after finding out what she called sludge was passing for coffee at the church. The topic had been mulled over more than once in their emails. Charlie had even mentioned her thoughtful gift from the pulpit, promising his small congregation that their new recruit would soon be a blessing to everyone.

"You're not foolin' me, Charlie. I see right through you and through that smile of yours." She told him with a slight tilt of her head. *"I brought the case, and in it, you'll find that not only is Seattle's Best owned and made by Starbucks, which I don't support, but it's a good blend. I picked up a half case of medium roast at Sam's Club and another half case of dark roast."* She told him. *"I did it for the people and put it on a bi-monthly schedule. We'll need to keep an eye on it to see how much we're using."* She smirked.

"You'll love it, but more, so much more importantly, the congregation will love it, and they'll never go to 7-11 again before service." She said. *"If I have to, if it's my mission in life, I'll get up early enough each and every Sunday to man...or woman...the coffee pots. If you don't have two, I'll buy you another one. I want the people of the Superior Word to have the Superior Brew to go along with their spiritual feast!"* Hideko chuckled under her breath,

smiling at her husband. *"I like this woman."* She said quietly.

Two

Leigh Madsen bought lunch for Charlie Garrett and her new friend Mathew Conner at the Thai restaurant Charlie had suggested, the one he repeatedly suggests whenever anyone asks him where he'd like to eat. She couldn't believe she'd stuffed herself to the point of nearly regretting the last dumpling, but Leigh wasn't one to back away from the table when it came to food. No one would know from her near-perfect form or how she carried herself that one of the 2006 runners-up for Miss Sievers County would have been able to do as much damage at the buffet, but she could.

Taking the opportunity to engage the two men into her web of interesting interests, Leigh began the conversation where they had left it back at the church; she reiterated why it was the lives of those who had a penchant for committing crime were so alluring to her. *"I find criminals utterly and over-the-top fascinating because they consciously choose a life outside everyone else's expectations; they break all social norms. I'm not saying I agree with it or that I would want that in my life, but to do it and to do it daily is...well, it's fascinating. I know I used the word twice."* She laughed under her breath, trying to read the faces of the two men staring back at her. If she were honest with herself when asked about her hobbies during the interviews at the pageant, she would not have mentioned her fascination with organized criminals; it could have cost her the crown.

Leigh mentioned a created behavior among Americans, mostly Americans; but she had observed the same behavior overseas when she lived there. *"Unless we're helpless cynics, we default to the irrational behavior that anyone of authority, law-abiding or not, is presumed to be correct. They are given that position by those of us who were intrigued or believed in their plight as much as they did. Until we are shown differently, we'll support the antics of a pirate simply because it's a romantic notion to do so."* She stated flatly.

"Take Al Capone. He's one we all know. Everyone knows Al, and if you say words like 'Chicago' and 'mobster,' his name is the first to pop into your brain, but dozens of hooligans made the Top 10 list for that city. If we go back far enough, there were probably hundreds, but here we have Al Capone, a limelighter.

"He reveled in the spotlight! You couldn't pick up a paper and not read about him in those days. Why? Why would someone breaking the law and doing it so openly want to be seen? Wouldn't it create

29

a whirlwind of cops surrounding him? Wouldn't he have been richer, quietly making more money, if he had been less obvious? I don't know. Would he have lived longer? Sentimental value means more than money most of the time." she concluded.

To Leigh, it was the chase that seemed to catch her attention. Capone wanted to be seen, he wanted to be chased, and he put the word out where he was going to be just to see if cops would show up to arrest him. When some did, they either met with the fact that he had never intended to show, or maybe he did, but so many followers and supporters surrounded him that even the cops were afraid to make their move.

"People like Capone, they see the world as belonging to them. Someone, maybe everybody, owed them something. They believed their lies about themselves, and eventually, it all ends; eventually, but no one knows, do they?" she asked again, hoping one or the other men would care to contribute. She recognized the chatterbox that she was or could be. She openly invited others to share in conversation; she valued everyone's opinions.

Charlie looked at Mathew to see if he would speak next. Still, when the quiet man's eyes met those of his preacher, Charlie knew it was his turn to hold the proverbial microphone and say something, either in agreement or in opposition so that the conversation could continue.

"What I find the most or at least quite interesting about men like Capone, or even more modern-day thugs like we have right here in Sarasota, is that they don't realize the gravity of their actions against others. They take and take, never once thinking of the pain and suffering they instill or permeate on the innocent. It's like their brains are shut off to everything that isn't about themselves."

He continued, *"...they're narcissists at best and beasts. I guess, yeah, I can see where they'd be an interesting study, but I don't want to get so close to them that I start thinking the way they think."* Charlie's words were true; Leigh and Mathew agreed, giving silent nods to the man before Leigh took the invisible mic back to talk more about the lives and lifestyles of the more compelling gangsters, mobsters, and simple thieves.

Men such as those who ran with the Doolin and Dalton gangs and those running with Jesse James or his cousins, the Youngers were clannish and tight. They came in all different shapes and sizes, but history has a way of telling only part of the truth; and usually the truth from the point of view of anyone claiming to know more than anyone else. *"History has done a pretty good job of recording most of the stories relating to their heists and undoing; I'm talking again about the Doolins and the Daltons. Lawmen destroyed both bands; still, people tend to rally for these characters as if they were heroes."*

She lamented that the wars and civil unrest winners always wrote history the way they saw fit; it didn't seem fair to anyone. No one got around to writing about the sad cases where a criminal may be a boy who stole some food to feed himself; if he were a little black boy or a Native, God rest his soul, he'd be hung for taking a penny's worth of anything. There was no justice; the rope had no sense of fairness – only equality.

"Edward Teach! Blackbeard. He wrote most of what we know about himself in journals. Now, whether or not what he said was true is anyone's guess. We know he lived in the time that he said he did; we know he did the things people said he did. He didn't take the time to record every murder, every rape, every romp he took with another man's wife, or the men he wounded for sport to watch them bleed.

"Still, we do know that he murdered, raped, caroused, and maimed people because he took pride in writing about it so he could later read and remember what he had been involved in. Certainly, we can't say all of his work was non-fiction, but there's a good chance a lot if it is true." She stated.

"He's another one who, like Capone, who wanted to be seen. He would walk down the middle of the busiest streets of towns he and his crew were plundering. He'd goad the law to come and stop him or to try. He was a real mouthy guy!" Leigh explained.

"In the end, of course, he met his, and he got his, but why didn't anyone stop him before he did as much as he did? It all boils down to self-preservation, safeguarding others, maybe their family.

"As far as why some are known, and others are not, it also boils down to self-hate and self-loathing from those who didn't believe in themselves and couldn't see themselves as heroes. When someone doesn't have the confidence to stand up for themselves, they certainly can't stand up for others." She spoke, but this time, she knew she was speaking from sheer experience, the experience of her colleague, the one who took his life rather than robustly standing up for himself when bullied by the boss.

Charlie took the mic back. He fixed his fatherly eyes on hers long enough to draw her full attention to hear what he had to say about who and what people who seem so dynamic are often anything but. He explained how a person's perception of themself could force someone to live their life under self-imposed guardianship, something akin to being held accountable first to others before considering what they must think of themselves.

"When a man or a woman, because women are just as apt to behave poorly as any man would when a person chooses to live in a way that is, as you said, contrary to the social norms, it's for gain or shame. They either want more for themselves, or they may expect to bring the world's weight down on someone

else, like what happened to you at your finance firm." He started.

"You were the one who was being seen; you weren't a Capone or a Blackbeard, but maybe a Norma Ray or someone who saw what should have been brought to light in the darkest corners. When you did that, when you brought down their Capone, he hit back with the force you should have expected them to hit back with.

"We're all delighted that man decided to use his clout and power over you instead of a Tommy Gun. Still, yeah, he drilled you and ripped you to shreds both personally and professionally until such a moment that after the smoke cleared on all of it, you were able to regain your footing and take inventory of what was left." He said, extending his hands across the table to hold hers, letting her know she landed softly, even if it took a while to connect.

Mathew hadn't heard the full story of what had happened at Ingram Horce and Driskoll. Still, he had heard Charlie and another member of the church talk about Leigh's impending arrival and what seemingly devastation she must have endured at the hands of the very powerful once she had decided to inform the Securities Exchange Commission about the shortfalls of several members of the Board of Trustees for the firm.

It wouldn't have been a long leap to assume that the same members and others connected to the firm would be angry enough to retaliate and annihilate the one they perceived as Enemy Number One. Leigh Madsen became their Persona Non-Grada immediately. He knew her story; in some ways, it was his, too. She had suffered at the hands of the same men and women who had hired her to better their own goals; then to be betrayed by them could only create a fight-or-flight reaction in her.

"Well," Leigh assured both her pastor and Mathew, *"...it's not like I want to study Capone, Teach, or even Benjamin Kincaid Driskoll with any anticipation or hope to become like them. It just goes through me to no end how people can strut around in the fanciest of garb, drive the most insanely obnoxious cars on the planet, and throw money away that could be used to help. That money should be used for help, but they are being lifted and even heralded by the very people who could have benefited from their generosity if they had used half as much energy in giving as they did in all the taking."* She said.

"Do you miss it?" Asked Charlie, trying to keep her talking so he and Mathew could finish their soup. *"Do you miss the haughty life you had up on Wall Street, making snap decisions that made some rich and others regret their choices?"* He looked over his soup spoon at her to see if she had taken the bait. He

knew if he timed it correctly, they'd have at least three more minutes to gulp down as much as possible.

She answered the pastor with a nod and almost said something about it, but instead, without taking a breath, Leigh leaped a few inches out of her seat when she remembered a thought she had forgotten, *"Oh...there's one more, another one, Pretty Boy Floyd! His real name was Charles Arthur Floyd, and he's from where I lived, or thereabouts anyway. He's another mobster gangster type from the '30s, you know. He's buried not 140 miles north of where I lived.*

"My sisters and I did a whole grave searching thing a few years ago, and he was our last stop before coming home." She explained. *"Floyd was a hero in that part of Oklahoma because the banks he robbed took land and mortgages from the good, clean, decent folks who fell on hard times. He'd go in and rob a bank, casually ask for the money, and walk out the door, knowing the local police wouldn't stop him. He was doing them a favor in some ways by thumbing it to the very bankers who put the shaft to their constituents.*

"It wasn't like Floyd was giving the money back to the farmers; he kept it, but his brazen, outlandish 'look-at-me' attitude paid off until it didn't. Those boys in Ohio weren't impressed with him when he tried the same thing up their way." She laughed, finishing the last bite of Khao Pad rice in her bowl.

"Don't even get me started on hangings right here where we're sitting, or I guess a little closer to where I come from; the hanging judges pretty much all came from Arkansas, Texas, and Louisiana." She said, wiping her smile with the corner of her pretty cloth napkin.

Before the others could ask her exactly why she was so interested in public executions, she mentioned that the last hanging in the U.S. had been a man named Rainey Bethea. It was on August 14, 1936, in Owensboro, Kentucky. Why she knew the date off the top of her head could have been more interesting than the fact itself.

"He raped and murdered a woman old enough to be his grandmother!" she exclaimed. Not much was known about Rainey, but because he was on record as being the last man or woman publicly hanged for his crimes, he would go down in history, she told them, for the evil that he was. *"I hope they spelled his name correctly in the papers so we know who he is now. I'd hate to get something like that wrong and then go off telling people about him."* She laughed.

"Everyone said the woman he killed was the epitome of everyone's friend. She was a quiet woman, a decent soul. The only thing he wanted from her was a little money or something he could sell. All he had to do was ask! She was a giver – he took that from everyone. They found him because he left his own prisoner's celluloid ring in her house!"

Leigh quietly shook her head and waited for the others to finish their meals before adding, *"They hung him in the parking lot so the green grassy lawn wouldn't be disturbed by all the foot traffic of the more than 20,000 spectators who waited outside in the summer heat for hours to see the man hang; it just goes through me."*

Three

The small Thai restaurant, owned by a small but boisterous Indian man, Sunil Patel, and his much younger Thai wife, Tassanee, appeared almost like an oasis amidst the urban landscape. Its vibrant, lucid colors and enticing aromas starkly contrasted the surrounding concrete jungle beyond its threshold. Mathew glanced up at the faded red and gold sign. The letters seemed to dance and shimmer in the warm Florida air that danced its afternoon reel around them.

Though he had walked past the place many times over the last year or so, it seemed too meaningful today. Perhaps he felt the difference between eating alone and eating with a beautiful woman. Even if she wasn't his, she was there. She was certainly there; every cell in his body sensed her presence. When he tried to stop thinking about her, his mind reminded him of who he was and why he still thought what he was thinking; he wasn't dead! That's why he still felt the way he did and thought the things he was thinking.

When they stepped inside earlier, Mathew noticed the quaint interior design—a mix of traditional Thai customary ornamentation with a more modern

Americano touch—begging someone to call it out of its inconsistencies. During the lunch hours, wooden tables were draped with checkered blue and white tablecloths aimlessly scattered across the open square room. Sunil and his wife covered each table in fine white doubled linen in the evenings for a more elegant appeal. The buffet was only served during the lunch hours.

The walls were painted with rich, earthy reds, rusts, golds, and silver paints, flecked with intricate tapestries of woven fabrics depicting romantic recreated scenes of the Thai ancient stories and folklore. He couldn't help but notice the distant chatter from the cooks' kitchen and the owners speaking in their native tongues. Their language only helped solidify in his mind that whatever they were brewing in the back would be authentic and delicious.

"Do you miss it?" Charlie asked, looking entirely into Mathew's face, trying to draw his attention from watching Leigh. Do you want to go back into the kitchen and try your skillful hand at making Thai food for us today?" he asked. *"Did you ever make Thai food when you were a chef in Chicago?"* The question was more or less another clever and discerning way to make an unknown point; Leigh hadn't been told much about Mathew's past.

A nostalgic, slow smile played at the corners of his lips as Conner tried to repress the intensely anxious moments of when he had been a well-sought-after cook-smith in a city that never sleeps. His gaze drifted toward the ceiling. He seemed a little lost in the memories of his past life, as if they weren't his memories, just a time that he had all but convinced himself was only a dream.

"I worked at a few upscale dining places, to be honest with you. When Tia...when my former fiancé's father had promised me a spot as head chef at his Old Sicilian Style establishment, I thought the clouds had come down from the heavens to sweep me up and carry me away. Maybe it would have been better for everyone if they had." He suggested.

"I loved experimenting with different styles during my downtime, but when I worked, I had to create or recreate the staples of the long-standing restaurant. You don't mess with success; you repeat it as well and as often as possible." He said. *"Yeah, you could say I made a few Pad Thais in my day."* He added before quietly unclenching his fists under the table, smoothing his hands across his lap, hoping no one had noticed the gesture.

A small, petite waitress approached their table, her arms skillfully dexterous, carrying several plates simultaneously. As the two men had opted out of the buffet, and ordered off the menu, they were served at their table.   After taking a bite of the savory meal before him, Mathew gave a satisfying nod to the smiling, attentive server, letting her know instantly that she had been successful in her efforts to please her first customers of the day. Charlie's nod was equally received, sending the reserved attendant on her way.

"Funny," said Leigh, quietly under her breath so that other patrons would no hear her complaint, *"She didn't wait for me to test my food. She just...she just waited on you guys."* Even before she had finished her

sentence, Leigh's mind swept back to the categorically packed away knowledge of her mind, realizing instantly that the culture of those who served her that day was accustomed to pleasing men over women, as it was usually the men in their lives who ordered, paid for and critiqued the food being served.

A genuine smile returned to Mathew's face, *"And that is why Charlie and I come here, Leigh. You had to know there was a reason. Charlie, here, is used to being treated like the king that he is; his wife won't let him alone; she's always doting on him, bringing him things, fussing, and mussing over the man.*

" I don't get that treatment anywhere else but in this place. It's my secret place of male-dominant indulgence, and I'll thank you very much for leaving me to my toxic masculinity for a meal now and again, if you don't mind." He said, somewhat calm as well, so that no other patrons would have heard him and no one would ever have taken him seriously.

Leigh had promised the men not only to return to the church in a week to join the two of them along with several others, to go to the neighboring projects to serve, but also to be available to either of them should the need arise. Charlie, for his part, knew that his dear wife Hideko would always be the one to make sure he was rarely in need of anything, while Mathew gave no hint of even the slightest desire to be assisted by anyone for any reason. Leigh felt her offer was good, notwithstanding the obvious; before bidding them adieu, she took herself to the front register, paid the bill for all three meals, and even took care of the tip.

Mathew's interest was piqued when he realized that Leigh had treated the three of them to lunch and also taken care of the tip. He tried not to show his surprise, attempting to play it cool while keeping his thoughts silent and buried within himself. Even when being flush with money, he had never made the effort to be as generous as he could have been. Now that he didn't have money to speak of, it was one of the most important things on his mind to be both kind and generous when he could be.

Noticing the man's gaze, the way he questioned her without saying a word, Leigh shrugged and turned before her retreat, *"I'm nice like that,"* she giggled, *"When I treat people, I never expect them to pick up the tip. Why would I?"* she asked, *"...if it's a gift, it's a full gift, I don't do anything half-way; you'll see."* She promised as she disappeared through the lunchtime throng of tourists and locals who had begun to pack into the small establishment.

Mat fell silent, thinking again in a manner that Charlie knew was his own. When Mathew went silent, it usually meant his mind was anything but quiet – he was thinking, and something was beginning to gel. To bring his friend back to the present reality, Charlie mentioned that for the next few days, Leigh would check into a hotel close enough to stay in touch. Her beachfront condo was being both sanitized and painted for its new tenant. Hideko had texted him to say Leigh had decided against purchasing just yet, giving her the time and effort she'd need to be sure she both wanted to stay in the area and made the right choice of investments. A home is perhaps the most significant purchase anyone will ever make.

Leigh's fingers crisscrossed her cell from inside her room at the Radisson Inn, skimming over her contacts' names before finding her best friend's last name. She knew she had changed her name from Sarina Kelly to Sarina, something other than Kelly, but she couldn't remember how to spell or pronounce Deschanel to save her life. She asked herself who in their right mind would trade an easy-to-spell name like Kelly for something you'd always have to spell out for someone, anyone, and everyone who ever needed to have it spelled out for them.

"Sarina?" Leigh questioned once her best friend managed to answer the call. *"It only took you six rings this time, woman. You're getting so much better at juggling your cell, kid, and whatever else you're dragging around."* She teased. Sarina, a fiery red-headed woman with piercing blue eyes, had always kept one of the best *"skinny-glass"* figures even after giving birth; her last, an eleven-month-old son, had been her fifth. *"You have a way with you, almost like you're a dang octopus. You don't even need that tail Darwin took away from us, do ya?"* Leigh laughed.

Between a solid marriage at a younger age and her childbearing, Sarina went to college and graduated top of her class at Tulane. She'd completed her Bachelor's degree before her twenty-first birthday, taking a year off to rear her first. Then she returned to law school, where after only a brief medical sabbatical, she had passed the bar sufficiently enough to land a work-from-home job as a contractual lawyer for one of the country's leading food corporations. If it looked easy, it wasn't, but the smile on that woman's face always seemed to make its way through the receiver of her cell to find the ear of her high school rival and best friend.

Their friendship was one of those rare constants in an otherwise tumultuous world. They shared a bond that seemed to transcend both distance and time. *"You are the ying to my yang, Sarry, and don't you let anyone else tell you otherwise. I wouldn't sell you for a million or pay another nickel for one just like you, but you are the reason I don't go looking for another best friend; I want you to know that, OK?"* Leigh stated flatly while practically dancing across the spacious hotel bedroom with its tiny kitchenette, two-burner cookstove, miniature fridge, and what had to suffice as a sink since it had hot and cold water coming out of a minute little faucet.

"Why are you so happy today?" asked her hometown friend, wondering what could have been even more exciting than living under the open skies of the Sunshine State, right on the beach nonetheless, and with seagulls and waves to keep a body up all night. *"What gives you the right to call me up and brag about all you've got, knowing I'm stuck here thinking about having to go back to Wal-Mart because I forgot dishwashing detergent, and that was the reason I went there in the first place?"* Sarina faked a complaint.

Leigh couldn't help herself and teased her friend, asking if she had come out of the store with six plastic bags of groceries, toiletries, and diapers, even though she had only gone to pick up a bottle of dish soap. She would have been harder on her friend, but she knew exactly how guilty she was of making the same mistake—sans the diapers. That was never going to happen.

"I don't know, Sarina, it's really weird. I can't put a pin in it, but I think I just met my husband." Leigh blurted because when she felt incapable of explaining herself, she would often do that. If she blurted it, she told herself, it would either happen because she put it out into the universe, or it was nonsense, to begin with, and it would be forgotten by the time the ladies got around to talking about something else, something that made sense.

Four

There was just something about the smell of a thick and hearty, warm homemade buttermilk biscuit that kept Leigh wrapped up tight in her terrycloth dressing robe that next Saturday morning; it could have been the heavenly scent of the soft, savory heated dough rising, or it could have been the pillowy soft texture that she remembered from her very early years running around her grandmother's kitchen every Sunday morning before the whole brood would break free from the long hardwood table where they gathered, to dress before going to church.

Whatever it was, memory, nostalgia, or just bated anticipation, every inch of her tiny kitchen was filled with the aromatic symphony of what she had managed to recreate using her grandmother's favorite recipe. She wasn't sure she could pull it off, but there wasn't anyone around or close enough to challenge her. Granny wouldn't lean out of Heaven long enough to chide the woman, so she felt relatively safe telling herself that what she had created had been a culinary success.

Being out of that uncomfortably cramped living space she shared in DeQueen with Sarina and her ever-growing family felt so good. Though grateful for it, she hadn't thoroughly thought through it when Sarina and her husband invited her to hole up in their place rather than to try and bounce from home to home and from one family member to the other.

When retreating from New York, Leigh's decision not to buy something permanent was the best decision possible. Waiting for her settlement to kick in and to be deposited took a while. Nearly five weeks of stuffing herself into the guest room of a house that didn't have a guest room was next to impossible. She hadn't purposely woken up before seven o'clock since she had left Arkansas; a girl could get used to sleeping in, Leigh thought. A girl could get used to sleeping in if she hadn't already promised her pastor she'd accompany him on her maiden trip to the city's lowest economic district, an area of town known most simply as *"the projects."*

"Tell me a little about the projects, Charlie." Leigh began, picking off a small piece of one of her golden-topped biscuits before offering a few extras to the man standing at the door. Turning the key to unlock the front door, Charlie never made eye contact with her but assured her, as he pushed open the glass door, that he would have been more than happy to help her feast on whatever it was that she brought with her, had it not been for the amount of bacon and eggs he'd stuffed down himself minutes before making his way to the church to make the first pot of coffee.

"Hideko won't let me walk out the door without a full belly, I assure you. You'd think I should be a heftier man the way she feeds me. I think it must be all the tree climbing and the miles I put in on the beach, walking from one end to the other every day, picking up trash, and talking to folks. I'm bound to relax someday, maybe gain a pound or two, but those days are long in the future. I'm pretty sure I'm sticking to the same size I've been for the past forty years, except I think I was thicker in high school." He added, after thinking about it.

Charlie hadn't been in the building more than a minute or two before the others began gathering outside, one or two chancing to return to the back of the church, where they knew the brew would be soon enough. If he could count on anything about his flock, Charlie knew they knew the Word, and they continuously enjoyed challenging him when it came to it. And they loved their coffee—a lot of it.

"Tell you what, Leigh, I'll let Dempsey tell you about the projects while I start the pot; he's been going with me for about five years. He's got it down to a science. He keeps me posted and up-to-date on all of it." Turning to the big fella beside him, Doug Dempsey was built like a mountain! Despite his tough and sturdy exterior, anyone could see that years of working in the fire field had given the man a particular physique, an imposing one.

Charlie paused. His eyes reflected a sadness at what he knew would be a harsh reality to explain; he tried to smile through it, to show that inner strength again, but some days were more challenging to face than others regarding their weekly trips. He lowered his head as if to tuck it away, turning from the others to give a particular instruction to this one of the best of the flock.

"Doug, can you give me a hand with this one? Leigh here is from Arkansas; she's our newest recruit. She's been up in New York City for the past several years, making it big in the Big Apple and rubbing shoulders with the hobknobbers who make the world go around. She's willing and able to dig her heels in and help us with all we do when we go to the Hammons; would you let her in on what she can expect? Don't beat around the bush now; she deserves the truth, and she'll know it too quickly if you try to sugarcoat it.

"Tell her exactly what you would tell a man; even though we don't usually take women with us, this week will be a little different since the Hammons are having their bake sale, and I know a few women wanted to be a part of that. Leigh brought us biscuits, not to sell, but for us – for now, she's got a few with her now, and we'll see if we can get a few more women to go now and again if they know someone else will be there too."

Fire Chief Douglas Dempsey had been one of Sarasota's bravest for over a quarter century. He and his wife Carianne founded the first annual Hammons Bake Sale a few years back; they had organized the event, creating a deeper city-wide awareness of the projects. It helped to have others understand what it was to live sparingly.

Chief Dempsey asked if it wasn't too much to ask; he wanted everyone in the stationhouse and every cop in the city to bring their families by the front gates of the Hammons on the first Saturday of October to buy a loaf or two of sweet bread to help support the year-end home improvement projects at the Hammons. These bake sales were a way to show the housing development that they weren't forgotten and that there were genuinely good people willing to lend whatever they could to help, even just for a day or so. It made people feel good for a day.

It also gave others a way to see how others were forced to live right under their noses, in the same city, without the benefit of resting and being at peace. If the cops or firefighters could come to buy a few baked goods, they could get caught up in a makeshift pickup game of basketball, chess, or flag football. It was only $10 to enter the tournaments, and if one wanted, if they wanted to go that extra mile, they could volunteer to help turn a wrench or a screwdriver, maybe pick up a paintbrush, and help a family make their homestead that much better.

The bake sale event was when and how the Dempseys met Charlie. When Charlie and another pastor in the area made routine weekly visits to the projects to assist with cleaning up and clearing projects in and around the stoic brick and stucco housing units, Dempsey's Engine leader Bud Watkins made a point to point the two in the same direction. Charlie wasn't into sports, but his buddy sure was. Before long, the two opposing teams met up on a bi-weekly basis to challenge those who lived in the projects to rotate into their respective teams.

Good people tend to find one another when other people steer them in the same direction. Chief Dempsey took most of the first cup of coffee from the pot before it had stopped brewing and gave Leigh a broad smile with his eyes as he very openly gestured that a biscuit could just about fit perfectly into his mouth at that very second.

"Here you go, Chief," Leigh said as she placed a warm biscuit in front of the man, pulled up a folding chair to seat herself, and prepared to hear what she knew wouldn't be easy to understand. Dempsey took a few bites of the soft, savory bread after covering it with a generous amount of homemade strawberry preserves Charlie kept tucked away in the pantry with the rest of the hidden gems known only to a few.

"Don't let anything I say to you this morning discourage you from returning to help; I want to clarify that part right now and first out in the open. You will see and need to know that the projects, or the Hammons Housing, are not a pretty place. We keep it clear and clean for the most part every Saturday, but by Monday, it's right back to where it usually is, with trash thrown around aimlessly, broken glass on top of last week's broken glass, on top of last month's broken glass. Once a month or so, we take a backhoe, a mini-excavator, and dig up what we can to keep it safer for the folks living there."

Dempsey finished the biscuit, nodding his way into a silent thank you to the cook, and continued what he needed to say. His gaze was intense and sincere; he didn't want to let Leigh or anyone else listening in on their conversation to think that where they were going would be easy to handle.

"It breaks my heart every week. Every week I go into the Hammons, I get a thick ugly lump in my throat and a hard knot in my gut, telling me that there's gonna come a day when I can't go anymore. I work so hard, we all do, at making the place a better and safer haven for the folks who want to be better, but we're not enough; there are just too many homeless who can't qualify to live inside one of the units, and those who do qualify aren't any more trustworthy than those who lay about the place day and night without a hope to hold to."

Dempsey looks past Leigh; his eyes softened and almost moist as he mentally recalls a recent suicide he and others were called to at the Hammons; the fire department had been instrumental in bridging the massive trust gap between the residents of the projects and law enforcement. It wasn't unheard of for the 9-1-1 dispatchers to send a fire and rescue unit out to do what ordinarily would have been considered police work if they believed a couple could be spoken to rather than being carted away. The people of the Hammons trusted Dempsey and his crew.

When the young man was found in the bathroom of his neighbor, a place he had used from time to time to shower since he wasn't part of those who were considered tenants, his body was carried out on the shoulders of three strong firefighters rather than being first examined or detained by the medical examiner; another city official not considered welcomed past the broken, unhinged gates of the housing authority. It wasn't strict protocol, but some regulations were flexible at the Hammons.

"That's why we do it, Leigh. We do it for people like Jerome Boyd, the kid who died, and Roscoe Shoemaker, one of the older men of the place, who was found just about a month ago in the foyer of the first block of houses. He had spent at least the last twenty years living on the streets so that his spot could be given to a mother with a few children. His place was next to nothing, maybe four hundred square feet, including the single closet between the living area and the bathroom, which would constitute a hallway.

"Shoemaker had been a barber in the sixties; before that, he was a Navy man; that's where he learned the skill of his trade. He was honorably discharged in 1954 after serving time in San Diego outside the tuna factory in a shipyard and living the dream in South Korea on a longer-than-usual tour of three and half years; he was an electronic technician before one of the Admirals grabbed him quickly off his duty station to give the officer a needed trim before the inspection.

"When the commander realized he'd just been given the best cut of his career, ol' Shoemaker had a new duty! He became the barber, and apparently, he got better at it because he used every penny he could find to rent a booth again, off the side of the beach, but this time in Sarasota. The housing authority gave veterans first dibs back in the day, unlike now. Shoey gave his unit up when he turned sixty-seven years old and his granddaughter needed a place to raise her brood. He stayed in the hall mainly, ate with the

family, and used the facilities; no one said a thing about it, though everyone knew his girl wasn't supposed to be there." The Chief finished.

"Why couldn't she apply for a place?" Leigh asked, not realizing the Florida Housing Authority had long been a harsh and uninviting government entity that chooses who will and will not qualify. Carrying a felony, any felony from any year after a person's eighteenth birthday automatically disqualifies a man or a woman from making an application. There were other authorities and other housing projects for that. They weren't any easier to work with and often took years to come through.

Dempsey finished his breakfast, cleared the dishes, and took a cup of hot coffee as he and Leigh tucked away the last of the morning's food fest, which resembled crumbs and more minor remnants of Confederate hardtack. Making their way past the others, Dempsey took Leigh by the elbow to lead her through a few would-be talkers; he understood the social routines and requirements of genteel Southern women trying to approach Leigh to introduce themselves, but he also realized the true and real facts regarding a typical Southern hello and how a good Southern good-bye or see-ya-later wouldn't come about for at least half an hour.

The way the Chief put it to Leigh, *"If we don't get out now, you'll be forced to find out where all the sales are, what so-and-so is doing with her new sewing machine, and whether or not wax paraffin is the way to go in modern canning...we gotta go!"* He told her, and with a gentle tug towards the door, the

The

Chief turned his charge around and pushed her gently
out the door toward his truck.

Five

She couldn't rest after her shower or even after meditating for over fifteen minutes; her brain wouldn't shut off. The images inside her head wouldn't stop; they wouldn't even tame down to the point of understanding most of what she had been exposed to that day. Leigh realized what it must be like to feel discombobulated after only being in and around the projects for a few hours on Saturday. She wondered what it would be like for the people she didn't get to meet.

Some of the people she was introduced to seemed aloof initially, barely welcoming her into their realm and only doing so because she came *"recommended"* or was in company with some of the people they knew already. If Charlie Garrett vouched for the woman, she had something going on; she was worth a look anyway. One woman in particular only stared at Leigh, who had worn less meticulous or bright clothes after being consulted by Charlie, telling her to keep it pretty muted.

"Keep it simple; you don't have to wear rags, but you can't expect anyone there to have matching tops and bottoms. Most, because it's later in the

morning, they may have switched it up a bit and put on their jeans or sweats, but you'll see a lot of pajamas, slippers, and maybe a hoodie over a tank top, and nothing much under that.

"Don't expect a lot of brand names, and if you see something that looks familiar, don't say something like you have one too; that won't impress them; it's likely to cause them to give it away. You're there to serve and listen, but if they ask you about your life or your things, that's your chance to bring in a little about your story; you're there to listen and to try and help."

He added, telling her that the people he knows who look for brand names in thrift shops are the same ones who want to stand out because they found something worth keeping; in other words, they want to be seen, not mimicked. He knew she would understand the concept and would undoubtedly respect what he said, knowing it was true. She did, however, know where she would donate her clothes in the future. She would probably have to send them through the Fire Department, but they would find good homes and be used much longer than she would have worn them.

One woman struck a chord close to Leigh's heart, if only because of her name. Though the spelling of Jamee Leard's name was different, Leigh once had a childhood friend named Jamie. Jamie was black and from the other side of town, from what folks around the neighborhood called *"Frog Level."* A creek ran through the whole north and south border of DeQueen, splitting the two sections of town with some natural border.

Those who lived on the north side of the creek were primarily white, and if they were old enough, they had jobs. Some worked in family businesses such as the sawmill, the dairy farms, or general stores, and some worked for others, again, mostly white folks of European descent, who ran the civil offices, the post office, the bank, and other financially oriented offices.

The people living on the southern side of the banks of the Cedar Ridge Creek were more than likely black, and when or if they were employed, it wasn't for someone over on the other side of the creek bed. There wasn't nearly as much opportunity on that side of the creek, and there was not nearly enough help or means to make a needed difference in the lives of the good folks who called that side of the county their home.

To even cross the creek was a daring feat for anyone on either side; like the Arkansas River, Cedar Ridge Creek had its broad and narrow spots – most of them running steep, rocky, and rapid. The years of the older, more dangerous civil unrest had long since aged away. This is precisely why Leigh had been horrified when her great Aunt Salley refused to allow Jamie Washington to play inside the house with Leigh when she went home with the elderly retired school teacher after church service.

Trying to explain to an eight-year-old the ways of life in the South seemed a little overwhelming to the Marm, who had taken the simplistic approach and said it wasn't done. *"Jamie understands; she knows she's not supposed to go into my house, youngin'. She knows her mama would give her the whoopin' of her days if she did."* Coached the older woman, glancing over her shoulder at a seemingly calm and reserved young friend. Jamie's sweet nod gave Aunt Salley all she needed to be able to ask her little grand-niece whether or not the two girls wanted to stay a little while, maybe outdoors; she'd rustle up a couple of sandwiches, and they could play *"picnic"* with a few dolls she kept around the house.

Not allowing a child into a house because of the color of her skin didn't make sense to young Leigh; it was something she never understood and swore she would never accept for herself. Each time after that, when she and her family would visit with her great aunt, Leigh made a point to be the braver soul and cross the creek bed to the south side of the town to be with her little friend. Maybe the whites weren't so giving, and maybe their rules were harsher and more unforgiving, but Leigh was never given the same treatment when she crossed to the other side of Cedar Ridge; there, she was family.

Jamee Leard was born in Chad, Africa. While they were standing at one of the tables at the Hammons, offering baked goods to those who had come to donate what they could. Charlie hadn't noticed Leigh's eyes before, but as he glanced at his newest recruit, he saw that she had been rubbing at and dabbing at the corners of her eyes when she believed no one was looking.

With outreached hands, he greeted Leigh, who had now made a nearly permanent place for herself near the new Jamee in her life, having gained enough trust to be included in a conversation between herself and another resident. Taking Leigh aside briefly, Charlie nodded to Jamee and her companions, letting them know he'd only take their friend from them momentarily. He wanted to share a brief background about Jamee Leard to give Leigh a deeper understanding of why she had been asked to join them this weekend.

Charlie's face turned pale when he thought of all Jamee Leard had been through, what her life must have been like the first fourteen or fifteen years of near squaller and deprivation in the old country. His fingers opened and closed around those of Leigh's. He almost seemed to be fidgeting while looking for the right words to use to explain. Looking back at Jamee, he almost sensed that she understood what was happening. She smiled somewhat hesitantly and lifted her chin.

"Chad, Leigh, is a place that has been through more than its fair share of pain and suffering," he tried to say without breaking into tears himself. *"It's one of the world's poorest nations, and the people there struggle every minute of every day just to survive, not only from famine and disease but from each other."* He continues before glancing silently toward Jamee for a second time, who now stood alone, but she remained close to them; about fifteen feet away.

"Jamee was called Derib; she didn't have or know her last name when she was brought over from the country through the Catholic Charities, whose missionaries had to buy her from her parents so they could make up what she would bring to the family in terms of 'employment' if you know what I mean." His words caught in his throat as he said it.

"Women and young girls have it the hardest there. They face daily violence, poverty, lack of education, and indecent ridicule when they have their monthly cycles. It's almost as if the older women forget they ever went through the same thing. Too many of the women become pregnant to stop their monthly flow, and when they have children, the babies often die within weeks of starvation. They end up doing the same thing over and over again to have what they believe to be a better life without the pressures of being forced to have sex if they are showing enough and prove their condition.

"For Jamee, she was one of the unlucky ones whose menstruation had come upon her at a very young age. By the time she was twelve, she was pregnant; however, after only a few weeks of being so, she miscarried, and it wasn't the last time that would happen. Still, as she has told me, being pregnant for a few months made it possible for her to at least not be bleeding when she would be forced to earn a few dollars for the family to survive."

The thought of what Charlie was trying to convey was devastatingly crushing for Leigh to hear. How could this young, small woman beside her be so calm and placid about what she had been through? The idea of someone being trapped inside their own home like she was, so foreign that it began to create anxiety within Leigh's mind. She wanted to wrap her arms around Jamee to comfort her but knew doing so would have the opposite effect.

Charlie looked directly into Leigh's face, his eyes full of determination and compassion for his mission at the projects and beyond, his promise to each soul living at the Hammons. *"I come here on my own, not expecting anyone else to join me, but I have been incredibly blessed by you, by Mathew, Dempsey, and the others. We're up to fifteen good hearts who want to make some difference now.*

"You are the first person I've seen Jamee speak to; honestly, I wasn't sure she would even want you near her. Being closer in age may have much to do with why she has accepted you. Jamee has a daughter herself, and if you see her, you'll swear to yourself that she's Jamee's twin, not her offspring. I think Amara is a little taller than her mother, but they have the same skin tone, and they have the same face and body as one another. I teased Jamee once and called her Amara, but I found out that was not something anyone should do. Her jealousy for her daughter is real."

Leigh couldn't understand his last statement. *"Jealousy?"* she asked, *"Why would her mother be jealous of her daughter, Charlie?"* Leigh asked, with apparent confusion in the tone of her questioning. *"Oh, you must have misunderstood, or maybe I didn't put it as I should have."* He answered. *"Jamee is jealous of Amara like God is jealous of us! He will not let anyone or anything take one of us from Him; we belong to Him and Him alone. This is what actual jealousy is.*

"Jealousy isn't when you covet something or are envious of something; no, it's when something or someone belongs to you, and you aren't about to let anyone else have it! That's the true meaning of the

word. Jamee is formidably jealous, meaning she will protect her daughter with her own life. She will die before she allows her to be harmed." He said, *"Keep an eye out; you'll see what I mean."*

With that, Charlie released Leigh to return to the table. For the next few hours, she and Jamee used the patience they had mustered between themselves to talk, ask questions, answer the other, and genuinely try and understand where the other fit into the world around them. Leigh's mind spun in circles as she tried to relax, make heads or tails of it all, and comprehend where life took its turns. She couldn't fathom living in such deprived and traumatic conditions, not for a day, let alone for over fifteen years.

Coming to America would have been, or perhaps should have been, a life-changing miracle for Jamee. Still, in some ways, taking the fish out of the waters she knew and placing it into the unknown created even more desperation for the young mother. Leigh knew she couldn't fully relate and would only offend the woman if she tried to compare their experiences. Unlike most women her age who had given birth at younger ages, Jamee was incredibly stoic and long-suffering; she was also very intuitive.

Six

Mathew knew he hadn't been able to spend as much time with Leigh as he had told her he would, not with Dempsey taking the lead with her and with Jamee being so willing to include Leigh in her life and conversation. He knew that everyone who had ever visited the Hammons had been unable to make headway with the woman they often referred to as *"Little Jamee"* rather than using just her name. The woman stood possibly four foot ten inches tall if that, and in every sense of the word, she was petite. Her voice often carried a sing-song way of speaking, as if she needed to express herself through lyrics rather than committing herself to any particular word or tale. Not wanting anyone to break into her closed world, Jamee Leard had successfully created and lived within a hardened invisible bubble, one she never left unattended. Mathew, perhaps more than anyone else who worked with Charlie on the weekends, knew why the bubble existed. He had only recently, perhaps over the past few months, been able to allow more people into his own space.

When he decided to do so, he texted Leigh on the church's social media app, the Church Link. It was a means for members to reach out to each other if they didn't know each other's telephone numbers. It worked like any other social media platform without photos and videos of kids and cats. This one used minimal effort and was rather basic by design; putting in a notice to ask if she was available for an evening stroll along the front beach walk, Mathew let Leigh know he was in the area or would be soon enough. He'd rap on her door to signal he was there; she didn't need to make any effort to answer if she was resting. He'd wait for her response.

The man remained calm or as quiet as he could, considering his experiences in the past with uninvited anxiety. As the Sarasota uniformed police officers approached him, their expressions were as stern as any actors that may have portrayed them. Mathew used the few seconds to compel himself to inhale and exhale slowly. He understood their caution – a large, bearded, obviously homeless stranger in the hallway of an upscale condominium complex would undoubtedly have drawn attention to more than one or two of Leigh's attentive neighbors. His appearance, unattended by a tenant, would have thrown up a few red flags.

As they questioned the man, he kept his answers short, honest, and concise. His quiet nature and mannerisms didn't go unnoticed by the cops. *"They'll see I mean no harm,"* he thought silently, maintaining eye contact with the white shield female officer who had been the one to take the lead. Her partner, an obvious rookie, stood back a couple of steps from his partner, his hand ready on the strap of his holstered Glock.

Mathew's honest answer wasn't met with much compassion or understanding when asked why he hadn't called the tenant on his phone. *"You said you know her; she's a friend from your church, and the two of you just spent several hours together at the projects at Hammons, is that right?"* drilled the stout and sturdy officer before reaching behind her back to draw a pair of metal handcuffs for the man she believed was more than likely, a stalker. She heard the part about the tenant spending hours at the Hammons but thought maybe this one followed her home afterward to get to know her better. *"She's your friend, but you don't know her number."* She repeated.

"I'll knock again, maybe she's taking a nap. She was exhausted from the event; maybe she was resting. She probably didn't get my Church-link message on her phone about coming over. We have a Teams thing; I thought she had the app downloaded." He said, *"You guys don't need to drag me off; I live outside and around toward the entrance of Turtle Beach. I mean, we're not exactly neighbors, but you know Charlie of The Superior Word. He lets me stay there; I watch the place."* Mathew explained again, trying to keep his voice down so as not to disturb Leigh's rest.

When the door of her new condo opened, Leigh stood in the doorway, half opening the door, half hiding behind it, as she hadn't fully pulled her dressing robe over her mostly naked body. *"Officers?"* she questioned; *"...what's going on? I know this man. He's my friend. We go to the same church. Did he do something?"* her words trailing as she spoke.

The silent partner, Officer Buck Edwards, stepped forward to make his introduction. His eyes opened a little wider than he had expected them to. *"This man says he knows you, that the two of you spent some time together today at the Hammons, the projects off Heron Avenue. Is that true, Ma'am?"* he asked, his eyes involuntarily surveying the woman from the top of her shoulder downward, trying to remain professional as he did so.

"This is Mathew Conner; yes, he's a friend of mine. Yes, we were at the Hammons today, and yes, he's OK; you don't have to cuff him or take him to the station; he's one hundred percent harmless, and I am in no danger, I assure you." She said, then, because she had been raised in the South, she thanked the police officers for their due diligence and service to the community. *"We need good police like you, those who take the time and care enough to follow up even the smallest of leads. I appreciate everything you do for us. I mean that."* She said.

Relief flooded Mathew's heart as his blood began to settle to a dull roar, allowing him to return to a normal state of humanness while he tried to keep his breathing under control. As the officers exchanged glances between themselves and the man and woman, who by this time were both standing on the inside of Leigh's threshold, Officer Edwards tipped his hat toward the couple and made his exit, with his more experienced partner tailing behind, making sure she wouldn't hear any wild cries for help the second she left the hallway.

"Thank you, Leigh." Mathew breathed, *"I didn't mean to cause your neighbors any trouble. Seeing a man like me in a place like this could stir up a little gossip; you don't deserve that. I think in the future, if you allow me to come back, that is, I'll wear more...well, something less...you know,"* he said, stumbling for the right words, before being asked to sit, relax, and whether or not a cup of tea would help.

Turning to Leigh, Mathew offered another quick apology before smiling and thinking out loud what it must have seemed like to anyone with x-ray vision, who could stare out their doors to see him in the hallway. *"Do they have cameras? Is that it? Is that how they knew I was in the hall?"* he asked. Leigh pointed to the camera and the device mounted on the wall, which served as a seven-inch monitor in every unit to show anyone who viewed it the entire length of the hall on either side of their respective doors.

Leigh's unit was at the end, with the door facing the hall's east side. She couldn't exactly see everything taking place several doors down, but if someone were to come within three doors of her unit, a chime would sound, alerting her that someone was, in fact, in the hallway.

It wasn't loud or obnoxious, as that would have annoyed every tenant on the floor. It was just a chime or note or two to say there was movement in the hall. Every unit's owner could change the chime or tone and lower or raise the volume of the notification. They could turn it off completely, but when nothing good was on the television, a good home-to-home look-see couldn't hurt.

"I can only imagine there's a few, shall we say, 'interested' parties on the floor, who, if anyone at all walks into the hallway, their little chime bells go off so they can grab their popcorn and bottles of wine should the show be worthy of it." She laughed, thinking primarily of the older man across the hall whose partner had already alerted Leigh to Don Stanfield's nosey ways. He had told her that he and Don had married when it became legal to do so in Florida, but after a couple of years of following the Covid lockdowns, he wasn't sure if he had made the right choice or if he'd perhaps created a scandal.

"Chet says he kept his original surname of Waverly because it was too close to the Waverley novels by Sir Walter Scott. With Don's last name being Kenig, he told himself not only would he have to spell it every time, but he'd be confused with the coffee makers. I laughed, of course, to think the two old geezers were so vastly different, but there they are, married!" she giggled, trying not to look at the monitor when she heard the tiny chime go off. Someone else was making their way through the gilded hallways of the Stratford Manor, daring to make themselves known to everyone on the eighth floor.

Turning suddenly to Mathew, Leigh realized, for the first time, that she had been standing in the living room of her place talking to a man she didn't know very well, that she was undressed and exposing herself from just below her thighs to someone she had maybe had lunch, two cups of coffee and a little conversation with. In a modest sort of hurried embarrassment, she made an excuse to retreat to the other room where she could throw on something more appropriate for what was now considered their first time alone.

From inside her bedroom, she called out to ask Mathew a question, more out of gentile, hospitable habit than anything else, given the circumstances. She didn't want there to be that strange and awkward awkwardness that could crop up in situations such as these. She could only imagine that Mathew, not unlike herself, wasn't opposed to an occasional dalliance if or when the right moment arose, but again, not only after so short a time of knowing one another. Where were her manners? She wondered.

"Mathew, I heard you saying something to the police officers just now; you said, 'you guys' instead of saying, 'y'all.' You do know and must realize, sir, that you live in the South now, right? Gone, gone, gone are those Chicago days and nights when you would say 'you guys' when a good old-fashioned well respected, 'y'all' will suffice."

Her words and behavior caused Mathew to blush under his collar. He hadn't thought about it, but if he had, he would have come to the same conclusion; the two of them didn't know one another well enough or long enough to be seeing one or the other without the socially commonly accepted amount of clothing to cover themselves. He chuckled, took a gentle peek toward the door of the woman's bedroom to see if he could see anything, and then answered her with the promise that he would give it his best efforts in the future to be more Southern in the future.

Seven

It wasn't much of a sacrifice in Mathew Conner's mind to be Leigh's protector as they walked along the north-bordering shorelines of Mascot Beach. In this area, Leigh's newly developed condominiums had risen to unimaginable heights in just under two years. The developer had petitioned the area for years prior, of course, and there were contracts, discussions, permits, and more to go through, but when the first golden shovel dug its way through the sandy shell-fragmented rock bed, even the headstrong developer had second thoughts about what he had committed himself to.

The initial concept for the condominiums had been to have four uniform towers, each under ten stories, nearly making a semi-circle design to give every tenant the best breathtaking view possible; naturally, the higher the floor, the better the overall view. Mathew couldn't help but think about the countless hours those unseen and unnoticed laborers spent as they fought the elements to create something as beautiful as the Stratford Manor had become, an icon of sorts. When finished, the project was in fact four uniform buildings stretching the earth as if they owned it; however, the first-believed ten-story dream grew exponentially into each towering edifice being no shorter than eighteen floors a piece.

The workers fought through the hot, humid heat of the days, which always stretched into the evening hours when there was light to be had, which always seemed to hover a little longer than it naturally should be allowed to do. Other hard-hatters milled about like hundreds of ants on a mission, some carrying lumber, others worming their way through a maze of materials, men, and madness so diligently, determined, and dedicated to their plight. The soil surrounding the new builds took on a resistance of its own, interspersed with roots of deep palm trees and other thick-stemmed tropical plants, clinging stubbornly in place, refusing to budge simply for progress.

"Makes me appreciate what I have behind the church," Mathew began. *"I can always count on maybe one or two people walking around after dusk, but nothing like this place. Even before the construction began on your building, the last one to be built, I couldn't tell you how many souls passed through this place; tourists mostly, but anyone and everyone in town had to push past this busy street and intersection to get to the three most popular beaches. It may take me seven or eight minutes to walk to leave the pavement behind for sandy shores, but I wouldn't trade it. I like the peace in the back of the building."* He concluded.

Their walk was relatively quiet in some ways; Leigh pointed out something now and again or asked a question for clarification, but both knew the other had a lot on their minds; time was good to share, but it was also good to savor. *"I guess everyone has their kind of grind, huh?"* she asked, not really having a point to the question but just mentioning it to have something to say. It may have been something she saw, and she suspected that Mathew had seen the same.

Whatever it was, her question was far more rhetorical than genuine; an answer consisting of words wasn't expected or necessary. A smile, a nod, something slight was all she needed to know they were in step as they made their way across the less crowded areas along the natural curve that separated one beachfront from the other. With the gulls looming overhead and the tangy salt air in their lungs, words weren't needed as they may have been in another setting.

Mathew instinctively put his hard, calloused hands into his pockets as they walked, something he did intentionally as well, to silently let his companion know he hadn't agreed to walk with her to ask her to become more familiar; he wasn't going to take her hand into his own. It wasn't that sort of walk; they both knew that to be true without saying it. She had mentioned wanting to see the connecting beaches, and she knew he knew them well. He had been the one to suggest the tour; giving her the text gave her a way to say yes or no. She never answered him, so he took the initiative.

As they strolled through the thick blanket of sand, every tiny sliver could be felt and even appreciated on her bare feet, choosing to hold her sandals rather than wear them. The grains of sand shifted just beneath Mathew's worn leather boots, a stark contrast in fashion to the unforgiving pavement of his former life. He stopped for a second to admire the horizon as the stark golden rays were just about to kiss the rosy hues lowering in the skies above them both.

The sunset painted the sky in a breathtaking menagerie of color, gently rippling from one end of the beach to the other. He paused, taking off his footwear to feel the cooler granules cascading over his feet and between each of his toes. The sensation of it sent a veiled tinge through the veins in his legs, and he sighed contentedly. It had been more than a minute since he had allowed himself to feel this free, so abandoned in thought. That he wasn't alone did not escape him for a second. The crispy, brisk air filled his lungs and, in doing so, soothed his soul.

This, he thought to himself, is true freedom. This means not having to put a deadline in place or subject himself to the need to be somewhere at any particular time. If the moment could somehow last, he could live precisely where he was, as he was for the rest of his given days. He allowed himself the privilege of gazing to his side to catch a glimpse of the woman who had chosen to stay beside him. It had undoubtedly been a long time since he had purposely made time to be in the company of a woman, let alone one with such grace and natural beauty. He swallowed hard quietly, thinking if the moment had to end, at least he had it; it would remain with him for a very long time. He had to mentally pinch himself more than once.

His gaze lingered on her face, illuminated by the fading of the sky's light; he felt a warmth spreading through him, filling him with peace. Despite the seeming hardships he had endured over the past several years, and in some way, because of those experiences, Mathew knew he had come to appreciate the small, quiet moments that found their way into his days recently. He knew he hadn't intended to think about Leigh as often as he did. He knew or told himself anyway that doing so could potentially ruin whatever they were about to have: a friendship.

Life, at that moment, in that place didn't need to be qualified; it needed only to be appreciated. He knew life wasn't about being rich or having something stand on a platform to announce to everyone just how much he had achieved for himself. It was about standing barefoot on a beach just before the gulls swooped their last, standing beside a friend who mattered to him. This was a moment he couldn't dream of releasing, but one to breathe in for another few long seconds.

Their journey continued along the fading edges of Mascot Beach, turning their strides southbound a little ways to cross an imaginary boundary, taking them over the threshold of Turtle Beach, where they could see the edges of a small outdoor bar and grill that was just about filled to capacity on the inside. There were few outdoor tables, but one was on the outer edge with their name on it. Taking the lead, Mathew removed his hands from his pockets to clasp onto Leigh's to run so that they would quicken their chances of commandeering the best seat in the house.

Upon reaching the wobbling bright, colored stainless-steel stools, Mathew released Leigh to allow her first choice of seating; she had been raised by a father who had always told her never to put your back to the door if you sat in a public place. She wondered out loud what her father would do in this particular case. *"I guess I have no choice but to put my back to the bar if I want to see the sea, but which way is the door in a place like this?"* she laughed. Mathew surveyed the area cautiously at first, taking note of the chaotic energy pouring from the crowded interior of the bar. He preferred solitude for sure, but for the moment, sharing the tiny table was as close to perfection as he had been in years.

"Do you want to hear a story, Mathew? If you do, and listen," she told him, *"...you can say no, this one is a long one, and if I tell it right, you'll end up wanting to borrow the book I just bought maybe a month or so ago from an author you may find rather interesting."* Her words were both intriguing and comforting. Listening to Leigh's southern drawl could sustain the man for days; it wasn't the same dialect as the women's voices he was used to hearing either in Florida, where some would say isn't considered the South, and it wasn't the nasal-tinged forced Chicago tones he had been accustomed to. Of course, he wanted her to tell him a good story.

Leigh's smile lifted the man from one level to the next; he had become interested in seconds, knowing whatever it was she was creating for him in terms of a tale would be satisfying to hear. Leigh's method of writing, she had told him, was to talk out everything she would commit to ink before committing it to her keyboard. The story would be said, felt, and experienced. Every tiny, well-thought detail would extend and live within each syllable of her voice through lingering Southern charm as it made its way from her heart to her mouth, to swim in the air before reaching his ears.

"*Before starting the story, I have to tell you the backstory. If I've learned anything at all in my life, in the years I've spent writing, it's to know the end of the story before you start to tell it, but if you don't have a good backstory to start the whole thing off with, your audience may never know why this piece fits into that piece, or how this peg ended up in that hole. Do you know what I mean?*" she asked, herself nodding, knowing that she could expect the same reaction in return by doing so.

"*You have to know why I ended up in Sarasota in the first place. I overheard you talking to Charlie's wife, Hideko, about it when we were working this morning, so I thought I would let you in on something, but maybe Hideko wasn't told. It's not a big secret or anything, but because it's not a big deal, Charlie may not have explained it thoroughly to his wife. I came to Sarasota after my cousin introduced me to Charlie when I visited with her one past summer; I guess it's been three years.*

"*Jude Stringfellow is an author. She's my cousin, but I'd say we're third or fourth cousins if I had to figure it out. We're both related to Collin Raye and Betsy Brake, the ventriloquist, for that matter. I don't know if you even know who I'm talking about, but Collin is an amazing singer; that being said, Jude is an amazing author. We're, you know, one big talented, amazing family.*" Leigh laughed before raising her hand to get the attention of the first waitress who had meandered close enough to their table to be considered close enough to their table.

After ordering their dinner and a fresh round of iced water with lemon for both, Leigh continued telling her backstory about how she came to live where she was. *"Jude was touring with her latest Nick Posh murder thriller; I can't remember which one it was; it took place in the 1930s and was based in Scotland; that much I remember. I didn't know we were kin until she blurted something to me. We do that, we blurt. I mean, I blurt.*

"She asked me if my family was related to the Brakes, Cates, or Hookers, and I had to laugh. Usually, when someone asks you if you're related to a bunch of hookers, you don't get too excited about it, but I did! I got excited about it because I love the Nick Posh series, and here I am, there I was, standing beside the author, and she's asking me if we're related. She said she saw a family resemblance in my eyes and forehead. I didn't ask her if that was a good thing or not." Teased Leigh.

"When Jude told me who her daddy was, Reuben Wayne Stringfellow, I knew immediately that we were kin because I had heard the name around town for years. You can't be a Hooker, a Brake, or a Cates without being related to a Stringfellow, not in our neck of the woods. Her daddy was born not three minutes from where my daddy's mama was born, and they're first cousins, so what does that do for Jude and me? I guess we're...well, we're related."

Leigh's backstory telling took much longer than she had expected; it survived dinner, two rounds of water, the call of the cicadas, God's lullaby after explaining their familial relationship, and how, after a few bites of ice cream together, Leigh explained that

Jude had shown her the true secret to her success as a writer of fiction. It was prayer! She told Mathew that he could believe her or not, but that is what the author had told her, and she had been quite successful at her craft.

"My cousin Jude told me that prayer would remain the one constant that would always remain steadfast even if money vanished if readers stopped reading, and if something happened to her to end her career, prayer would remain. Jude shared another fact with me, too: the website of The Superior Word: Charlie's website! That was the first time I even knew he existed. I had stopped going to church when I got to New York; I'm a Baptist, but I was raised down here, where Southern Baptists exist. You can't find the same type of congregation up North; it's just not the same.

"When I first started listening to him, I was at Ingram Horace and Driskoll, grinding away on caffeine at the desk of an unappreciative position, and though I knew I had it better than most financially, I was stuck so deep in depression and thoughts of quitting due to the long and grueling hours I was keeping just to keep my position; it was those breaks I'd take listening to Charlie preach through the Genesis sermons that kept me upright!" she admitted.

"When I broke free from that joint, I nearly tripped over myself to get away from anything related to high-stakes monopoly to get back to basics and find the foundation I knew I needed. I decided to meet the man in person when I left the finance world; maybe take a week's trip and see the ocean. I knew I wanted to make a difference in someone's life, and I

knew Charlie would know where to put me and what to do with me. I thought maybe he'd give me advice and I'd go back home to put it to use - - but I decided to stay."

The author recently shared another more profound, intimate moment with her cousin. She told her she was planning to write a book about people experiencing homelessness, especially those in nursing homes who are often forgotten. In the middle of the book, she'd add stories about people who were utterly hurting and hadn't the strength or energy to pull themselves out of the deeper depressions they had allowed their souls to fall through. The book would be titled *"The,"* just *"The."*

"When I asked her why she'd choose such an unusual title, she said it was because the people she wanted to focus on were always given labels, and those labels always began with the word 'The.' She said it slowly to me, 'The homeless,' 'The forgotten,' 'The unseen,' and 'The outcasts.' They were more than nothing to Jude. They were the reason for needing to become aware in the first place." Leigh's eyes met Mathew's in the dark, just enough light from the moon cascading its silvery face over the waves to make out his weary expression.

"She told me that she wanted to write 'The' because when it was published, and it would be very soon, no one would know what to do with it. They won't know where to put it in the library or on shelves because the word that defines it is the same word that is always ignored when they shelve a book or put it up for sale. The word 'The' is the most ignored thing. She wanted to bring awareness to that fact." Leigh

scanned the man's face to see if he understood her or if he was just happy to let her talk.

Eight

If one thing could be said about the way Mathew had been forced to learn to be human again after what he had endured, it would be that he never lost sight of what it felt like to prepare a good meal for someone who, yes, was paying for it, but who would always appreciate the craftsman for his art. In the kitchen, Mathew was not only at home but in paradise. Pots, pans, measuring cups, wooden spoons, and other utensils became extensions of his hands, mind, and soul. He wanted to share his experiences with her; and waited for the right moment to do so.

To steady himself as the two of them made their nearly two-mile trek back to the condominiums, Conner thought constantly about the recipes he had created for his portfolio; he was a master chef, the author of his biography when it came to the palate. Listening to Leigh took the edge and rawness out of his mind long enough to squelch most of the anxiety trying to build up inside of him. He was fine after they got going after they were in their strides along the sand, but slowing down to the point of realizing their evening would end created unnecessary havoc in his thoughts.

Leigh went on about her cousin, the author, and how the book she wrote had a theme within it, almost a theme within a theme. The thought of it reverberated at the back of his skull; perhaps he could ask her another question or two to keep her talking, to keep the moment quiet and still. Mathew's usually quiet, calm demeanor began to crack ever so slightly as they neared the Stratford Manors, revealing the nervously beneath the surface. He was all too aware of his clenched fists inside his pockets but hoped she hadn't noticed; had she seen?

The knot that began to develop before he reached her place earlier had returned; despite all of his attempts to equate what Leigh was talking about to food, to its willful preparation, he was unable to make the connections last as long as they had when they were further away from the entrance of her home. Mathew glanced at Leigh; her excitement about the new book was palpable; he told himself if he wanted to know her better or if he wanted her to think he cared about her as a friend, he'd need to read the book. It wasn't out yet, not for sale, but Jude had asked Leigh to read it for mistakes and suggestions.

"The book," he said to her, *"...you said it had an odd title, it was..."* He glanced at her once again with eyes too curious, too honest to ignore. Leigh smiled and faced him. She slowed their walk to a stop, took his left hand in hers, and led him over to one of the teal-painted benches just outside the front door of the third building, her building.

"The book is titled 'The' for a good reason. It's unlike anything you'll ever read, and if you want to, I'll lend you my copy. I know you're not much of a reader, really, and I completely understand it when people who have full lives say that; you can't always see yourself taking time for just really relaxing, learning, and thinking, and yeah, the book is fascinating, but only if you have the heart to become as aware of your surroundings as I think you've proven a hundred times over that you are. I think you'll like the book, Mat...can...can I call you Mat? I guess I just did." She laughed.

Mathew took a deep breath and let her see it. He drew as much sea air as he could into his lungs and allowed himself to exhale with a genuine effort to slow himself down slowly. *"Because I am your friend, you can call me Mat."* He said. *"You are one of just a very few who have even wanted to."* He said. *"Most people I used to know don't talk to me at all, and those who talk to me now have started calling me 'T' since I only have one, not a spare."*

Squaring his shoulders as he ran his hand through his close-cropped hair, he mentally prepared himself for the next question, which he wasn't sure would be *"Would you like to come up for a cup of tea?"* or *"Can you wait here while I go get the book?"* He had just about decided that taking things too quickly would mean ruining everything; his preemptive method of suggesting that he wait for her to return with the book seemed the best choice.

Leigh wasn't gone for more than four minutes, and when she returned with the book in her hands, she couldn't stop smiling. Extending both hands toward him, he stood from the bench and took the book, his hands briefly grazing her fingers. He could feel the book's thickness and noticed a familiar smile looking back at him from the back cover. Could it be that the author, Jude Stringfellow, was such a close relation that even her smile proved their kinship? *"She looks almost exactly like you," he said, "I mean, without the hair; you have such...such beautiful red hair."*

There. He said it. It had been on his mind for about two weeks since the moment he saw her at the church, but now, he's put it out there, and there was no taking it back. Would she notice? Again, he wondered if she would have even imagined that he would have imagined that she was anything other than just another member of the small congregation; the knot in his stomach seemed to lower a little and was hard to ignore.

Leigh blushed, but it wasn't enough to see in the dark, and she was thankful for that. She was backlit at best, knowing that the entry lights of the condo building were directly behind her. She thought that if he had been closer, maybe he would have heard her heart beating a little louder, but that was probably just her imagination. It was probably, she told herself, just that she was getting the opportunity to share something reasonably personal with Mathew in hopes that he would find it reassuring.

She knew what the book was about, and to be honest, if she had to be honest with herself, it was almost as if her cousin had spent time with Mathew James Conner in both his out-casting and his rebuilding processes. How was it, she wondered, that

Jude's fiction could somehow manifest itself in the man standing before her? It was an odd sensation. *"The man in the book has many layers. He's been through the wringer a few times; he's even contemplated taking his own life. Thankfully, he doesn't...spoiler alert; sorry. I'm blurting again."*

Leigh's eyes filled with hope and expectation; she told him to start off reading just a chapter or two a night, don't rush it; the book had a way of sucking you into it once you get started, and she didn't want him putting off anything significant so he could spend time alone in its pages. Mathew's shy smile said all he needed to say. He hadn't read an entire book in too many years. This one would take time, but it could be what he needed in a few ways to fill the void he was hopelessly aware had permeated him to the core.

He thanked her and promised to do precisely as she had asked; he would take his time so that he could read every last word. If the photo on the back of the book indicated how family ties bind, maybe the words inside the book would also reveal a familial connection. He hoped they would. Anything he could learn about Leigh would help him settle the questions his mind was conjuring about her.

The evening had ended for them; Mathew felt a tightening in his arms and legs; he hadn't stretched enough, he told himself. He'd probably feel that long walk through arduous sands tomorrow; every muscle in his body would remind him that after forty, a man should take some ibuprofen before trying to hike 10,000 steps all at once. Torn between his penchant for isolation and the desire to spend another minute with her, he rubbed his thumb over the back cover photo and repeated his words, only not out loud; he repeated his words to himself.

"Leigh," he started, glancing at her again, *"I should probably get going."* He paused, searching for the right words in the moment. *"I wanted....I wanted to say I truly appreciate you agreeing to walk with me tonight; it gave me something to do and something to look forward to."* She smiled again, and she drew a long-aired breath before speaking.

"No, Mat...Mat, thank you. I know it's not like it was years ago, and in the present, we can't just go traipsing out on the beaches alone, especially at night. It's not safe. It's not even smart, so no, thank you for asking. I know I must have talked your ears off about things, and I hope that's OK, I just...well, I like to talk." She said, her eyes dancing the way she knew she couldn't stop if she tried to.

Again, she used that voice he could listen to endlessly if she allowed it. His penchant for being alone stung deeply inside his chest; he had questioned it before, but now he was outright arguing within himself, wondering how he'd ever pull off whatever it could take to be the person he needed to be to keep up with what normal or civil societies expected of men his age to do when they make a conscious effort to be with someone for more than just meaningless pleasure. Anyone could do that; he wasn't anyone – and neither was she.

A man could pay for the type of companionship his body craved with no ties or strings attached. Society has little if nothing to say about how a man could or should behave if that were the case, but to want to be in her company forced him to reconsider a year's worth of forging on his own. Was it that hot outside, or was there something else going on inside his heart to keep him warm? He tried to listen to the little voice inside his head, but even that was couldn't fully be trusted now that he saw Leigh as something other than just another woman.

He stood straight, his movements slow and deliberate, reluctant to sever whatever connection they had made together. *"I appreciate you thinking of me, too, with the book. I'll read it, and yeah, I'll get it back to you soon, but if you want me to take my time, it won't be next week; it'll be a week or so after that if that's OK with you?"* his crystal blue eyes asking at the top of their ability while his words were gently whispered. He wanted nothing more than to delve into her world deeper than he had ever cared to venture before, but he knew every clock in the universe would tell him he hadn't spent enough time to bear out the privilege to do so.

Leigh spoke again, engaging him in one of her Southern goodbyes that could linger if allowed. *"You promised you'd teach me how to make a proper omelet. Right there on that beach, you promised. So, the way I see it, you can do one of two things: come back tomorrow morning and teach me, or you can be a nice guy and let me sleep in, and we'll have Southwest omelets for lunch. Them's your choices, Mister."* She said, almost catching herself flirting before she realized how it might sound to someone who hadn't known her very long.

Mathew watched Leigh's figure disappear into the light before crossing the threshold of her building. He felt a strange mix of relief and disappointment, which was soon replaced by another wave of nervousness, anxiety, and even hardline drops of depression when he considered that even on his best days, the only good clothes he could muster would be those he found secondhand at the thrift store. He owned one pair of boots, and they had to make it through at least another six or seven months. Another worry for another day, he told himself; right now, he had to make it through another sleepless night with too many thoughts racing through his head.

The man was no stranger to hardship; he had long ago learned to find solace in his own company. It's just now; it could somehow feel even more lonely than before because he knew he had allowed his thoughts to dance and swirl aimlessly, creating tendrils of hope in his heart, making their way through every vein held in place inside his body, every vein indeed. *"Thank you again,"* he whispered to her, knowing she was too far away to hear him. As he walked away, he glanced over again at the door of her building to see if she had made it into the building safely.

Back in the privacy of his place, the makeshift shelter he called his own, Mathew opened the book Leigh had given him to read. She was right, he noted; it was signed by the author, her cousin, and the words written in kinship meant the world to him as he remembered better days spent up in the Chicagoland area with a few of his good friends and cousins before the hammer hit as hard as it did in his life.

They're all married now; they have children not only in high school and college, but one of his closest friends was about to become a grandfather for the first time, a solid reminder he thought of how things never turn out how you think they're going to. No one wakes up at the age of seventeen and says they'll end up living in the back of a store room in the back of a strip mall in the back of the world somewhere without two nickels to rub together.

As he opened the book, a small piece of blue-lined paper fluttered from the pages. He quickly grabbed the spot where the paper had been resting to hold his place if that's where Leigh wanted him to start. She had mentioned a particular story that she wanted him to read first, then start at the beginning of the book, but only try to read one or two chapters at a time—make it last!

The paper was a bookmark, but it also had Leigh's cell phone number written on it. It was scribbled a little hastily but was in good enough shape that he could make out all of the numbers. His heart did that thing where it skips a beat as he stared at the digits, realizing the significance of what he held in his hand. Mathew ran his finger over the face of the paper a few times, memorizing the sequence of the numbers. It felt strange to care about something so minor; it felt good to care about something so big.

He told himself he couldn't and he shouldn't become too attached to anyone, anyone at all. He wondered to himself and spoke to the walls, asking how he could even think about what he was thinking and how he could manage the heartbreak if what he wanted wasn't what she wanted. The big man sighed deeply, tucking the bookmark back into its place before pulling it out another time to look at the numbers, to think again about thinking. When he turned the paper over, he saw that Leigh had written a short note.

"Mat, I don't want you to be arrested trying to stand outside my door again, waiting for me to wake up. Just call me when you're on your way, and I'll have time to get ready for the omelet lesson." Had she written that in such a short amount of time? Had she walked away, taken the elevator, walked the hall, opened her door, found the book, found the paper, found a pen, and then taken the time to write the note and give him her number, only to leave the unit, walk the wall, wait on the elevator, and come outside again all in such a short amount of time? Eventually, he gave up trying to figure the timing out in his head and sat on the bed to begin reading what he knew would be something he needed or wanted to read.

Despite his exhaustion, he determined within himself to at least finish half of the one story Leigh wanted him to read. Maybe, he told himself, if he did, it would help him relax and carry him into dreamland, where he wouldn't see himself being chased or toppling off the cliff while trying to win a wine-tasting contest.

His dreams were never the kind he could share at dinner parties. His dreams were like something one may read about in a Tom Clancy suspense thriller where he's hiding inside one of the ship's cannons about to have his guts blown out of him with bullets shaped like fish sticks while candles made of sticky tar paper lit up the room to show everyone where he was hiding; he couldn't see himself sharing those visions with anyone.

As he turned on the little light beside his bed to see the words better, he couldn't help but ask himself if what he was about to read was going to impact him as much as Leigh thought it would, or was it just some anomaly she thought up to appease the moment. She said the author had some sixth sense when she wrote the book, as if he would relate to its words quicker and more profoundly than most. He turned the pages to the ninth chapter and read it to himself.

Nine

Mat picked up the book, turning it over in his hands, flipping edges of the pages, as if feathering them; it helped him become familiar with the process. It had been a while since he had read for the sake of reading. Leigh must have had a reason for placing the little note where she did; it was placed at the beginning of Chapter 9; a chapter titled, "*The Blanket*".

The Blanket – by Jude Stringfellow

The day I moved from my home in America to Scotland, I really didn't have an elaborate plan, and I was going there to escape not only my family; well, not my kids, but what was left of a childhood entire of both good times and honorable times that somehow, and for some reasons had turned so ugly that I didn't even recognize it let alone call it "*family*" anymore. I love my kids; I won't make excuses about any of them when people ask me about them or want to know more. I'll just pause a second and let my heart fill up with overwhelming joy; joy warm enough to light a fire. I was going to need a good fire; it was colder in

Edinburgh than I had actually imagined it was. Oh, yeah, I saw the photos and watched videos. I did my homework before moving, but that wind took me by surprise and weirdly reminded me of the very place I had left: Oklahoma.

I found myself quickly volunteering for just about anything and everything I could to find new friends, meet new people, and be a part of the newest of new communities that, if you think about it, are ancient by my standards of what is new. In Oklahoma, we thought the buildings being renovated downtown were "*old*" because they were built at the turn of the 20th century; I didn't know what old was. I was just about to walk into a building over two and half centuries old, and it was sitting squarely in a place the locals refer to as "*New Town.*" Yeah, there's that. I walked into the Thrift Store, aptly named "The Thrift Store." You gotta love a good, catchy name for a storefront. At least I found it quickly enough.

As I walked around the store, taking in all the new smells from newly sprayed disinfectant and old clothes that could probably have been washed another round before being hung out to be sold, I realized that there must also be a cat in the little building. Even though the smell of a two- or three-day-old litter box was evident, but it didn't bother me.

I'd say it had a calming effect on my soul; I knew if nothing else were to come of the day, I would at least count on meeting at least one new friend. Cats aren't dogs, but anything friendly would be significant. So far, I had managed to track down and meet a few online acquaintances who agreed to meet me once I landed in their neck of the woods.

We had been cordial enough, and the coffee was good—one of them told me about the Thrift Store needing help. Sure, I know it's volunteer work, and I won't be paid, but I will be paid another way, right? I will make friends, I will be a part of the community, I will see things, learn things, know things, and just maybe someday actually fit into my new surroundings. This was a starting point.

I wasn't in the store very long before meeting the first level of administration, a chap called Lucas; he was a regular volunteer who had been nearly knighted for his hours of servitude. One could only dream of one day being so revered by the others; I nodded to Lucas, and he showed me to my position, explaining to me along the aisles that things didn't put themselves back onto the shelves after "*visitors*" (that's what we were to call customers) had their moments with the "*bibbles and bobs*" as he called them.

After years of experience working at the Thrift Store, he was fairly certain that I would have no problems folding t-shirts and linen and rehanging removed coats or jackets, some of which he assured me I would find in the oddest of places. He was not wrong.

Somewhere in the third hour of my *employment,* I reached the well-swept floor to pick up what appeared to be unfolded and tossed about dull colored blanket that was either knocked to the floor unwittingly or perhaps someone had picked it up and opened it, thinking they'd possibly buy it. Still, when they realized it had holes and was a bit oddly shaped, they set it down and forgot about it. I walked past it myself, saying I would return to redeem it after my afternoon break, a bit of coffee from the Wee Café. Again, I loved the name. It was, in fact, yes, a very small café - - a great name for it.

When I returned to the Thrift Store, I found the floor where the blanket had been was empty; or instead it was clean, there was no longer an older rough blanket lying about. I should have thought nothing of it, but my heart pricked thinking it had been sold and I had not presented it well to my new visitors. I had possibly failed them. That wasn't the case at all; no, the blanket had been tossed to the bin and was lying out on the open dusty black pavement just outside the back door of the Thrift Store, not quite fully out of sight and sort of hanging halfway in and halfway out of the dumpster outback. Again, I really should have just thought nothing of it, but my heart would not leave me alone about this damn blanket. There was something about it. What?

Before asking Lucas what he may have thought about it, I walked to the back door of the store, propped open the door so it wouldn't close on me (I had heard a rumor about that), and reached into the big blue metal dumpster and retrieved the old, torn, misshaped cloth.

Indeed, it would have some worth to someone, wasn't it donated? Where did it come from? Was it now just too old, perhaps too worn? I don't think I thought about that when I had examined it; sure, it was tattered, but nothing a bit of mending wouldn't fix. Maybe it was dirty. I hadn't taken the time to smell it or give it a natural look; I just walked away – well, I guess like others had done before me. It was done before me; anything that had happened to the thing happened before I found it. It wasn't all that impressive; perhaps that is why Lucas finally decided to rid the store of it; it wasn't worth much to anyone.

I remember returning the blanket to the front of the store and finding my new boss to see if he would mind if I fixed the blanket. His words were harsh but not necessarily wrong; he said it was not worth my time, but I could if I wanted to do it. He didn't even mind if I did it while working at the store because it would give me something to do during those lull hours when nothing much was happening.

Volunteering at a community thrift store can be a bit dull at times. You see the merchandise a few dozen times and walk the aisles repeatedly, helping or assisting visitors; it doesn't take long to learn the layout and know just about everything under the roof!

When there wasn't anyone to help, and I had nothing else to do, I decided to pull the old blanket out from under the desk where I had kept it safe from being discarded again. I held its long and thick mass up as far as my hands could reach above me. It seemed to be a double-sized bed cover that was good at once and probably kept at least two people warm simultaneously. I allowed myself a bit of a free-for-all all when it came to thinking about where the blanket originated, what its real purpose was, where it was purchased, who purchased it, and how long they owned it before either giving it to someone else to use or more likely storing it in a cupboard for years before deciding to donate it to the Thrift Store.

I ran my fingers along the edges again, wondering and asking questions about how the tears were made and why no one tried to patch them; they were just left to grow bigger. Everyone knows if you leave a tear long enough, it will just fray out and eventually become impossible to mend; was this the fate of my new...wait, was I just about to consider a worn-out blanket a "*friend*"?

I guess so; I hadn't found the hide or hair of a cat! I knew I was going to ask Lucas about something. Still, I got so busy, and then the break, and now the blanket - I know a cat is hiding in the store somewhere, but right now, my thought was with the possibility of possibly mending the old cover and making it, I don't know, somewhat helpful?

It did stink. Now that it was closer to me, I could smell it, and I was holding it up against my face. There was a smell to it, and maybe the owners didn't wash it because they thought doing so would leave it worse for wear, causing it to unravel, and then they couldn't even donate it. Best to hand it over to the clerk when you drop things off, no questions asked; maybe it was at the bottom of a paper sack, and no one would even know about it until it was either too late to reject it or perhaps too late in the day to make the trash run – whatever the reason, it couldn't have been at the Thrift Store very long or Lucas would have found it by its odor and tossed it, which is probably exactly what happened now that I think about it, and yeah, I thought about it.

I decided that this was my new mission. I don't even know why I chose that. I think it had something to do with the sad way it was discarded onto the floor when I first found it, or maybe it was just something calling to me from inside the woolen fibers, saying.

"Hey, we used to be on the back of really cool sheep (or two), and we walked this Earth! Save us! We spread our love over people and unknown people, and we kept them warm from the weather and safe from the storms outside. We deserve more than this!" OK, you can see that being a writer and working in a

super eclectic place like a Thrift Store, where memories and history collide, could be a bit of a playhouse for one with such an imaginative imagination. I thought so; it was fun. Just me and Blanket getting to know one another. I was all he had left now; I just called it he. I was getting into this, wasn't I?

I counted 11 holes and a torn corner. The corner that was torn was also the corner that seemingly was tugged and pulled out of shape, causing the entire blanket to appear to be mangled. God help me; I was going to accept this new assignment. I'd need God, I'm sure. I thought an excellent cold wash would set that, but these holes must be mended and repaired first. I set my detective skills in motion and went about the store, through each aisle, up and down each row and shelf, trying to find perhaps a sewing machine that someone had donated, but the best I could come up with was a repair kit, from the Scottish Army in fact, and from World War II.

This store was quietly surprising with its strange mishaps of properties once belonging to so many people. Now, these things, they rest unnoticed for various amounts of time on clean, organized shelves, lending themselves to "*visitors*" who may or may not wish to acquire said items. In my opinion, a Scottish Army mending kit was something a college drama club could have in their prop collection; I would want one if I were a stage manager. Who knows?

The blanket had a little tag sewn to the back and in the opposite corner of the torn, pulled corner. The tag read 1980; it was blue and had white letters, well, numbers. I suppose with this new clue; I was to assume that the blanket was about 40 years old—quite old for a blanket, but not necessarily so since it was first made of remarkably pure material.

God Himself had made the sheep, you know, and man had sheared them, carrying the fibrous fluff to the manufacturer who then stripped it, dyed it, blended it with strengtheners, and wove it into the miraculous masterpiece that I'm sure it was at one point. It had to be. It was just too something to be anything else. Still, I couldn't put my finger on it, even though all of my fingers and thumbs were utterly lost in it now, as I found a new thread from yet another box of do-dads and began making my way through the dense, plush wool with my ever so exciting needle; I can call it a needle since that's the closest thing it resembles, can't I?

Oh, the resourcefulness in me! I found a bit of steel and took almost the rest of the afternoon trying to fashion it into what would be used as a guide to lace the new threads through. Though the new thread wasn't the same color as the blanket, it would lend a bit of reason as a conversation starter whenever someone asked me about it. I fully intended now to keep the damn thing. I had grown not only used to it being in my hands, but now I was fond of it for some reason. I am such a romantic at times, and this blanket was my patient in terms of me healing it and restoring it to usefulness.

Fashioning the needle took a long time, and it wasn't easy either, as I had to find something to file the thickness of it down to a sharper point. This point would be hazardous indeed if someone were to prick themselves with its tip, but for me, I wanted it to be smooth so it could carry the thread through the wool without snagging it, causing yet another tear or perhaps worsening one that I was working on, to begin with. The needle needed to do the job correctly; I saw to that. I took tremendous and steady aim when I bore a hole at the top of the hammered top; I used an old wooden handled ball hammer to flatten the top, and then a tiny nail bore a hole so I could thread it.

Was I really this mad? What the hell had come over me; it's an old, worn-out blanket, and I was giving it the attention Florence Nightingale gave to one of her wounded patients on the battlefield – that's it, this was a hero; it must be. I was devoting too much time for it to be anything else. My mind was made up; this blanket would answer questions once it felt better about itself. I knew it.

Lucas called from the back of the store to thank me for my time as a new volunteer, and he told me to leave a bit earlier than the actual closing time because he was the only one he trusted with the finances, and he'd see to it that the doors were locked. I could come back, he said, if I wanted to. I left, waving good night to his back as he turned to lock up the rear door. I made some mention about taking the blanket, and his wave or gesture let me know he was OK with me taking it, and his chuckle let me know he thinks this American could use a few more screws in her head. Well, he's not wrong. I seem to obsess when I get something in my skull that I can't shake. I don't know if I'd call it a pit bull with a bone, but I'd go with Chihuahua any day. I don't give up easily, that's for sure.

I could make a bit more headway with the repairs at home, where I had more light, more thread, an actual needle, and a good pair of cutting scissors. I turned on the "telly," *as they call it here, and started watching a "football" game, which,* of course, you may have guessed, is actually soccer, but yeah, when in Rome. I'm not about to try and convince anyone that the sport they call football isn't football because I'm not in my backyard now, am I? Nope, grin, laugh with them, walk away, ask me questions about it, and that's the plan.

Meanwhile, back on the couch, the blanket and I were beginning to get a little friendly. He was keeping my feet and legs warm while I was poking him and drawing my hap-hazard needle through his skin. I didn't find a strong enough needle in my belongings to do the job, so I just stuck with what I had made. It was working, and it gave me satisfaction to know I had made this happen in the first place.

Eleven holes. Done. Eleven various shaped, various pulled, variously various holes that could have been explained if my new friend could talk, but one was caused by being burned. That was unmistakable. Someone had either fallen asleep with the blanket and burned it, or maybe they were just too close to someone who was smoking, and things got rough. Whatever happened, the blanket took the brunt of it, and weirdly (I say that word often), the burned hole was the one hole that didn't need mending as it was cauterized and wasn't spreading; it was just there. I couldn't fix that one without pulling the material and causing a gather or pucker so that one was left as it is, tattooed forever into the flesh of the blanket close to the tag bore his age. Tattooed. Interesting re-thought.

I was finished with the repairs, and the commentators were about to end their rants about Scotland's national team at the same time. I will never understand how a 90-minute game can go on for an hour after it's over, and the deciding goals or points can be determined by penalties rather than actual play on the field. In REAL football, a penalty is dealt with right then and there, you move the ball back a few yards, and you move on; none of this time added and bickering over who gets a yellow warning and who gets a red card. In our game of football, the only cards being played are the aces up the sleeves of the quarterback as he steps into his pocket to see where he'll end up throwing the damn ball – with his

HANDS! Hands all over the ball; you know, football. Never mind. No amount of complaining was ever going to change anything.

With the brightly colored mending thread lying across and inside the older, duller-colored blanket, I had to ask myself if I should have waited to find a closer matching thread to make my repairs. I mean, given the time and effort I put into it, there's no way I would undo the work and start over; it was going to have to be OK the way it was – something inside me said the blanket really wouldn't work less, feel less, be less, or even care less if I had used rainbow thread; it was fixed! It was useful now or would be after I had given it a good soak in some cold, soapy water.

I decided to hand wash it in the tub rather than chance it being damaged in the washing machine. Besides, having my hands all over it, rubbing it, feeling it, and loving it made me realize that it really was mine now. I hadn't paid for it, but it was tossed and thrown away, and I had been allowed to redeem it. Redeem. I thought about that word. Hadn't I been redeemed? I was.

The dirt and filth that came off that blanket when I drained the bathtub! I decided to give it another bath just for good measure. I wondered where it had laid and on what surfaces. There must have been at least a half-pound of dust and dirt hidden within the woven stitches, unseen but detected by my nostrils to a degree. I knew something was there, but I had no idea. I was both surprised and pleased when I lifted it out of the final rinse and began slowly wringing it, massaging all of the water from its grip - - massage, that's an odd word to use, but that's exactly what I was doing to it. I was massaging it.

Being an American, I had determined not to use a *"green line,"* what we called a clothesline when I knew I was moving to Scotland over a year ago. I had made plans to buy a dryer at their equivalent to Home Depot, a store called *Screwfix,* and buy a dryer I did! I bought a big, fat, heavy-duty, expensive dryer that I knew I would use every week if I needed to. Still, I was not about to be someone getting caught in an unexpected serial rainstorm and having to bring my laundry in after having hung it out only 15 minutes beforehand. This being winter, and the skies deciding not only to rain but to snow and blow wind simultaneously, I knew I had made the right decision.

Throwing in a few scented dryer sheets was a given for this project. The blanket's fluff would be restored soon enough, and to be honest with you, I was looking forward to seeing just how wonderful it could be given the love and care it deserved. I wondered how much it may change (if at all) with the heat from the dryer – I decided to turn the temperature down a smidge, but I wanted the blanket to feel fresh and toasty since it would be sleeping with me, in fact laying on top of me tonight. That wasn't my initial plan;

it wasn't like I ran out to the dumpster and grabbed the old thing to force it to do my bidding, but something told me that the blanket, once returned to health, would want to repay me with kindness; the type of kindness he was created to give. I was right.

When the bell from the dryer dinged to let me know my charge was finished, I looked up at the clock. I don't know why I did that; it was just that maybe the bell sounded a bit like a chime. I looked up, and it was one o'clock in the morning. One ding, one o'clock. How fitting. The blanket and I made ourselves newly acquainted; me with hardly any clothes on, mind you, and he with his freshly stitched scars being amply displayed for anyone to see and notice.

There was no hiding the fact, the truth, that he was broken, hurt, marred from years of abuse and wear. He may have been thrilled to be given a new assignment, or maybe he was feeling open and exposed because everyone would see his painful past being covered up, and perhaps I was overthinking this a bit!

My bedroom was upstairs, and it was time to say goodnight to the house plants, put the coffee in the maker, and prepare the alarms for the night to secure my house. I should have done that when I first came home, but the blanket kept my mind from routine thinking. It was going to be OK, I told him. He would be with friends and never be discarded again; he would never sleep rough again, not if I had anything to say about it, and I did have a say in the matter. He had a home now. He was loved, and even though I don't know everything about his past, and he certainly has no idea how many blankets I've slept with - - I don't think he gave a damn; he fit right in on top of my other comforters, and no, I didn't even try to hide the fact that he was patched up; I let my night-light light up the colors on him, and on everything new about him - - and now, well *"everything glows."*

Ten

Charlie's text wasn't exactly ominous, but it was vague enough to make her wonder what was happening. She hadn't even considered there ever being a reason not to volunteer at the Hammons on any particular day, except the hurricane that had kept them from their work, but there it was, right in front of her on the little screen. If she misread it, she at least wanted to know what Charlie had meant. All he had said in the text was, *"Not today, there's been a situation. Fill you in later, thanks."* Mathew, Dempsey, and others received the exact group text.

"I didn't even realize I was in a group text," Leigh told herself; it must mean she's part of the overall group on a more permanent basis, but what could have happened at the projects that would cause Charlie to cancel a routine weekly visit to help, she wondered. This was the week she and Mrs. Dempsey, Carianne, had promised to show her a faster and more efficient way to restore broken blinds. They didn't need to be replaced but refurbished. It may not be something her old self would have been interested in; she would not have been willing to even think about such things when all that mattered was building her portfolio, but it mattered now. Everything changed; everything.

His chest rose and lowered repeatedly with the weight of what he was about to relay to Leigh. Charlie Garrett, pastor, and friend, rubbed the bridge of his nose with his thumb for no other reason but to buy him more time before answering. He wanted to choose his words. He inhaled hard before nodding his head as if to give himself the go-ahead while signaling to his wife that this conversation may take a little longer than he thought it *might*.

"I'm afraid we won't be able to go into the Hammons for a while yet." He started. He looked around the room, his gaze falling on the box of donated items Hideko had arranged and the new stack of inexpensive bibles that had come in from Amazon; again, more donations for the people he had hoped to meet and help that day. The donation boxes were filled with supplies: bandages, washcloths, simple household cleaners, and small brushes to be used to clean. Where the old brushes ended up is anyone's guess, but they always seemed to need more.

"The authorities have asked anyone who isn't an actual resident of the place to stay clear for a while until they can sort it all out. It's mostly for our safety, but I wonder if we're not there to shed a little light on those being questioned and if they'll be taken advantage of.

"You can tell someone all day long that they have the right to remain silent and not to speak, but the uneducated tend to sound off when maybe they should shut up." He said, realizing he was becoming emotional over the matter. Charlie was more than just a pastor; he was a friend and a community leader, and his military training in the Air Force was constantly

reminding him that his role was more than just to volunteer his time; he was a shepherd; he was to protect as well.

"I don't mean to sound harsh, not that, but when people get nervous, even when they're not guilty of something, they can blurt out something, and it may or may not be used against them. Once you're arrested, you're there to expose what all happened. I've seen plenty of folks arrested who weren't guilty, but the police question them, knowing they'll talk because they don't or can't afford an attorney to tell them to keep their mouths closed. I'm not an attorney, but I can at least.... I could have told them to wait to speak until they got one." Charlie lamented, looking heavily at Leigh, who held one of Charlie's dogs in her lap.

"Tosha! You picked a good one. She's Hideko's favorite. She's liable to lick you to death, though; you've been warned." Charlie laughed, scooping up another tiny black and white mixed breed Chihuahua before continuing. *"There was a fire, and when they got to it, there was a body, or someone they thought was dead; I think I heard over the scanner that they took the person to the hospital alive. We'll certainly want to pray for them. If we don't know exactly who it is, God does."* Charlie's heart beat faster, his eyes closed tightly, thinking about the heartache and the chaos that must be swirling around the family of the one who was injured in the fire.

"Dempsey hasn't told me; I got the news from another fireman, Kenny Foyr. He doesn't attend here; he's the junior pastor for the new church on Shore

Road; like Dempsey, he's been with Sarasota Fire for many years. He told me that they arrested someone and that they, I think, said it was a woman; now that I think about it, I think he said she would be arrested for attempted murder as well as for arson. If that's the case," he reasoned with himself, *"...the person didn't die; otherwise, it would be murder, so yeah, they must have survived. Maybe they'll be lucky, and it'll just be smoke inhalation."* His words tapered as he spoke.

"I know how much you were looking forward to going today, and I hate to disappoint you, but we'll make it back out there soon, and we won't be there to muddle up any evidence they're shifting through now to figure out what happened." While Charlie and Leigh talked, a rap on the door indicated another would-be volunteer sought information and instruction; this time, it was Carianne Dempsey. She had more intel to share and didn't want to do so over text.

After the four of them spoke, the three women resigned to the small dining table off the side of the kitchen to have tea and discuss the families of the Hammons and what may be the best plan to continue their limited involvement as most of the time Charlie and the other men who had volunteered had kept women from joining them on their weekly practice of helping. Maybe there were families nearby, the women thought, who needed assistance with a less physical element, just perhaps a talking thing – someplace they could meet and have open discussions like one might find at an AA meeting, but for people hurting from life.

Leigh's mind began to wander during their conversation; she began thinking intensely about what it would look like to start up such a place. She could see how much passion and care it would require to pull it off, and it touched her deeply in a way she hadn't been familiar with before moving to Sarasota. Leaning forward in her chair, resting her elbows on the table, Leigh interrupted the flow of the ladies as they chatted; she tapped her chin and made a little grunting noise to indicate she had something to say.

"Just thinking out loud here, but we could even organize workshops or classes to teach them skillsets such as cooking, cleaning, sewing, writing, whatever each of us has to offer. I think Debra Tilley mentioned she taught art classes at the community college a few years ago. That could be something some of the women would enjoy."

Her words began to take on a new life of their own. Hideko smiled excitedly, saying that volunteering her cooking skills would be so satisfying. She had always wanted to train others how to prepare Japanese cuisine, and this idea, if it took flight, could be her chance. She hadn't given it much thought before, but if someone were willing to give her the opportunity and have a place she could set up, a place other than her own home, she would be happy to try it.

Quietly, with a distinct purpose, Hideko let her thoughts be known. She felt confident with Carianne and now with Leigh that she had something they could hear and agree with. *"I wouldn't mind training them how to cook; just a few lessons would be all it would take. We could start with the basics and build up from there. We could do a dish a week after everyone was familiar with how to prepare a meal to be efficient."* She added, *"I'd love to do it; let's try. Let's see what we can do. I know Charlie will help us find a place; we couldn't have them come to our houses; that wouldn't be safe."*

After some brainstorming, the three women mustered a plan that included finding a place to host cooking and crafting and having an area where children of different ages could rest or play. At the same time, their mothers communed, studied, and learned. *"We could rotate the classes or have two or three choices going simultaneously,"* Carianne boasted. *"I can teach simple home economics and how to save money but make a house homey and comfortable. I've been doing it for years,"* she added that she had a penchant for clipping coupons, too, but in today's world of app-this and app-that, she hadn't been able to find as many shopping flyers.

"Now that I said that out loud, I think maybe I would want to start by teaching them how to grab the best parking spot and the art of trying to find a buggy that didn't rattle as badly as all the rest," she laughed.

Excitement bubbled within Leigh as she listened to the women's eager commitments coming to life. They agreed to meet again in a week at Charlie and Hideko's to plan out the bare bones of what it would take to make it all happen. Each woman promised the others to think hard about the project and put in enough time and thought to see it through.

Leigh leaned forward to speak, her eyes catching those of Charlie's courageous wife. She knew a man who could influence her the way Charlie had over the past few years, must have a light shining in his heart. Leigh knew it sounded a bit cliché to say it out loud, but she believed that behind every good man was a strong and confident woman, helping him to become who he needed to become.

"You're an amazing woman, Hideko Garrett." She stated. *"I'll reach out to my contacts as well, find someone who may own property in the area that we can either rent, or maybe I'll just buy something we can use and consider it my contribution to the whole thing. That may make more sense now that I think about it. I can't make promises, but if we're going to do this, and I think we will, it's because we have different gifts to offer.*

"I do cook; I'm not bad at it, but you're right; learning to cook differently would be something every woman would be interested in doing if they believed it could build a bit of confidence within them. I see that. I could teach finance, the basics. I wouldn't want to lead off with investment strategies when the folks we're talking to need to know how to open a checking account and keep the books balanced."

As they sat back against their chairs smiling, all three women seemed to glow inside themselves with hope as they shared their unique ideas and thoughts about the future of their project. Their combined energy was infectious, to say the least; the room was filled with a palpable sense of hope and camaraderie. Hideko smiled as she turned from one woman to the next, her eyes beginning to fill with warmth and compassion. She couldn't speak, she couldn't say another word.

Leigh took a moment to savor the sight of the three of them before realizing it was almost as if a tiny light had illuminated the scene. Here she was, a typical American woman from the South, white, nearly middle-aged, but on the younger side, sitting with two women of color or minority. Both women were older and wiser, yet they had two very distinct things in common: they believed in themselves and hoped to help others.

Interrupting the moment, Charlie entered the room excitedly, accompanied by tiny nails rattling on the tile. He swung open the back door of the beachside house to allow the herd of dogs to scamper outside for a few moments of play and relaxation. As he stood in the kitchen, holding the door for a lingering moment, his eyes fell naturally to the women just a few feet away. *"No, no..."* he said laughing, *"... something is goin' on here. There's no way three women are in the same room, and there's no sound coming out of at least one. If it's this quiet, something big must be happening!"* He wasn't wrong.

Reaching down to pet the last dog who hadn't entirely made his way out the door, Charlie ruffled the fur of the smaller dog in the pack. His fingers automatically found the worn blue leather collar adoring the dog's neck. Looking at the tiny bone-shaped I.D. tag, he laughed. *"It's been a minute since we had that phone number, buddy. If you ever got lost, they'd have a hard time trying to find us. I wonder who they'd reach if they called it."*

Taking in another few seconds of the morning sun before closing the door to give the dogs their me-time, the pastor silently sighed to himself, somehow realizing that his life was about to take another involuntary turn, which would no doubt revolve around volunteering.

Eleven

HMP at Burmington, London, England, continued to execute prisoners right up to the middle of the year 1961, when Edwin Bush was hung for the crimes he had committed earlier that same year. On March 3, 1961, the body of a shop worker had been found in the back of the store, brutally murdered by someone using at least two distinctly sharp weapons, and perhaps a third. Two knives remained inside the body of the elderly clerk, who some said had never known a stranger; she was the epitome of hospitable. Her murder shocked the city to its core.

Dr. Emilio Castille, a London-born man of exciting background and makeup, stood in the center of the commercial bookstore on Broad Street talking about and hawking his first book, *"The Art of Psychosis."* As Dr. Castille explained it, Edwin Bush, the murderer in the case at hand, suffered from an uncommon but not completely rare disorder today known as scopophobia, a fear of being known or seen in public places.

Castille quickly explained it in layman's terms. He had taught long enough to realize that every entry-level student coming through his classroom door would learn at a completely different level than anyone else who may walk through the same doorway on the same day. For years, he had been able to reach his audience using his expressive eyes and facial reactions, underlining and punctuating whatever point he was trying to make. His strong British-tinged Cuban accent didn't hurt his chances of holding his audiences captive.

"The intriguing subject of scopophobia, as you may or may not know, is the intense fear of being looked at, watched, seen. Someone glances at you; it's not that big of a thing, but if you suffer from this very real disorder, someone staring at you may as well have laser beams for eyeballs!" Castille said, his eye widening as he leaned forward, awkwardly trying to pierce the air with his exaggerated stare. The audience, quite divided by their reactions, were very much in his control from that point forward.

The doctor explained that this feeling, this disorder, can lead to severe anxiety in a person who has the slightest bit of self-hate or another social ataxia. The opposite of scopophobia, it would seem, would be something akin to narcissism, a compulsion in a person to force themselves on others, to be the center of attention at all costs. This, of course, was not the case for the last man to be hanged at Burmington in the summer of 1961.

"The year itself, 1961, is an odd one as well. If you look at it, you see it for what it is: 1961." Dr. Castille said. *"Look at it while standing on your head, and believe it or not, it is still the same year!"* he said laughingly while demonstrating his point. With the agility of a man half his age. The prominent clinical psychologist, Dr. Emilio Rafael Castille, bounced himself into a fantastic headstand right there on the carpeted floor before the eyes of over three dozen witnesses before adding,

"Clearly, you can see, I have very little scopophobia going on in this head of mine." Before he could stop laughing both at himself and with the others, he noticed from his unusual position that someone was trying to ask him a question. Climbing downward and managing to straighten himself with the grace of a gazelle, Emilio Castille, once again balanced, stepped forward to introduce himself to the interloper.

"From that side of the world, your hand looked like it was digging into the ground rather than being raised," he stated. *"How can I help you? Do you have a question?"* The woman couldn't help herself. She found herself turning, bending in the middle, as the man repositioned, straightening himself to his full height, several inches under six feet tall. His unique coloring was enhanced by the amount of fresh blood that had rushed to his face and neck a moment earlier.

"You're Dr. Emilio Castille," she said, almost as if he wasn't unaware. *"I'm sorry, that was dumb; wow, you're Dr. Emilio Castille!"* she boldly commented, this time making more of a statement. *"I read all of your work while working on my thesis during my MBA. We*

had to do a few hours in Psych, so I chose your work to study. Let me thank you," she said, offering her hand.

"Your take on the unseen and the seen are exactly what I'm here to look up today. I was going to go to the library, but since I purchase everything now instead of borrowing it, I assumed I could pop into Barnes and Noble and find a book or two on the subject. I had no idea you would be here in person." Leigh's mind was blown.

After a few moments spent excusing himself from the others, Dr. Castille offered his hand in reciprocity to thank Leigh for *"saving him"* from the masses. *"If I had to be completely honest, sometimes crowds get me a little nervous. I'm OK with them when I'm teaching, and there's a natural barrier with the podium, but sometimes, being in front of just a few can make it seem like a stampede is approaching. I hope you'll let me buy you coffee or tea."* His words caught her off guard; she was just about to ask the same of him.

When Leigh ordered a tall unsweetened tea rather than something full of sugar, as most Southerners swore by, the good doctor was quick to take notice, mentioning that a person's preference, especially one so starkly independent of the social mores, was what set each person apart from the others. *"It's what makes you, you."* He said before adding that even though it was hot outside, he would always be a hot coffee drinker; none of that iced brew for him. *"I'm not a complete snob about it, but I won't lift a Maxwell House to my lips. Life is just too short for that nonsense."* He stated, and with that, the two of them had an understanding.

The next hour was spent exploring their opinions regarding topics such as exhibitionism, self-esteem-driven behaviors, and even atelophobia, or the persistent fear of being imperfect, not being what others expect of someone. *"My mother, a proper English socialite, expected me to follow in my father's footsteps and to become a mail carrier. I had the body for it, and we Castilles can walk for days without becoming exhausted."* Emilio stated.

"My father, being one of only two mail carriers in the small Cuban community outside of Manchester, where we were all raised, took me on his routes, hoping I would catch the bug to want to take over so he could either retire early or he could count on me to do most of the heavy lifting. Instead, because I don't suffer from atelophobia, which, as you know, is the fear of being imperfect, I decided to do my own thing; I studied the brain. There's a reason for it." He wanted her to know.

When Emilio was a teen, he had first read about the murder of the shopkeeper in London, the one he talked about in the closing statement of his monologue when he promoted his book. *"People said things like she was the epitome of niceness, no one hated her, she got along with everyone. No one could believe she had been brutally murdered, so viciously attacked by someone who no one had ever heard about.*

"She had lived in the area for maybe five months, yet everyone knew her; the killer had been there his entire life! He was there every day, working,

attending school, not being seen. See the difference?" he asked, trying to bring to light how a person is perceived, which has or could have much to do with how they behave. Because the shopkeeper was so chummy and outspoken, she was received well. The contrast between herself and her killer couldn't have been more severe.

Leigh tried to think harder about it, remembering the sixteen personality traits accredited to the research of the Myers-Briggs team. She tried to put two and two together, realizing that the murderer must be an introvert while the victim is an extrovert. It had to be more than just the *"I"* versus the *"E"*; there were other factors. Myers and Briggs were a mother-and-daughter team inspired by another study of human behavior, which indicated that natural-born traits are literally embedded into a person's makeup: his or her hardwiring.

The killer, Leigh knew, would have exhibited similar traits to people who became frustrated, enraged, or angry enough to kill. In contrast, the shopkeeper would have instinctively had traits in her personality that closely resembled countless others who were outspoken, easy to approach, trusting, and trustworthy. There were always two sides to the coin, every coin. No one is all good, and no one is all bad; then again, things considered normal are neither good nor bad. They are deemed expected behaviors.

Why, she wondered, would or could it happen that a random man walked into a random store, much like the one the two of them were sitting in, and openly attacked someone who had never wronged him in the past? There must be more to the story. When she asked, Castille explained that she, the keeper of the store, didn't have the authority to haggle prices with the man.

He told the police after he was arrested for her murder that in his country, it was customary to ask for less, and then the shop owners or workers would come to an agreement. The man became frustrated when the woman refused to play the pricing game. He relied on an old custom that was normal for him but foreign to her. This in and of itself wasn't the only reason for his attack, but it was an underlying and foreboding current of built-up steam that had to release itself, and it did.

"There's a term for it in Psychology. It's called 'Traditionalism,' and we're all guilty of it; we're guilty of doing it, having it, and forcing our customs or norms on others. We're all traditional about something, but when you allow it to take over your mind and add an intrinsic value to it, to the point that it rules your behavior, a person can become manic."

His words thumped hard in her mind as she inhaled another breath, and she remembered all the times she had either told someone she had always done things this or that way or when she wanted to break from a tradition but could not do so for fear of being outcast for her desire. It was the same when she tried unfriending someone on her social media platforms. She couldn't go through with it because doing so would upset someone else she was connected to; someone who wouldn't understand why she had let their other friend or relative be cut off from the etherland of followers. Or worse, the person she wanted to unfriend could cause trouble or embarrassment for her; either way, it was nearly impossible to do.

"I understand completely. I may know more today than thirty, sixty, ninety days ago. I worked in New York City as a financial advisor for a top firm. I was there almost six years, and when you say things are traditional, you're talking about nearly two hundred years of doing things the same way because so-and-so did it that way, so it's good enough for everyone else.

"Sure, we used the most up-to-date digital means to get the intel we needed, but to the last breath of the last minute of the market for the day, we relied on good old-fashioned traditions which have been proven right and wrong so often no one even knows who to trust; so we trust ourselves," Leigh confessed.

Dr. Castille let his reader in on another unspoken secret in Psychology. He told her people with lower incomes, the down of luck, often relied on their employers or immediate supervisors to be genuinely correct about almost any subject matter; their position warranted them being regarded as untouchable. His words rang clear; they hurt, but they were necessarily spoken. If she was a student of the studies and truly wanted to know why some people end up repeating the same unfortunate patterns, he was apt to let her in on the more likely reasoning.

"Leigh, these people you've been telling me about at the projects, those at the Hammons, they have a community, and it's not unlike what you'll find in a typical prison system." As he spoke, Leigh found herself nodding in agreement. It wasn't forced, but

126

something she knew to be involuntary. This was precisely how she felt about them. They were isolated, some by choice, others by situation and circumstances. They had to weave their lives accordingly to survive.

"If a person comes into a prison, they will go through a period where they are tested, and sometimes they do the testing, to see where it is that they fit in with the pecking order of that place as opposed to where they had just come from; be it another prison, or wherever they may have lived. They had to earn their new slot no matter where they came from or their position.

"No one will step aside and simply give them the top slot without cause or reason. Oh sure," he said, *"there will be those who step aside, even hurriedly, giving up their spot because they saw in the other person something they didn't want to confront, but there will always be another ladder for the newcomer to climb.*

"He, well, or she, in cases of women going to prison or living in these types of housing units, will never pick up exactly where they left off. It can be debilitating, crippling to the point that they never recover, and, to the contrary, they may see it as an opportunity to finally be the one in control if they have the moxie to force the incumbent off their throne, so to speak."

Dr. Castille's words and generosity remained with Leigh for several days. Reading and rereading the notes from her old courses led her to recall the various stages of these disorders mentioned in the recently published book by Castille. Conditions such as zero-sum bias played a role in everyone's life. The birth order of a child could force a kid into having the feeling that the parents loved another sibling more; thereby, it makes sense to the one that there must be less love to share, which is never true, but the bias remains, creating and recreating feelings of lower self-worth.

Zero-sum bias is real. The one sibling will ask, why keep trying if it will only bring the same results? If children can't earn the love or respect they crave because they believe they aren't allowed to prove themselves, they often fall short in many other situations. Could the shopkeeper's murderer have been a middle child, perhaps? Studies show that more people are murdered by those born as middle children than by any other birth order. According to another survey, middle-child birth order children are most susceptible to other irrational behaviors such as suicide, self-injury, and other threatening behaviors.

Females, it turns out, are even more likely to self-injure, while males are more likely to kill someone else other than themselves. Leigh thought about it. She was the first of three girls, and yes, she could easily peg her sister Macy as a serial killer; if Teddy bears and Barbie dolls were any indication of the facts related to the syndrome, Macy was a simple statistic just waiting to walk into the wrong place at the wrong time, while their littlest sister Jewel couldn't do anything wrong; ever.

Twelve

The following weeks passed with enough busy work regarding the plans to create a new space for women and children, not only from the Hammons but anyone and everyone who needed or wanted a place to come and stay an hour or so to learn a lesson or two, maybe just playing board games, or shooting pool if they could find a couple of old tables that could be refurbished.

Mathew was flattered when Leigh asked him to assist with the women's resort, asking him to consider teaching the women or the older kids how to play guitar. *"That's a great idea,"* he said, his voice steady and trying to remain calm. *"I'll do my best to find some second-hand guitars to use, but I won't be much help buying them once I find them,"* he added. *"I can check Craigslist and Facebook Marketplace for sure. There's a small flea market on Superior, too, so I'll hit it up if you like."*

Before doing so, Leigh ensured she had not drawn anyone else's attention. She handed Mathew a small roll of cash he could open at another time; she knew she could trust him not to use it for himself. He hesitated momentarily; accepting the money went against everything he had ever believed. He may be poor, but he had principles and couldn't see why he should start changing his ways now. *"I won't use it for anything but the guitars, and I'll bring you every receipt,"* he told her. He needed her nod and smile to assure himself they were good; this wasn't about him, and he knew it.

They had all gathered at Charlie's place to discuss the storefront resort and the plans each woman had worked on for the past week or two. When they had met for the second time, they discussed the collective idea to put their thoughts in writing, to organize them, and to give the others a sort of shadowbox preemptive peek at what they had come up with, assuring one another that they were all thinking along the same lines. Each woman had a different perspective and looked forward to learning new things.

"Before we get too excited about it, we must eat!" Mathew said, standing up and brushing off his pants in a make-believe attempt at being a little posh and pious. *"It's my turn to cook, Hideko; you've done enough this week. I have something in mind that will bring everyone back for seconds, and if you're perfect and fortunate at the same time, I'll even let you have a sneak peek while I'm in there spinning my magic. I'd ask if you have any preferences, but I've already decided on a dish. We're having Cacio pepe tonight, a classic Roman pasta dish from long before Jesus took up reading in the Temple."* He mused, glancing over at Charlie to see if he could get a rise from his landlord and friend.

"It's not as simple as you think," he told them. *"The cheese can become rubbery and almost tasteless if you don't do it right, so I want you to pay close attention to the details; some of the best Italian chefs I worked with in the past considered this dish to be complicated but for some reason, it was never hard for me to do. I guess it's just that way regarding anything in life. What one can do another can't, which makes this the best dish for all of us."* He said, giving a nod to Leigh for all that she had shown and proven to him.

It was Carianne who did most of the searching when it came to the necessary supplies for the resort. Within an hour of clicking through Facebook Marketplace, she found four or five guitars within a few miles drive. Mathew went with her to pick them up the day before to handle the price negotiation and ensure they would be suitable for future play. Mathew's golden touch helped with restringing, tuning, and performing minor repairs needed to bring the instruments to the point that the one playing them would feel confident in doing so.

Within another week, the musical department of whatever it was that they were planning was complete. Mathew was excited and hadn't been so in quite a long time. This was his opportunity to showcase another side of himself, one that didn't involve food prep, which was, in fact, his first love but one that challenged him to use other skills for the greater good of others.

"You can teach them how to drive a stick shift, Leigh." Mathew teased, chuckling softly to himself, blushing under his beard. He had driven a shift when learning to drive, but as most people did, he learned on a car with the gears lower and to the side. Leigh's 1960 Chevy F-100 half-ton pickup had been through several transmission changes but had remained a manual driving machine. The fact that the gear shift was on the column made the thing that much more of an iconic dream mobile than anything else about it.

Mathew told Chief Dempsey and his wife that driving a car with a manual transition wasn't difficult if that's what you were trained on to begin with. Kids these days, he told them, would never have the lessons in life that an old car or truck, in Leigh's particular case, could teach them about using a lighter touch while forcing your weight into something that needed to be manhandled to manipulate it into doing exactly what you wanted and expected it to do.

"I guess it's a good thing I never became a father," he told them. *"I equate driving with survival. Who's to say I wouldn't throw one or two of my kids into the ocean to see if they could swim or not?"* He laughed before returning to the kitchen to check on his cheese and boil the pasta.

Leigh caught the awkward smiles being exchanged between the fire chief and his wife. The two had raised two highly energetic and intelligent girls, twins, who had both graduated top in their class, been accepted to prestigious colleges, and were both members of the university swim team. The couple were incredibly proud of their daughters, speaking of them often while hoping to see them more often than they did.

"I know you guys didn't throw them in head first when they were babies, am I right?" Mathew teased while measuring out the aged pecorino Romano cheese and determining the exact temperature of the open-flamed natural gas burner using his sense of smell and the way the heat approached his nostrils. Everything had to be precise; it had to be perfect, and this was one instance in his life he knew he could control if nothing else.

When the topic of the women's resort came up again, as Leigh expected it to, she was quite prepared to give her ideas and plans over to Hideko for approval, only to see that Hideko had the same thoughts; she was just about ready to hand over her ideas, typed and organized, to Leigh to see what she would think about them.

The resort, or what they often called the resort, would be small but not too small, small enough to manage. Leigh mentioned that if it took off, they could open up a second or even a third one closer to the projects, so the people at the Hammons wouldn't need to ride the bus to get to the first one. After making such a statement, Leigh was immediately struck with the thought that something so basic could take on such a life, requiring planning, permits, building contracts, remodels, fixings, fixtures, and more.

Each woman, including Carianne, had created a portfolio of sorts, outlining the details of what they believed would be the best-case scenarios with structured thoughts on who would teach what courses, how the layout of the space could be best utilized, and all without the foreknowledge of what the actual space would even look like. They all knew, without the others saying so, that the location couldn't be too close to the area where the Hammons were constructed. There was at least a two-mile radius surrounding the place that remained too dangerous to set up something like they had imagined.

Their plans were formulated out of mutual and exclusively independent faith in what they believed would become a reality. Dempsey mentioned the safety issue, while Charlie discussed the logistics of how to get the patrons to the place. It was great to see everyone thinking and making plans for it to take shape and become reality.

"Eventually, we'll need to develop a business plan if we're going to do it," Carianne suggested. *"I'll be honest: Doug and I are not keen or interested in digging into our savings to make something like this happen. We're OK with being silent partners and working with the groups, but we're unable to do more than we can. I hope I didn't lead anyone to think that we would be funding the project.*

"Doug's about to retire in a few months, and while he'll be officially out from under the Sarasota flag, he will consider working as a consultant for the State of Florida. Since I gave up teaching, I won't be tied to the house. We have plans to move about and see the state; take in what we can in our golden years...sort of yellowing years since we're only in our sixties." She laughed.

Leigh appreciated Carianne's honesty which came as a respite for Hideko, who had not needed too much of a reason to say that she, too, would be helpful on a once-a-week basis; she could afford to do that, and it would bring her much joy to do so. Still, with finances the way they were and how she often becomes overwhelmed when in the middle of many faces, she couldn't commit to more than she had mentioned regarding the cooking courses. The details were in the plans she had typed.

Mathew had been listening to the women as they exchanged notebooks and plans, as they talked about who could contribute to the resort and what could be expected of them. Knowing that it was Leigh's idea to open such a place, it wasn't the least surprising to him when he heard the two older women give their reasons for not becoming more closely involved. Within a few minutes of their conversation, he had pieced together enough from what he could hear to make the assumptions he knew would become facts.

He watched as Leigh took charge of the situation; not a single heartbeat skipped as she did. She hadn't become despondent or shown any sadness or disappointment; to his surprise, he saw the woman's mouth curl up into a sly, tiny smile. Her demeanor hadn't changed; it had been enhanced. She somehow knew that she would be the one to make the project a reality. She had the means, the motive, and the opportunity; others were there to assist. She knew that. Somehow, she knew that the others knew it too.

Mathew watched Leigh shift her weight in her chair before she spoke; she was just about ready to step off the edge of the proverbial cliff of life, it seemed, but she knew the waters below her would be deep enough and free of any obstacles - she had found a calling that at the moment seemed overwhelming to the man, but in that other part of his brain where he kept all of his secrets, he knew she was going to not only survive the ordeal but bring it to fruition in such a way that nothing else as it had ever been done in that part of their world. Knowing he would be a part of it filled him with unmeasurable pride, even if he had no business to feel the way he did.

Mathew divvied up his masterpiece as they continued to discuss the logistics of it all. The simple dish stirred the souls of anyone trying to make it; why was something so basic so hard to pull off? Life, as it turns out, was the attempt to create and recreate one's own Cacio pepe repeatedly. It's simple, yes, but when done right, it makes the most lasting impression on anyone privileged to be invited to the table.

"There's something comforting about it. It only has three ingredients, the sauce, I mean." He told them. *"You have to choose your pasta. I prefer spaghetti most of the time, but I also know that folks don't like eating long, stringy noodles in front of others, so I went with penne instead. You can dive in with your fork and not feel as if you have to decide when to cut it off before stuffing it into your mouth; all the while, you're watching to see what everyone else is doing."* He laughed. *"All I'm sayin' is if you analyze the best data when you have it, you can make a better decision when you need to."*

He looked around the group and found seven faces besides his own, all smiling, knowing that what they were about to enjoy would be memorable. When served with salad, fresh fruit, and a sprig or two of mint, the meal created an orchestra of senses between the smells, the sight of it, and, of course, the tastes. When it all came together, no one would have imagined that a meal such as they were being treated to could have been crafted by an unhomed man living behind their small church; the cold thought hit them collectively, but no one said anything about it.

The pastor, his wife, the fire chief, and his wife were known to Leigh, as her presence in the church had been nearly constant, but there were others present who had been conversing for quite a while, having never bee introduced. *"Oh, Leigh, I'm sorry,"* Charlie said, almost forgetting himself. *"This is Alessio Gallo and his friend and colleague Elena Conti. Both of them are from a couple of counties over from us and are into foo-foo dinners. I pull them over whenever Mathew wants to cook something special.*

"Eleana writes for a magazine, and she's been trying to get Mathew to give her an interview about his life, but you know him," Charlie said, giving Mathew a quick bump in the rib with his elbow, *"So maybe if you ask him nicely, he'll give Eleana a chance to tell a story or two about the greatest chef this town has ever seen...or hasn't seen...whichever it is."* Charlie smiled, and as he did, he caught Mathew turning on his heel. However, he could hear him laughing as he walked away.

"That guy! He's not ready, I guess." Charlie added, *"Maybe you start with something easy, like asking him to join us while we eat. He's been known to sit alone because he's not sure he can handle what others may say if they don't like what he's made. I keep telling him we'd love a bologna sandwich as long as it's given in love. This man, this guy, he's something else. I wish...."* Charlie said, and the others looked on, *"...I just wish he knew how very much we appreciate him."*

It seemed like hours had passed, but in reality, it had only been a few minutes when Mathew appeared from the other room; he had missed their initial expressions as they each took their first bites of the wonderfully crafted dinner. However, he managed to bring himself back, seating himself between Hideko and Leigh, facing the food critic as he did, and smiling, offering her a hope that she may be able to ask a few questions at least.

Mathew watched intensely, studying each of their faces for what he called slight reactions; some would call them *"tells"* if they were playing poker in a high-stakes game. As they took a few more bites, their expressions of delight and deep satisfaction brought a certain warmth to the man; he found himself relaxing into the moment.

"So, Leigh," he asked, turning the woman beside him, catching her in mid-chew as he did to draw attention away from himself, *"What do say you take me for a spin in that mint green jalopy of yours after dessert, so you can explain to me why it is a woman*

who could drive anything she could ever dream of, has decided on an old relic...er...vintage classic, I mean."

All eyes were fixated on Leigh as she tried to gain her balance in her chair. She had indeed been caught off guard by the statement. After a few seconds, allowing herself to think about it, she silently assured him with her eyes that his masterpiece had been greatly appreciated and that his decision to return to the table to be with them meant a great deal to her. When she could, she opened her mouth to ask, *"There's dessert?"*

Thirteen

The smaller, stale, sterile room was designed to put off anyone considering it. It was called an interrogation room for a reason. All but one wall was painted in such a bland grayish-tan color that even a framed photograph would complain of being associated with it if left hanging on them too long. To prevent any visual distraction, the room wasn't equipped with any external view, only a large plated glass window that showed one's reflection; someone was no doubt watching them from behind its façade.

The place could not have been more uninviting. The window allowing others to observe was foremost on the mind of Jamee Leard, the small woman of deep, rich color; the woman from Chad, a country without distinction other than no matter who said it, they typically said the name under their breath. Hadn't Chad been a place of hate, most recently talked about after several dozens of women and children's bodies were found burned and mutilated in an unmarked mass grave?

Poverty and malnutrition are rampant in most of the continent of Africa, but somehow Chad seemed to have it worse than most of the other often talked about countries. To exacerbate their issues further, gender-based violence was so common that usually, when a woman gave birth to a daughter, she or the midwife with her would terminate the newborn's life to give it a chance at peace from the beginning, not being willing to allow the grave to slowly suck her into it through the same cruel pattern of vicious actions forced upon most young girls and young women of the country.

Trying to remember the inmate's beginnings, her first and most formidable years, Captain J'Anna Bonet-Thomas brought her most sympathetic heart to the room to question the young mother and survivor; only this interview would have nothing to do with her days in Chad, but what led up to her decision to set fire to her apartment unit at the Hammons a few nights before. Why, the Captain needed to know, was Jamee Leard bent on ending her own life through the act of deliberate arson, but also the life of her nearly seventeen-year-old daughter Amara. Both needed to be taken to the hospital with severe smoke inhalation. There had to be a reason; most killing decisions aren't as spontaneous as the press or Hollywood would have us believe.

Captain Bonet-Thomas started the interview by offering the suspect a few snacks, giving her a blanket to wrap herself in, and a cup of hot coffee with sugar, no cream. She remembered meeting Jamee under better circumstances a few years back and celebrating her twenty-fifth birthday at the café where both had been privileged to call their first job. A teenage J'Anna Bonet, high school prom queen, twenty years before, had landed a job as a hostess up front, seating guests, while for Jamee, shortly after she had arrived in the States, was a backroom position of dishwasher but an opportunity to have a better life. The women were about the same age, but J'Anna Bonet had been promoted from hostess to assistant manager after a few years at the bakery and before she graduated college to pursue a career in Criminal Justice.

The Clark Bakery and Café on Main had been a staple in the community for several decades. Though most employees were admittedly of color, the clientele was anything but; it was a haven for anyone and everyone who passed to or from the shorelines of either of the two close beaches. The early and later hours meant more part-time employment was available to kids looking to earn a little to help their families. A young J'Anna had hired Jamee Cane, a young mother, before she had married briefly and changed her name to Leard. The two had kept in touch for a while before life intervened.

Being hired to work full-time meant freedom from her life on the streets of Sarasota; it meant Jamee would qualify for a housing unit at the Hammons. Being separated and on her way to divorce helped her cause. That was another time, a lifetime for one woman and only a few short moments for the other. Jamee was a hotbed for psychological study. Any given day, the woman could be watched, observed, even picked apart by those putting their mind and thoughts through the wringer trying to pinpoint exactly what she was suffering from, what could be the underlying motive for her next decision.

Access to education or healthcare in her home country was not only limited, it was nil for those who had no status, whose families were members of the lower chaste classes, as Jamee's was. Too often, there was talk of some intervention or potential awakening just on the cusp of happening; yet again and again, the hopes of most lives living in her community were dashed.

Until a good-intentioned missionary from Crandon, Ohio, had nearly abducted her to save her, Jamee had been used in the most unspeakable ways: trafficked for sex among those who lived in her community and the next at their whim when they chose because they chose. She had no defense; even her parents and her family were helpless while trying to protect her.

"Jamee," Captain Bonet-Thomas began the interview, swallowing hard and taking a moment to process the words she knew would be hard to hear, so uncomfortable to think about. *"You are not invisible. You are not disposable, either. I know you've seen your share and more tragedies in your life; I'm going to consider all of that, I promise."* Bonet-Thomas said.

"It never gets easier to face or to try and put it behind you; what you've been through is devastating. I know that. I want you to know that I know you've been mistreated, so very badly, but we have to discuss what you did," she told her, *"...and I know that your past played a large role in your actions."* Bonet-Thomas led, leaning closer to her subject, turning her

back to the two-way mirror. *"I want you to tell me what you were thinking, why you did it. But I also want you to look up,"* she told her.

"Do you see the red flashing light?" she asked. *"It's recording us. The microphones are pretty good, too, so I want to make it a lot easier for you to tell the truth; I think you'll understand it in a few minutes. I need to ask someone to turn off that camera first."*

Jamee couldn't face the Captain. Shame had mustered its way through and around her, consuming her in its wake. She could not face the window because she believed someone, maybe a few others, was staring at her, watching her, and waiting for her to say anything to give them an idea of what she was trying to stop from happening. She wasn't trying to kill her daughter or herself; she was trying to set them both free from the inevitable.

When the Captain came back into the room after a short absence, she asked Jamee to take another look up at the camera in the corner of the room. It was dead. There were no lights and no microphones. *"Jamee, I know some things that happened to you in Chad. I can't know how it was because I wasn't there; only you can know that. Still, I did read about some of the things women go through, and I tried to watch a documentary on it, girl, I promise, but I couldn't get through the first few minutes without losing my mind; it was so terrible the things you must have suffered.*

"All you wanted to do," the Captain encouraged, *"was to be unseen, to hide, to never be known or shown, but they forced you to be publicly used and humiliated. Your file says you were gang raped more*

144

than once by soldiers of the brutal opposition who came through your village, and I can't – I won't try to think of what they forced you to do. It's insane, to say the least. It's barbaric, and to be honest, it isn't even human. Those men were animals!" she told her captive.

The officer wanted the suspect to listen for several minutes and to follow her instructions to the letter. When it came time for a pause, the Captain waited, giving Jamee the time and space she knew she needed to try and open up to her regarding the night in question. There had to be a reason, maybe a few, and they most assuredly involved a pathology of depression, anxiety, overt self-hate, and probably a few more specific psychological theories yet to be determined.

Though the Captain and several others in the Sarasota Police Department had worked extensively with other survivors of similar atrocities, it felt helpless for them in cases like Jamee's, where the actions of others embedded such fear and caused such deeply seeded anger that the following action could be explosive or implosive; no one knew which. They tried to prepare themselves for whatever she would say or confess.

Since Jamee was given a nationalized citizenry after being rescued several years back, she fell under the same rules, laws, and regulations as any native-born American; the laws were the laws, and breaking them came with severe and swift consequences. The penalties for arson and attempted murder were not simple punishments to be administered in her particular case. Before Captain Bonet-Thomas would turn Jamee over to the system, she wanted to know a little more.

"We're talking off the record, Jamee. I know you've been arrested, and the officers at the scene told you that you had the right to remain silent, and you did yourself a big favor by adhering to that. Now, I want to extend to you something we call 'Queen for the Day'; it's not a pass or a get-out-of-jail card if you remember playing the game Monopoly; that's an American reference to an American game, but I think you understand what I'm trying to tell you.

"You'll have at least an hour to let everything off your chest and out in the open. You can say whatever you want to say, whatever you need to say right now, and nothing you say to me will be held against you." She told Jamee. She took out her tablet to search for the term *"Queen for the Day"* on a search engine. While scrolling through videos and other media, she finally came across the term as it was written about in a New York Times article, explaining that to be Queen for the Day meant that a subject could say anything they could say or wanted to say in their defense, and nothing could be used to harm them at their trial.

The Captain showed the digital article to Jamee, reading it to her, asking her if she understood What it was she was doing for her. *"Jamee, listen to me; I'll even put it in writing. The first thing I'll do when you say you understand me is to have the two men behind that window first turn off their camera too,"* she said, pointing to the black tinted window behind her, *"...and*

146

I'll ask them to leave the room they're in so no one but you and me are talking.

"No one Jamee, no one will hear what you say other than me. I won't record it; I won't repeat it. Do you understand?" The flushed and compassionate policewoman asked, hoping she would at least get a nod from the small woman beside her.

Uncurling herself after a few long silent minutes, Jamee Leard faced the Captain. Her dark, penetrating eyes were full of pain and redness. She couldn't cry another tear if she were forced. All of her emotions had been spent to the point of sheer numbness; the past seventy-odd hours had been as hard for her as the first fifteen years of her life. Jamee gave the Captain her hands and gave her a quick nod, indicating that she would accept her terms and tell her everything she could since not one word would be held against her.

"I know I'm going to jail for what I've done. I don't think I even thought about it before because I thought I would be dead. I thought the smoke would kill us both before the fire raged as it did." She said she had seen television shows where it happened that way, movies where people were trapped in rooms surrounded by fire, and minutes or seconds later, their bodies were found by authorities. *"I thought it would be like that,"* Jamee confessed. *"I thought I would just go to sleep and die; Amara was already sleeping. She would never know, and we would reunite with one another before the gates in heaven, up there, where there is only peace."* Her words cut deeply and without deceit.

An hour passed; Jamee could read the face of the old clock on the wall. It was 9:13 p.m.; she had been talking with the Captain as Queen for the Day for over an hour, but she had so much more to say. *"You'll be OK, keep talking. I'm not even looking at the time. We can stay here all night if you want to, Jamee. I want you to tell me exactly what happened and why you thought it was the only way to improve things for you and your daughter."*

The captain asked her subject to tell her more about Amara, about her birth, about finding herself pregnant when she had been rescued, how that could help her in the long run, and why she had chosen to keep the baby when in America, she could have given her up for adoption. The questions poured out of the policewoman and were answered as best they could be.

When Jamee asked J'Anna what her name meant, more of the story began to make more sense. *J'Anna* is mostly a new or modern name, she told Jamee, whereas the name the mother had chosen for her daughter Amara was older and more established. In Chad, where the baby should have been born, the child may have been smothered by the midwife before even being brought to her mother's bosom; she may not have been given a name.

In America, however, where Jamee was at the time of Amara's birth, the name was chosen and given to her by one of the nurses at Saint Anthony Hospital; it had a dual meaning: grace from bitterness and eternity. The baby was conceived violently and harshly, but she was received in love and given care.

"You said it earlier, J'Anna. I spent my life being afraid to be seen; the doctor I saw told me there was a word for what I did, but I don't remember it. I remember the words he told me about my desire to be accepted and do what I'm supposed to do because it's the right thing to do; something about going with the flow as long as it is on the right path. That is what I wanted for myself and Amara, but when the men who came to paint looked at her with the same eyes that I saw looking at me when I was her age, I feared the worst.

"They wanted her body. They came to our apartment pretending to be helpful but purposely painted our bedroom with two coats. They spent extended time looking at our things and discussing how beautiful Amara would be in a few years. A few years? I told myself no. They are trying to convince themselves that they will wait for her when I know what men do, and their eyes could not hide what they were thinking." She told the Captain.

"Two groups come to see us at the Hammons; the church people are welcome, and the others are not, but they come anyway we can't stop them. The housing people tell us that this is the way it is. First, Charlie's group comes to teach, to bring us hope, and to discuss our lives – they tell us ways to improve our situation, but then the Hammons send the others to do the painting and the pulling up of tile since we don't have carpet on our floors."

Jamee mentioned that these men they send are not from Charlie's church; they are usually high school boys or their coaches, earning points for social studies or something called D.E.C.A. Jamee wasn't sure what it stood for. She only knew that they came in packs of two or more grown men and usually closed the doors trapping Jamee and Amara in the apartment with them she mentioned.

Captain Bonet-Thomas knew all about the D.E.C.A. kids from Sarasota High School, as she was very involved in their programs, helping the juniors and seniors in the program with finding community efforts to achieve bonus points; this was one of many ways the nationwide school program, but Jamee was talking about grown men, the kids in the Distributive Education Clubs of America were anything but adults; they were high school students who were organized to market, manage, and create entrepreneurship among themselves. They were certainly not painters, carpet or tile pullers, or even community outreach folk; this D.E.C.A. she spoke of must have been entirely different.

"Let me look up the group you're talking about, Jamee because I think there could be a real confusion. You're saying that the men, not boys, not teenagers, but men who came to your apartment were there to improve it, fix it, and make it more livable, right? They didn't come to talk to you about work, your job, or finances, marketing, nothing like that?" she asked. When it was understood that the men who had painted the room and had said they'd be back had nothing to do with the school system where her young daughter was a student, the pieces began to fall into place for both.

What the captain found, after making a few phone calls, was that the D.E.C.A. Jamee had seen on the paperwork in her apartment had not been the secondary education program geared to build and strengthen the youthful minds of America's future but stood for the Disciples Encouraging Community Advancement; an extended family or branch of several Christian organizations such as the Salvation Army, churches, youth groups and more.

Their mission or work involved exactly what Jamee described: volunteer work for improving housing projects, picking up trash, providing food for the elderly, and even collecting donations of clothing and household goods to distribute for free to those in need. There could be a rotten egg among them; anything was possible, but Captain Bonet-Thomas took a note about the group, purposely meaning to check out who strictly had been assigned to paint the inside of Jamee and Amara's apartment a few days before.

Bonet-Thomas couldn't imagine what one or the other of the men had said to make Jamee feel as if returning to their apartment would mean whatever she believed it meant; they likely only meant that they had either run out of paint and would need to return later, or they weren't finished with the make-ready or remodel and needed Jamee to know they would have to make a second trip.

"You didn't feel safe around them? Did they say or do something that made you nervous? Could you just have reported it to their sponsor? What was the reasoning behind the fire? I don't understand." She confessed. To Bonet-Thomas, the acts of the men seemed typically normal and weren't threatening unless one of them had become suspicious once they began their work.

"Jamee, the D.E.C.A. we're talking about now are not just in Sarasota. They are a national group with thousands and thousands of volunteers, both men and women. I think the Hammons prefer...no, I know the Hammons insist on allowing only men to come into the units to do the work because of past experiences with the workers being the targeted ones.

"Are you telling me that no one at the Hammons has ever threatened you or your daughter but that these seemingly good souls who were there to help improve your life caused you fear the worst?" the captain asked. If one or the other man in the apartment had been less than professional, their sponsors should be made aware. Still, given the tiny captive's heightened fears and the mind set over what could be an impossible challenge to overcome, things started to click.

After explaining her reasoning, the mother found solace in having a friend to describe her feelings to, if only for an hour or so because she was Queen for a Day. *"J'Anna, I love my Amara more than life. Because of this love, I would have taken her with me to the other side, freeing us from any fear, pain, or hurt. I know her beauty – I see it every day.*

"No matter how hard I try to mask it by asking her to wear her hoodie in public or to consider lowering her face when we are in places, I know men see her. I cannot keep her hidden forever, but I could....at least I thought I could protect her from a future so sickening she would be scarred by it as I was."

Fourteen

It was a time of reckoning. Mathew leaned back against the seat of the old truck, where he had been admiring the new remodel from inside the cab. From his point of view, only the truck's exterior shape remained authentic and original. Everything else looked newer than new, brighter, smoother, in its place, and for that matter, a candidate for showcasing what could be done when one sets their mind to restoring something as unique as her grandfather's *"jalopy,"* as he called it.

Leigh faced Mathew from the driver's seat, her eyes filled with curiosity and perhaps a little concern. *"You promised me you'd tell me all about your stint as a top chef, what it took to get to that point, what you did while you were recognized, and all about the fall from grace."* She said while taking another scoop of her Sonic Oreo cookie blast; though full of sugary goodness, she knew it would catch up to her later.

Sugar and ice be damned, she told herself, she could take a brain freeze if it meant hearing the things she hoped to hear from him, so she could better understand him. He was like a jigsaw puzzle made up of many shades of any one color, hard to pinpoint. It's easy to get lost trying to figure the man out; she wanted

153

to try repeatedly. If probing open-ended questions were his love language, she was apt to use them.

"Tell me everything, and don't forget to leave out the part about the gangsters either; you know I love a good mob story." She told him. *"You can even embellish that part if you want to. They can take you out back, turn you inside out, and then hang you from the roof of one of the ten or fifteen-story parking lots on Michigan Avenue. I want to hear it from the horse's mouth!"*

His smile turned upward on one side of his mouth but remained a bit crooked on the other. Trying to find the right words would be difficult if he wanted to tell her the truth without taking the real chance that she'd run away, drive away, or somehow get away from him. He had become accustomed to her blunt and often aggressive way of expressing her thoughts; it wasn't something he had ever mastered, but he could always admire a woman, anyone, who could find a piece of ground they preferred and stand on it.

"That's more or less it right there: a horse's mouth, or maybe I'm the other end more often than not." He laughed, taking a drink and finishing the last of his tater tots. *"We've all seen pictures of horses on balconies in the middle of the French Quarter during Marti Gras or someone letting their horse roam into their house; we watch videos of it kicking the hell out of the glass shower, right?*

"Well, it's like that for me. I was never in the right place at the right time. I was always out of place and in the wrong place because I allowed it or maybe because I was invited. I don't know. It wasn't good,

and it took being kicked pretty hard to get it through my head that what I was doing wasn't working out too well." He began.

"It started back in Kansas City if I'm honest. I was raised in Springfield, Missouri, but attended college in K.C. I had always wanted to be a chef, maybe not necessarily one as popular as I became, certainly not one associated with the Chicago families the way it ended up being. I wanted to cook. I wanted to prep. I wanted to design, create, and be a master in my kitchen. That's it; I wanted to say 'this is my house' and let the world know that any mark I made was mine to make." Mathew took another sip before continuing his story.

When he had finished telling her all about his life as a student at Esteffoil School of Culinary Arts, he promised to *"circle back"* to the women and the night he was talked into running through Lee Summit naked as a jaybird for a prank. This particular story piqued the woman's curiosity to the point that she pointed out that in one of her college courses, she had been taught that the strong emotional pull of being curious was greater than most people knew.

"Did you know that a person given an envelope by a stranger with their name on it is far more likely to be opened by that person than if someone they knew had given them the same envelope?" she asked. He hadn't heard the concept but could wrap his head around it.

"Sure, that makes sense," he told her. *"If I don't know you, and you give me something, I'm gonna want to see what it's all about, but if I do know you,*

I'm far more likely to know you well enough to guess whatever you gave me. It's going to fit in with what I know about you." He said.

They both agreed, and Leigh stuffed her mouth again with another full scoop of her deliciously melted creamy drink, giving her captive the nod to coax him into continuing his story. He had become her entertainment, but somehow, the man didn't mind. He'd buy the next round if it meant she'd let him stay with her a little longer.

"There I was, working my way up in the world of cooking so I could eventually work for someone who could teach me the ropes, not what they teach you in school. It's never the same. The people who enter your restaurant differ from those on television or in the movies. They aren't usually dressed as well and don't leave their attitudes outside.

"They bring their rudeness, their narrow-minded idiot mouths with them, and most of the time, when I'm honest with myself, I found myself not making too big of a splash so no one would care to thank me. Remember, I had to make it good enough so they didn't want to call me out in front of everyone. People think, for some reason, that a chef can step out of the kitchen to be given a compliment or a scolding. That's not really what we sign up for; not really." He stated.

"Long hours and nights passed. I paid my dues, I guess you'd say. When I knew a decent food critic was in the house, I paid attention; I babied them. I met important people who ensured I had the setup I needed; they said it was a gift. Not like your gifts, OK?

They had a way of not paying the tip, if you know what I mean; I was expected to pick up the real tab — to either lie for them or die for them; my choice.

"It happened any number of times in Missouri's best restaurants, but if you are going to be a star in Missouri, you have to go where the fire burns the brightest. It burns bright where the big names and beautiful people are. It burns brightest where the money is and where they don't post the price of a meal on the menu. That was the world I was playing in, and I loved it.

"If you want to make it in the world of food, you have to go to Chicago, New York, Milan, Paris, London, Miami, and yeah, that's what I did. I chose Chicago; it was closer to my family and more affordable than any other city. I had a backward sort of quiet aggressiveness that lent its value in a city like Chicago, where, as you know, attracts a certain clientele occasionally."

Mathew knew Leigh's not-so-secret obsession with mobsters, so he was sure to bring it up in the open conversation as long as he could roll up the windows and keep the looky-loos from seeing him or hearing anything he had to say about anyone who may or may not still be living; anyone who could bring a world of pain to him even though he had resigned from the world over a year before; and should have done so a year or two before that.

"I caught the palate of some unsavory types...characters straight out of a James Cagey film. If it had been the '30s, they would have walked in wearing Fedoras. They had tailor-made suits, Rolex

watches, Gucci this or that, shoes that cost more than my rent, and at what I was paying for rent, that's saying something." He continued.

"They wanted to set me up and get me started so they could use my place as a storage closet for whatever they were shipping or selling locally. At first, I told myself it's none of my business what they do; they're paying good money, they get theirs, and I get mine. It was all just the cost and art of doing business until it wasn't." He paused to see her reaction. She hadn't stopped her stare long enough to blink.

"They wanted a piece of my action too. It wasn't enough for them to use the storage closet, the walk-in freezer, or the back office next to my own office; they set up a guy, made him the Matre'd, and gave him cart blanche over walking around my restaurant with whatever and whomever he wanted to; when he wanted to.

"I got a phone call from the alarm system one Sunday morning around 4:45 a.m. asking if I was in the restaurant. I said no, but I was supposed to say I was there. When I didn't say I was there, it caused trouble for the guy who was...I think you know what that could mean for me if I was telling the truth when a lie would have greased the gears." He said. Mathew's voice began to quiver involuntarily, and he took an extra few seconds to cough through the discomfort before continuing.

"I was threatened, of course, and I could handle that, but when my best waitress and her husband were gunned down leaving a show the next day, the family was sending me a message. I should have taken *the fall for them, not given the cop's permission to see what was happening. That was over three years ago; I stayed a lot longer than I should have, moving from one space to the next, thinking I'd be OK if I let them have more of the pie than I had let them have the first go-round, except the next go-round never happened.*

Mathew wanted to be more specific. He wanted to point fingers at his ex, telling Leigh about her betrayal and her fat Sicilian father's unique way of adding pressure to the man, forcing him to be tattooed with the number 43 on the back of his right wrist. It was still there, only covered with a stylized book – the Bible. He heard himself telling her that he would have been Gio Aiello's 43rd confirmed dead if he screwed up again. Somehow, he figured, his testimony took care of that.

"As you can imagine, if you give a man your coat, you may have to give him your shirt, pants, socks, everything if he lets you breathe another day. That's how I felt. Sure, I was being asked to be on television shows; who do you think runs them? I was seen. I was out there drumming up business and making the best Italian pasta and desserts this side of the big boot, but I was not living, and any air I took in didn't belong to me." Mat said.

"After a while, I stopped sleeping right; I began taking drugs to do that. After a while longer, I couldn't stay awake; I started taking more and different types of drugs and supplements for that. Coming and going, I had no clue. It was just how it was, Tuesday through Sunday; I somehow managed to sleep on Mondays. I looked forward to it." His words caught her deep within her gut.

"*Then there was the trial. It didn't happen for a full eighteen months after the first arrests were made. I learned a valuable lesson: never compromise your worth or who you are. Your mistakes are your own, but others can lend you their mistakes occasionally just in case you didn't have enough on your plate to begin with.*" He said.

"*No one ever hung me upside down from a parking lot,*" he said, and as he did, he lifted the corner of his shirt, pulling it from being tucked into the side of his jeans to expose an apparent wound on the side of his abdomen. "*That didn't happen, but this did. Aiello was in jail; they said he couldn't get to me. I didn't believe that, not for a second, but where was I gonna go? I was still engaged to his daughter, and I knew she was telling him everything I did: who I talked to, what I talked about. It was hell.*"

To her shock, the bullet's entry looked remarkably like the gunshot wounds recreated in movies: smooth, pinkish, and discolored. The edges of it pulled tightly into a filled space where once a hole had encased a lead bullet. This wasn't one of the stories she picked up in True Crime magazines. It wasn't a show-and-tell either; she knew it was his reality. He had been through this and so much more.

"*They got me. It wasn't something I didn't expect, but after the ninth or tenth time trying to break out of what I had gotten myself into, I found out why you don't accept offers to meet your partners alone on the pier. They could end up shooting you in the early morning hours with little to no traffic there to see or hear anything.*" He said, lowering his shirttail.

"You never know how you'll react to that until it happens. I fell to the ground immediately. I knew I was hit, of course, but something just told me to stop, drop, lay there, and not move. I don't know if it was the Spirit; I had become a Believer a few weeks earlier, and when I say that, some of the ones I was facing would claim to be Christians as well; most would say they were devout, but being born into a Catholic home doesn't cut it; it doesn't save you.

"We know that. I was more lost than you can imagine, living a life of heavy sedation, partying through the nights, using cocaine, sleeping throughout the day, using more cocaine to stay awake, cooking, and working the rest of the time. When I say cocaine, I mean the good stuff – it was in a flour canister, not in those little premeasured packs you see in movies. It was available in quantities unmeasured.

Mat turned a little in his seat, allowing himself to think about the following few things he might say, but as he did, he felt the pressure again not to say more, not until he had some feedback from her; instead of talking, he leaned in to kiss her. Mathew felt the weight of his past encase him again; this, he knew, was only fear, and when he couldn't remember all the things he'd trained himself to do when fear arose, he remembered the night he first met Leigh, how fear subsided immediately; it was weird, but it happened.

For a while, there was silence in the cab of the old truck, with neither of them saying a word to each other. Mathew raised his head off his chest and turned to face his friend. His left hand had already reached across the bench seat to find Leigh's. *"That's why I came to Florida, Leigh. I lost everything except my life. They owned my place, my apartment, all of it. They took it back, everything.*

"When I heard the sirens coming down Lake Shore Drive the night I was shot, I didn't imagine they were coming for me. I thought I was dead. I thought this was exactly how it ended, and I'm just going to lay here, and someone will find me in the morning. After he shot me, I think the punk knew I wasn't gone. He walked away; he must have called 9-1-1 because no one else was anywhere near to hear the shot." He said.

"It wasn't like I was smart enough to take someone to meet with the man; nope, I went alone. I expected him to be with someone, but he wasn't. It was just the two of us - three if you count Mr. Ruger." He tried to bring a bit of brevity to the matter. It had been three years since he'd talked about it; even Charlie hadn't known the whole story. Somehow, telling it to Leigh made sense to him, and it felt good to get it out of his head where it had rattled around for too long.

Leigh was hurting, hurting for Mathew, but also hurt that she had not considered the gravity of his backstory. She had gone over it a time or two in her mind, playing out what he might say, but she had no idea that he had paid for his wrongs with a bullet. It made the idea of romanticizing the gangsters characteristically insane for her to think of them now as anything less than diabolical.

"We do that, you know," she said, *"We, well, me anyway, we romanticize the pirates of the world like I told you guys once, giving them a following or some sort of place of prestige when, in reality, a thug is a*

thug, lower than most, and destined for the fate they deserve." She said, her other hand clenched in pseudo feelings of despair and an anxiousness that came out of nowhere.

"I'm sorry that happened to you. You said you'd tell me more about Tia; but no, I can't. I don't know what you're thinking of telling me, but listen, you don't have to tell me anything because she didn't know what she had." She said. *"Your story is enough that you're here now; it's my turn. You're not the same as you were, and no amount of money will persuade you to return to a life of allowing others to do their dirty work, making you seen so they can remain in the shadows. That is not going to ever happen to you again."* She promised.

Fifteen

Sarasota, Florida, wasn't Miami, but then again, not many of the people living there would expect or want their fair city to be as bustling or as hustling as the mega-popular and overly saturated city known for its high-ended drama, criminal cartels, and flashy cars. Within the city limits of Sarasota resided the less intrusive, organized parent-teacher conferences and family-oriented businesses. Laws were abided by, sermons were preached and heard, and the beaches were as beautiful at sunrise and sunset as any other Floridian city, even if one by chance wanted to throw Panama City into the horizontal scenic competition.

Choosing Sarasota was easy for Leigh; it's where Charlie lived. She knew she wanted to make a difference in people's lives by doing something, and since she had already come to terms with not wanting to stay in DeQueen, Arkansas, but to branch out to a more colorfully alluring, even a more fantasy-like place; the thought of moving someplace strange to her wasn't as tricky knowing that there would be at least one or two familiar faces. There would be ten if she included the faces of every dog in the Garrett house; she had seen them occasionally in his videos.

An easy, gentle breeze rustled through the palm trees while Mathew considered answering her question about why he had chosen to live in Sarasota. Before he came to the area, he had no idea who Charlie Garrett was. Meeting him was, in fact, an added benefit, but only after he made the move. He looked around at the sun just as it began to kiss the vibrant horizon before he answered.

"I chose Sarasota over any other city because it was in Florida, to begin with; at least I knew I would wind up in this state. I wanted to be far from anything and anyone I was associated with back in Chicago; you know why, that is," he said. He mentioned again that living in Missouri was rather dull, and nothing was too exciting to keep his interest. Since he believed at least two-thirds of his nights would be spent sleeping under the stars, he assumed a warmer climate with a greater population meant free abandoned food would be more accessible, and he could settle into some form of shelter.

"I needed a place to start over, to be me, to find out exactly what I had inside of myself to start the process of healing physically from what had happened to me and mentally too. I needed the air, the waves, the sea salt, and, yeah, the smells. I wanted that. Food is a strong strong drug of its own. Hearing bacon sizzle, watching bread rise, putting my hands into the dough to knead it; all of this is necessary. I don't have a kitchen, but I have people who let me get the tension out of my hands and heart and onto their plates." He told her.

"I wanted to hear those loud God-forsaken gulls every morning and evening. I don't know why that kind of thing stuck in my head, but when I'd watch an old show that took place in Florida, I remembered the birds. I think I thought pelicans were just made up, something you saw in books. I found one picking up my sock the first week I arrived. He got away with it, too. That, believe it or not, is how I met Charlie." Mat laughed as he finally got around to sharing how he met the pastor.

"It turns out the bird's name was Gus. Charlie had been feeding him for years behind the church. I was walking the parking lot looking for a place to ditch my stuff and hide from an impending storm. Somehow, I ended up behind the church, too; I didn't know it was a church, and I didn't know Charlie was a preacher.

He looked homeless like me. I didn't want to infringe on his spot, so I went a little down the sidewalk, maybe fifty feet, and set up my sleeping bag. I asked him if he'd ever turned the water on now and again to get a drink or wash up, and he said sure he had. He asked me if I thought the storage closet would be better since the storm was coming, and when he opened it with a key, I realized he wasn't from the streets, but still, I didn't know he owned the place. The man was barefoot! Mat continued, smiling and shaking his head.

"He gave me the key and told me I was welcome; that's how we met. The bird hasn't been around for a few months; Charlie thinks maybe he's moved on to better pastures, but I firmly believe he got *a few extra dollars for the sock and a new career selling things he finds on the beach."* The story made Leigh laugh, but it also gave her an insight into her companion's dry and dad-joke mind.

"Who doesn't know pelicans are real? That's like saying you never knew a hurdy-gurdy was a real stringed instrument; c'mon, you can't be serious." She asked, pointing out to the sands surrounding them. *"They're everywhere! I know I've seen them in most of the South; now that I think about it, there has to be some up on the Great Lakes. There has to be!"* She mocked him because she knew he was mocking himself, maybe trying to make her feel a little more sorry for him. Despite the levity of their conversation, Leigh was grateful for these moments of honesty between them.

There was something about the pull and allure of the ocean, too; it had a vast, unpredictable, yet calming way of putting Mathew's mind at ease after a stressful day or night. The waves, they never stop. They push, withdraw, lap, and carry themselves a few feet further, only to retreat and restart their processes. He loved the water – its rhythmic ebb and flow brought him an immediate sense of peace no matter how rough his day had been. He thought of it when he wasn't basking on the sands, putting his feet into it.

Mathew's journey, his running, had come to an end. He had either found a new beginning or was going to be content with the ending of the one he walked away from. It was his turn to make a difference, something most people only got the opportunity to do if they were wealthy enough to afford to hire people to make it happen. He was one of those people, and it wasn't going to be money that motivated him to push forward. This was love; love for himself first, which hadn't happened in a very long time, and love for others.

"When you're ready, I'll circle back, like I told you I would." He told her, *"But I don't want to just tell you about the women in my life; that's only a part of it. The real story, the guts of it, would have to be my beginning; what set things in the motion and direction they went in the first place."* Leigh promised to listen to every word when he felt ready to share. She told him it was time to get to know Sarasota since they had both decided to make it their home.

"For instance, did you know that Sarasota is one of two places in the States where they used to bury the elephants that retired from circus life?" she asked him. Mat's fake surprise at this knowledge was evident; placing both hands over his cheeks, he exclaimed, *"Well, I hope they were dead first! Because if not, that would be a terrible legacy to have."* He joked. Leigh couldn't contain the unexpected snort that expelled from her lips; it was as spontaneous as one had ever been.

"Not just the circus dead elephants, but other dead elephants from zoos and shows, even private owners who had the bankroll it took to feed the beasts...before they died, they, too, are buried underneath us! They were allowed to retire here, right here, and up the coast all the way to Panama City, I'm told." She verified the fact with Bay County Animal Control before writing to her best friend about it a few weeks back.

"Sarasota used to be the winter home for the Ringling Brothers Circus group; they wintered here, mostly on the little islands to the west. A whole area was set aside for them. John Ringling owned it, of course, but the people and the animals rested here for years. Can you imagine," she asked, *"waking up and seeing elephants, camels, tigers, and monkeys taking a dip in the ocean if you lived on Lido or Siesta Key Beach, where they lived? Maybe you couldn't; there were rules, but I like to let my mind wander when possible."* She admitted.

She further admitted to the man that from time to time, she'd buy a new minty aromatic candle, light it, and meditate for long periods on end, letting the scent rise and dance into her head as she inhaled. She began thinking of the circus, Sarasota, the carnival atmosphere, and another time. It wasn't unlike her daydreams or fantasies about meeting or being associated with the gangsters she once romanticized. Something about the sand, the smells, the call of those gulls; she could almost see them vying with the cheerful monkeys for scraps that may be found on the seashore at dusk.

There wasn't much left of the circus life there now; she knew this to be true. However, other places in and around Sarasota were of interest, too. An area known as Longboat Key was the vacation spot for many Native Americans for hundreds, probably thousands of years before the ringleader made his way up the sandy shores and bought his way to paradise. They probably didn't have giant mammals to tend to, but they had their own practices, ceremonies, and lifestyle.

Before Ringling came along, the French pirate Jean La Fitte had shipwrecked near the same spot; such history. Such diverse and exciting differences. She wondered out loud if she would rather see a wanton clown roaming the beachfront or a half-drunk pirate without any reason to attack if she wasn't a threat.

Around the same time, John Ringling purchased the rights to several other smaller and less robust circus groups, making his one of the world's largest. He bought over a hundred acres of the south end of the Longboat Key and uprooted many natural trees to plant giant Australian pines. Ringling went a step further and put on the Ritz; he built the Ritz-Carlton hotel there on New Pass; it was started but never finished.

So many small and what some would say insignificant stories beleaguer the area, but they are not all bad; some became famous rather than infamous. Some people who called the area home for decades were artists, poets, writers, actors, and engineers. Sarasota may not be Miami, but it didn't seem like it ever wanted to be. After another moment or two of silence Mat turned his attention back to the waves; he could just barely make them out in the distance. *"Let's park the truck closer to the beach and sit for a while; what do you say?"* He coaxed her.

"What do you see when you see the waves, Leigh? What does the ocean tell you?" he asked. Her eyes remained fixed on a spot in front of her, somewhere out on the water. She allowed the waves to crash, rolling as they did, caressing themselves and

folding over and over again. The thought of it comforted Leigh.

"The ocean…it tells me how to be patient; to wait on what is to be." She began, her voice barely audible above the incoming surf. *"It's been here for millions of years, carving out the coastline piece by piece, never rushing, never pushing anything too far unless it's riled by an outside source that forces it to make a stand."* She said.

"It teaches me to be humble, to listen, and to learn, not to jump to any conclusion, or decide that something must be this way or that way, but to let things play out the way they're intended to play out; to understand that things have their own way of working out – but that all of it comes from a higher source; not from anything I can do on my own." She softly ended her words.

Wrapping her warmly into a blanket she had remembered to bring, Mathew pulled her a little closer to feel the warmth of her body against his. The waves continued to speak, their words audible if not completely understood. *"It's a lullaby sometimes; that's what I hear. The waves, the rocks, the birds, the sun, all of it. It comes together again and again, repeating the same words in a language I feel rather than hear."* He told her.

"I don't tell people this, but I mostly sleep outside when it's dry because the ocean keeps me company; it understands me. There's a freeing about living out with it, a calming emotion that runs its course and holds me near it. I don't know and don't want to be away from it; maybe it sounds crazy." He

hesitated to finish what he was thinking because he knew where his heart wanted to be, and the internal battle within him was his to bear.

"I don't know if I'll ever be able to live indoors permanently now; I've been homeless for over a year, and I know it may sound as if I've given up, which I haven't," he told Leigh, *"Not paying rent, utilities, or buying groceries for myself every week has been strategically rewarding. I've not worked the entire time, not since I left Chicago. When I finally ran out of money, I had at least found a home, my little nook, as I call it. I eat what people don't, and when they let me cook for them, I eat even better, and so do they!"* he mused.

Leigh hadn't thought about it because to do so would be to say something rude or seemingly rude, even though she may want an answer to satisfy her wonder. *"You...wait, you don't buy groceries?"* she asked. *"How do you eat if you don't buy groceries? I mean, you just paid for food at Sonic for yourself. You wouldn't let me buy you lunch.*

"You have to have something going on if you're not working...I'm sorry," she said, shaking her head. *"That's too personal, too much. I'm sorry. I do that. I get way too interested, and that leads me to become way too nosey."* She admitted another tidbit about herself. One he was happy to find out about; it gave him cause to explore her other tidbits.

He held her gaze for a minute before answering, *"I even thought about attaching myself to some wealthy business mogul or a has-been celebrity; there are plenty of them here, you know. I could be their personal chef, have living quarters, and be out from the elements every night."* He said, pausing to think through his following admission. *"But, if I did that, I would have to submit to being caged again. I can't be tied down; it doesn't work for me. If I know anything about myself, I can't be told what to do or when to do it.*

"Whatever I do, I have to decide to do it alone." He concluded before adding one more piece of intel she might need to know. *"And as for food? Like I said, I eat what others don't. If you start thinking about that last statement, you may figure it out, and before you go off feeling sorry for me, I don't dumpster dive, I promise...I hang out at eateries, mostly those open bars and cafes on the sand. Let's say the pelicans aren't the only scavengers on Turtle Beach."*

Staring at him but trying her hardest not to do so, Leigh slowly shook her head again. She opened her mouth and was about to say something, but that little voice she listened to suggested that she let that one slide, at least for now. *"We'll come back to that."* She gave him one of the off-beat head tilts usually reserved for dogs when they hear a strange high-pitched sound somewhere around their heads.

There could be more to Leigh's choice to move to the city than what she told him. Maybe she had a secret. What could it be? Dempsey had told his wife, who had let Mathew in on the details, that Leigh was prepared to fund any project as long as Charlie thought it was good. Was she a devoted congregation member, maybe, having been an online viewer for years, having seen it all in person, and was she impressed to the point of building it up somehow?

"Why do you put so much faith in Charlie? Can I ask? Is that too personal?" Mathew Conner wanted to know. When the answer came, and he heard it for himself, he had to admit that a lot of truth was held inside her reasoning. Leigh Avery Madsen had been privileged, but the difference between her and others may be that she knew what she had been given and counted it as a blessing more than just a prize.

"After living with, working with, and nearly marrying into a world of greed and self-absorbed people whose only goals revolve around money and the status and power that money represented to them, it was absolutely and one-hundred percent fascinating to me that a man who preached barefoot on the beach, who didn't even have a church to preach in for years, wouldn't accept government money to build one.

"He didn't take money for preaching, either. He let God do what God does, and then, the same guy goes out and takes it upon himself to pick up trash around the strip mall stores where he's not even paid; he's paid by 7-11 to pick up and clean up their area." She explained, but Charlie wasn't on anyone's church payroll; his church didn't and wouldn't accept money from any federal funder because he preached all of the Word, not the sanitized version they'd make him say if he received money from them. He let it be, and it was.

"There he was, cleaning up that entire side of Superior Avenue, and when he took a long-needed rest, sometimes on the curb or by the dumpster, people would come up to him and give him a dollar or two. They'd see him barefoot; you know, he doesn't wear

shoes much. He's got that colorful hippie bandana around the crown of his head, and he's bearded like a Duck Dynasty character or a member of ZZ Topp!" she laughed.

"I saw that, heard about it, thought, yeah, that's the man I would listen to. That's the one I would put my faith in, my trust in. But listen," she told Mathew, *"I don't worship Charlie Garrett. Every single day, he's a man. He's God's man, but he's a man. I respect him; that's what I know and what I do. I respect him.*

"There's not a man on Wall Street who would do one iota of what our preacher would do for his neighbor, but the same commandment is given to each of us. Why would I feel comfortable around idiots like the ones I fought, sued, and took to the cleaners? If I was going to have peace, I first needed to leave those shady, biased, unethical people and chill by myself until I could figure things out." Her explanation made sense.

"Once I got back into listening to the sermons on YouTube as I had in the past, I remembered something Charlie wanted to do for the people in his community. I called him, and we talked; I packed up the old green truck and drove straight here - - except yeah, I didn't take the straightest way; I went the scenic route, but even that was meaningful. I got to see where Elvis was born!" she grinned, trying not to sound too much like a giddy fan.

Sixteen

The morning light burst through the shades before she had even had a chance to crack them open. If time had something on her, it was that she was unable to predict just how horrifically gleeful and shiny it had decided to be before she had condemned herself to that second cup of coffee. Pulling back the kitchen curtains required an enormous effort on her part, if only because she couldn't open her eyes to face the fact that six o'clock was, in fact, already staring her in the face with all its personality.

Kate Tisdale knew enough about morning to realize she couldn't control it, not when it showed up and not when it ran away, leaving her further behind that Monday than usual. Climbing back into bed wasn't an option, not any more than pulling the covers up over her head and forgetting she'd ever heard the alarm sound off when it did. Why is it, she asked herself, that the first hour of every day seems to race into oblivion, but the subsequent work hours rattled on as if they had nothing else to see or do; that is unless she had committed herself to a deadline and then yes, the hours whisked away at the speed of sound, leaving her in the dust again; not giving her a sliver of a chance to play keep up with the other adjusters she worked with.

"Worked with" may be an overstatement, considering Kate and anyone else at the company worked remotely from their homes; no one worked *"with"* anyone. They worked, at best, in the same unit, for the same company, earning roughly the same base pay, but she had made it a personal and professional goal to step out from under the heavy, wet blanket of what was considered a male-dominant position; to earn a place for herself where she, Katheryn Joanna Hooker Tisdale, a middle-aged married mother of two, would be either first, second or maybe at the very least, third out of eleven licensed auto claims adjusters who had called themselves employed for the Merrick Group Advisors.

Kate was determined to be a top player, and if that meant acting like a man from time to time, then pulling up her big-girl panties and putting the screws to anyone in her way wouldn't be too far out of the question as long as she had the evidence she needed to line the complaint she had planned to deliver to Human Resources the very next time that son-of-a-bitch manager decided to step out of line again; and mistake her for being the patsy he decided she was. Kate Tisdale was anything but willing to concede. What's good for the goose is good for whatever that man was.

Glancing down at her phone for the tenth time in as many minutes, Kate shook her head in disbelief at the carelessness of some people who seemed bent on being as private as they had positioned themselves to be. There was private, and then there was Eddie

Rogers, one of the managers of the adjusters at the company she had been employed for the past eleven months.

What she saw in her email inbox couldn't be described as anything less attractive or more disgusting to anyone else who saw it. Still, to anyone knowing what it was, the ramifications could take on an enormous life with just a little help. How dare he send her photos of himself to her private email? It had to be a mistake; he must have meant for them to go to someone whose name was close to hers.

"I'm going to need a couple of PTO hours this morning, Josh." She told her current manager, *"...something has come up, and it's family; I can't escape it. It won't take me an hour; I'll try to give you better notice in the future."* She told him. Kate furrowed her brow in concentration, thinking intently as she did. Her secret wouldn't be kept much longer. Secrets, she told herself, could be too heavy at times; they need to be unleashed. This one couldn't be sneezed at or swept under the rug. It may not be the kinder thing to do, but it was at least the right step in eliminating the competition, that's for sure.

When released, she jumped from her seat in her home office, nearly tripping over one of her dogs but recovering nicely – even making a comical dance out of the would-be failure. Nothing would get in her way that morning, and nothing would stop her momentum, not now. She had a big fat fish to fry, and the grease was getting hot enough to smell. With the kids making their breakfast and busying themselves before heading off to school, Kate's exit through the garage door was as seamless and as uneventful as any other gesture of any other day.

"First, I'm going to drive by his house and take a picture of the other car sitting in his drive this morning," she told her good friend Lynne Davis on the phone, who had quit the company less than a month beforehand after something similar to what Kate was experiencing had happened to her as well. Lynne wasn't like Kate. Most women weren't like Kate.

The same could be said about most men; there weren't that many people who would purposely plan their targeted revenge with as much zeal and hardcore drive as Kate Tisdale; then again, if people knew her well enough, they wouldn't be on the side of her that caused them as much grief as she was prepared to steer their way. Indeed, leopards don't change their spots, but it's equally true that a scorpion will sting when pushed into the corner every single time.

"That car, the little blue Z, belongs to Dylan Colbert, the boss' boss' boss' son – he has no idea his baby boy is bangin' the sheets with one of his employees, but when he sees that I've uploaded a few pics of his kid was possibly swapping spit with Eddie Rogers, with his car parked up close to the garage of Eddie's little house; he'll have to know something's up.

"He probably suspects it; this will seal it." She told Lynne, thanking her for the early morning pics she had given the former co-worker just before dawn. *"If his car is still in the drive now, at 7:12 a.m., and it was in the drive at what...5:35 a.m., when you started your shift, then yeah, Daddy Colbert is gonna have a sit*

down with our soon-to-be former manager.” She told her friend.

“Did you know Lynne that Eddie is a direct descendant of General Clark Walsh of Delaware? The same guy who stood with George Washington many times and fought beside and for him? You can't pick your family, I know, but to think that one of the greatest and bravest souls of our modern-day history was so gallant and well respected, only to have his great-whatever grandson pop up as a backstabbing piece of no-account runs through me.” She said.

Lynne Davis thought about it, wondering if she should have said anything, but it wasn't as if anything happening to Eddie Rogers would make any difference to her now that she had left the company. *“He didn't have to keep turning me into H.R. for all the silly things he did. I never should have trusted him.”* She said. *“We had a few drinks one evening at his place,”* she said.

“Which, by the way, couldn't be more pristine if you paid a truckload of maids twice a week to scour it, dust and fluff, and whatever else Mr. Twinkletoes has them do. God knows he's not hitting on any one of them; they're beneath him. He can't move up in the world screwing maids, but give him the son of the CEO, and yeah, he's movin' and shakin' baby... movin' and shakin'.”

Lynne knew what she did was underhanded in some ways, but then again, getting back at Eddie after she left seemed just as fair to her as what he did to her while she was under his command at the company. He was her manager; he should have managed instead of manipulated. Having invited her over with a few others for drinks, heavily hoping she would partake enough to unwind and answer a few off-the-wall veiled questions, which she did, put her at his mercy.

"I don't care if he's gay, I don't care if he's bi; that's not the thing. He can be both all day, but he has no right to lord his position over employees who disagree with him or who don't agree with his antics. He says and does things we couldn't do because of his tenure and because if they jump down his throat about something, he plays the victim; little Mr. Butthurt," Lynne added. *"He was perfectly fine with my language and my way of handling insurance adjusters on the other side unless he was pissed about something, and then he'd turn on me and anyone else he spoke to if he had the upper hand over them. He's a snake!"*

When Lynne was hired, she was unaware that wearing a MAGA tee-shirt at her desk at home, where the general public didn't see her, could land her in trouble with one of the managers. After viewing her wearing it during a Teams meeting, he chose to nail her to the H.R. cross. Eddie also allowed another adjuster, a man, to go entirely shirtless, claiming it was hot inside. *"What is it?"* she asked Kate. *"If I had been shirtless or a man, would that have been better?"*

Lynne asked what Eddie had over Kate to ensure she could feel better about having supplied the woman with the starting pistol she needed to send her off to the races. *"What did he do to me, you mean?"* Kate asked. *"He and I talked about a call I had. A woman I was dealing with made an off-color remark about me, and I didn't take it.*

"I swung back in my chair and gave it to her the way my daddy taught me to when I was little and bullied in school. Now, yeah, maybe I shouldn't have done it, but she not only used slurs to describe me, she called me stupid and said if I had a brain in my head, I'd play with it. Maybe what I said next was just as immature, but she started it.

"I didn't call her anything; I just said I was above all that high school nonsense, and if she thought I was a bitch, she should know it takes one to know one. It wasn't even offense; it was defense at best. Duckturd Eddie, or what my grandpa would have called him, 'Pansy-pants,' decided to tell H.R. I was unprofessional in my demeanor and that since we were on a recorded line, I had misrepresented the company somehow." Kate complained.

"First of all, and maybe you didn't know this, we talked about it in a meeting after you left; the recorded line is for quality control, not to be shared or even offered to be shared with anyone who may call in or who we call. We use it for us; he could have said what I said was unnecessary, but no, he reported me to H.R."

Lynne shook her head, but since the two were on the phone with one another, Kate hadn't seen it. *"Eddie told me, and yes, on the same recorded call, that I should have told the woman to you-know-what herself, and he called her something I won't even say, even if my kids would have been able to get away with it now, I don't do those things.*

"I try not to use that language, but there he was using it at work, and he had the...well, he doesn't have balls, but there he was turning me in when he was telling me to tell her where to get off. But you know he didn't report himself to H.R., did he? Nope...nope, he's not about to do that. He can't stand that my politics and faith are much different than his own, and I get slapped with a reprimand because he has the time in, and I don't. It's unfair, and I won't take it lying down." Kate's words burned in her head before leaving her mouth.

Once the photos of Dylan's car in Eddie's drive were uploaded anonymously to the company server, it was anyone's guess who may find them and anyone's second guess who would leak them to Richard Dale Colbert III. It was, however, a good enough bet for anyone that it would happen. Fireworks may not be on the menu today, but they were undoubtedly about to be lit to smolder for the gossip rings that tend to surface and make circles on Teams.

Clocking in at 9:00 a.m. on the dot, ready for the day, her first duty required both a smile and a plan set in motion; Kate had both ready to fire off the second the time clock accepted her morning time card entry. A quick email to Lynne before the day got underway read:

"Some people just don't want to be seen, and that's too bad when they are. Maybe those who shouldn't be seen should stay in their closets and play with their dolls instead of poking the bears as they do. Why is it that some people can't leave well enough alone? I wouldn't have been mad at him if he had scolded me; hell, I think I scolded myself; I told him what I did." Kate mentioned.

"I expected to be spoken to, but he goes off and does what he did; he gets what he gets for it. I'm not sorry, and I won't apologize."   Kate ended the exchange by telling Lynne thank you for the picture; hers alone wouldn't have been that big of a deal, Eddie could have played it off as some breakfast thing they had planned, but the predawn pics were going to put a monkey wrench right where he needed one to go – up his.

Seventeen

The next time they saw each other, Leigh and Mathew had been discussing people experiencing homelessness, who, for political correctness, were being called *"unhomed"* by some. To the amazement of both parties, the word *"unhomed"* seemed slightly more derogatory than the more familiar term. Still, they also agreed that it could be that their age and cultural experiences played a significant role in how they approached change, especially change that affected them personally and now professionally.

The unseen and seen of the world had a few things in common, in that they knew where they wanted to be; the unseen typically refused to put themselves *"out there,"* be it on social media or, even now, working outside the home, since working remotely had become so popular. On the other hand, the seen had a much harder time working remotely and had difficulty staying off social media.

Of course, all the shades of gray lingered between the two points, and the innuendo of these gray areas fascinated the two chatters that evening while sitting beneath an incredibly closer-than-usually close full moon.

Mathew began listing those he found to be unnoticed. He whispered them rather than speaking them, not wanting to disrespect the collective. There were always exceptions in his mind, but when he considered the majority of the groups, somehow, the individuals among them took a less prevalent stand.

"The undercover cop. He's seen, of course, but purposely not for who he is. Then some catfish people online, absolutely fake people who don't want the real them to be discovered. I could go on," he told her. *"Certain prostitutes, true orphans, people who get left at the bus stops, that mechanic in town who's probably the best, but he doesn't want more business. He's happy working the hours he has. Everyone's got an angle...even the Moon! It's bigger! It wants to be seen tonight."* Mat told her.

"It's perigee. It's bigger and brighter today than usual, as it's a little closer to Earth than usual; I think this happens a few times a year." Leigh stated she was embarrassed about not knowing about Perigee before her thirty-third birthday. *"Seems the moon did something around that time, too, and here I thought it was just up there shining away for me, but yeah, no. It was Science....Science. I can't take credit for it."* She sat down another carrot juice was on the rocks and passed it to the man.

Because neither of them drank alcohol, smoked, or used recreational drugs, there had been quite a few things to discuss that they seemingly had in common. It wasn't rare, but it was certainly uncommon for a woman with so much in the way of worldly financial experience to not be a connoisseur of fine wines; Leigh was, she told him, a little unusual, but if being unusual meant that she stayed sober, saved money, and didn't have to own a steam cleaner to get the couch cushions clean again, but she had no problem with being different than most successful women in her former line of business.

He had asked her before but found the opportunity to do so again if she had been written up in any articles for the fast-lane markets of money makers and financial baron robbers, who seemed to like to be seen between the slick cover pages of those overpriced rags that told anyone who was anyone how the other people in their set were doing.

"Were you on the cover or buried somewhere in the back where they talk about how you're planning your next move rather than how you've already made it?" he asked, then, almost instantly, recanting, pulling back and shaking his head to apologize for what could have been deemed vicious or rude. *"I'm....geez Leigh, I'm so sorry. I didn't mean that."* He said to her, lifting his glass to thank her and beg forgiveness silently at the same time.

"You may wanna take it easy there, buddy; I'm just saying you can drink too much of that and end up looking like Donald Trump." Her joke hit precisely where she intended it to; *"Touche,"* he laughed. Mathew hadn't voted for anyone since the second Clinton Administration in 1996, his first time to vote and the last time he attempted to do so. Tilting his head to the side, he accepted his alcohol-free cocktail before saying something sarcastic about the one man he couldn't stand but knew had the best laid-out plans regarding how a country could and should be run.

"I wouldn't step across the street to vote for him, but I know when he was in office, I had a better job, more money in my pockets, in my bank, and groceries were affordable. I shudder to think what I would have to pay now if I bought them. For whatever reason, I can remember stepping into the Aldi store we had up that way in Elgin, just outside of Chicago, where I lived, and I bought milk. I don't know why that memory hits me; I think Rogan said something on the radio about it, and it just stuck," He told himself, but it was just as likely that he knew she had just poured herself a half glass of the stuff.

"Milk was less than three bucks a gallon when Trump was in office, and now it's nearly twice that; I can't imagine how a man working forty hours a week to keep his family under a roof can afford to do that, pay the utilities, feed the kids, himself, and his wife, and own a car, pay the insurance and God only knows what else." He stated, tilting his glass to bring in the clinking of the cheers he intended to share with his evening hostess.

Leigh closed her eyes and took a deep, long breath, savoring the moment; the last slivers of light mingled with the breeze coming off the surf. The rhythmic crash of the waves not fifty feet from where they sat provided such a soothing backdrop to their conversation. She couldn't remember a time before moving to Florida that she had given in to such relaxation daily; it wasn't the same as living in a concrete city surrounded by glass and mortar, the various taunt expensive suits pushing past her on their way to the top rung. Florida oozed color; it oozed peace and tranquility too. She liked this new life – it fit.

"You can't say the moon always wants to be seen, but a few planets out there are not always so bright, bold, and brazen. Our Sun could probably take the prize for being the most extroverted, with Mr. Moon coming in second place. Pluto may have to be the least of the seen if he was still a planet, but certainly, he is talked about. He's a cold, uncaring sort, one who may or may not give a damn if he's mentioned in the journals, I don't know." She wondered.

"I can say this: many of the stars seem shy but seen nevertheless, while others strictly hold their place, refusing to budge or flicker. They have a statement to make." She laughed, pointing her half-filled tall glass upward toward Orion's Belt to seal her point. *"My milk's on that one there; Orion's Belt, as being the most commonly known, most likely to be seen celestial formation in the night sky; even over the dippers...everyone has to look around to find them; they're not hiding, but they don't stand out on their own with their head high enough for everyone to figure it out."* Her words made the man think; laugh, of course, but think again.

"What about the unseen and the seen that makes you wonder so much? You have brought it up a few times." He said, *"...and your milk is about to spill out of that thing, so you might wanna bring it in a little."* He said, moving his shoulder in just a tad toward her to avoid being splashed by an overly excited gesture that could have gotten out of control if she let it.

"Milk was under three dollars a gallon? I guess it's been a while; I don't remember that. I drink so much of it; I'm always buying it, so it's sort like the old

frog in the pot story, you know, the one where he's sittin' in the saucepan, thinking it's a jacuzzi or something, and the ol' cook turns up the heat slowly but continuously. Before he knows it, he's the soup!" She laughed again before asking him if he had ever served frog when he was a chef.

Because Mathew Conner was feeling incredibly good, he smiled to see if his eyes could answer rather than his mouth. If he were honest, he was afraid to open his mouth for fear of what he may say or do. She was close to him. She was closer to him than she had been; naturally, she was at her own perigee. He couldn't jinx it. His silence wasn't for the sake of being unnoticed but for being noticed only by one. He couldn't thank Douglas Dempsey enough for the donated clothes he was going to give to the projects; allowing Mat the chance to pick through them first. He was especially thankful for the new, or newer shoes.

They were seated, and that was good; they were mere inches apart from one another. He could hear her breathing. Mathew felt his heart pounding in his chest. He felt somewhat confused; he hadn't allowed himself to feel this way in years. He purposely, intentionally, hadn't put himself out there to allow a moment like this one to creep up the way it had. He was vulnerable, hopeful, of course; what if she wanted to kiss him as much as he tried to kiss her? He couldn't tell without asking but couldn't bring himself to ask.

He wanted to reach up and brush back the errant strand of her bright auburn hair that had fallen haplessly across her face, to feel her pulse against his own. The weight of his past and self-imposed solitude stopped him; it made him remember past experiences when he zigged when he should have zagged; how many times has he been in this situation and made a mistake he couldn't take back? He didn't want that for this relationship, not with Leigh. He wanted it to be what he had always wanted from life: *acceptance.*

The air between them crackled with tension; it was as if whatever happened would happen, and if it were to be, it would be, but then again, his mind raced inside his skull, asking, what if it didn't happen and there he'd be, worse than embarrassed. He could not change the instant; it would be forever written in their history. At the exact second, his mind refused to succumb to the dread; he moved toward her quickly, perhaps to seal the situation, making it impossible for him to change his mind.

He had to act and act soon before another nerve could inch through his veins to change everything. With a quiet determination, he lifted his hand, slowly moving it toward her right cheek. His fingers trembled, but maybe she wouldn't feel that; maybe all she would feel was his warmth; he touched her, not for the first time, but for the first deliberate time. *"Leigh,"* he whispered, his voice barely audible. He was committed now, he told himself, he couldn't retreat.

He paused for a second to see if she had heard him, and she had. He wanted to know if she could read minds or if she could tell that while his head was thinking, his heart was praying. At that moment, between the shivering silver ray of the moon against her form and the shadow of a sea bird finding its way to the shoreline to rest, he kissed her. Though time hadn't stopped, and the world was still probably spinning, Mathew James Conner had painted a picture inside himself, one that brought an unnoticed soul to light in front of God and everyone else. He kissed her, and she let him.

Eighteen

The plush auditorium in the center convention hall was impressive and enormous; the room could only be appreciated by opening the doors and stepping inside. From out in the hallway, it looked like any other ingress to any other conference hall. Inside, however, once she stepped into it from about mid-point, neither at the front nor the back of the room, Leigh could see that words such as *"opulent"* or *"lavish,"* even *"swank"* could be used to describe it.

The large auditorium with rows upon rows of thick, plush, comfortable padded seats was arranged in a semi-circle around a centered stage to maximize utility for all seated to hear the speaker. The walls were adorned with artwork from various foreign countries, depicting abstract interpretations of the human mind, thoughts, emotions, and relationships. The lighting was warm and to the point, often highlighting a specific portrait or image whenever the speaker directed it to do so.

A robotic light system was entirely controlled by the one commanding the room, Dr. Emilio Castille, a man she had met and spoken with on another occasion. Deciding to drive up to see him wasn't a hard decision;

she followed him on social media and knew his schedule. She hoped he would announce another book's publication; that would make her day.

Dr. Castille's presentation that evening at the behest of the University of Florida's Psychology department at the brand-new three-story convention center in downtown Fort Myer had been planned for well over a year in advance. Its topic happened to intrigue Leigh so much so that she decided, come hell or high water, as folks back home would say, she was going to make the conference and hear him speak about the very word that inspired her cousin to write the now Amazon Best Seller book titled *"The."*

The word itself, as Castille explained, held its place in many various societies. Its importance in the English language knows no end; however, in much of the world, where articles such as the word *"the"* were neither that important nor necessary. They lived and died at the whim of those societies. It is such a strange and exciting perception indeed. To think that an entire conference's evening program could be fixed around this one word was unimaginable, yet it was happening.

"Before we start, I will ask you to do a few things tonight that may make you uncomfortable. Believe me when I say I need your attention, and both things I ask you to do are for that purpose. First, before anything else happens, can I get you to turn off your phones or put them on silent now since we have that option?

"Can I ask you to do that so we're not hearing various ringtones and buzzers throughout the lecture? It would mean a great deal to me, and if we hear it

because you signed the waiver before you came into the room, we can ask you to leave if we think your phone or device is causing others or myself to be distracted." Castille said with a strong, authoritative voice and broad and welcoming smile.

"When I discuss psychological pathology," began Dr. Castille from the glass and golden-toned brass podium command center of the stage, *"I don't just focus on the clinical aspects of it. I delve into how societal norms, media presentation or representation, and cultural beliefs will shape our understanding of it and how it deals with the human mind and mental health. It's fascinating,"* he continued, *"...to see how certain behaviors can be perceived as being 'normal' to some and absolutely 'abnormal' to others."* As he spoke, he used air quotes to emphasize his chosen words.

"My goal here tonight is to challenge you to perceive what you believe is expected in another light; try, if you can, to imagine what you believe is expected, to be just the opposite; and if you can do that, you may begin to understand the reasons so many irrational people, or those we perceive as being illogical, will do what they do – the police go through these practices daily; as do other first responders, doctors, nurses, even teachers.

"To understand the reasons behind the behaviors being presented to us when they are presented, we can't simply expect the person presenting the behaviors to do so under our pretext of what is normal. A pretext is often not the truth; it's what we've told ourselves is true." His words hung

heavily; this was just the first minute of a nearly ninety-minute lecture.

As Dr. Castille continued to delve into the minds of the audience, he encouraged each of them to do what they had expected to be asked to do; he asked them to get up, move three or four seats to their left or to their right, and then make sure when they sat down again that they sat beside, in front of, and behind someone they did not know. As they stood to obey his commands, he graciously thanked them for doing so and for going along with his little exercise.

He knew this would jar them, but he would have them where he needed them, in a state of presence to think only for themselves without being subtly influenced by anyone they may feel comfortable with. He wanted them to be as independently minded for the next hour and a half as they could be without their own psychological pathology becoming interrupted.

Leigh had come solo to the conference yet immediately thought of Mathew Conner. How he would have been so very uncomfortable with this, the first experiment of the evening. Not knowing anyone in the conference besides Leigh, he would have been apprehensive about doing anything remotely singular. This thought clung to her as she took a seat, knowing that no matter where she sat, she would adhere to the wishes of the orator.

"Too often," Dr. Castille began, *"the unseen aspects of psychopathology – the internal battles and silent sufferings we have within our minds, go untreated due to our fears of rejection, abandonment, and separation from others. I'll go so far as to say we*

do things the way we think we should do things so that others don't stigmatize us, those others who society says are normal or better for some reason. They aren't better. They aren't even normal until and unless the proverbial 'they' say 'they' are." The doctor spoke.

"We accept this to be true when we change who we are to suit their normal; that's why I need you to be as independent as you can be tonight. There is no normal. No one is beside you, in front of you, or behind you to nudge you into thinking their way. This is you. This is just you tonight. You can agree with me, you can disagree with me, but what you can't do is say it won't make you think because I already have met that goal." He said, laughing into the tiny mic clipped to his lapel.

"We've talked about 'they' and how 'they' tell us what is and isn't. Let's dive into something a bit more foreign; this way, you'll understand a little more of what it is like to be both seen, unseen, needed, and not only forgotten, but purposely so, and you'll do this all at the same time when I tell you the word that creates such diversity in our lives; are you ready for it?" he asked his audience.

Leigh was acutely aware that her personal and professional position wasn't the norm for the group now gathered at the newly constructed multi-million-dollar convention center with all its bells and elaborate whistles. Surrounding her and the good doctor was an enormous group of over two thousand medical professionals, students of every medical discipline, and individuals most genuinely interested in studying the mind.

A mix of ages, races, and backgrounds could be seen at a glance: some wearing professional attire, others in more relaxed clothes depicting their youth or their position at the moment, or maybe they were also trying to fit in with what 'they' said their generation would wear. It was almost comical to her that she could pick out those considered *"boomers,"* people her parent's age, by the greater social groups who tend to categorize generations. There were at least dozens, even hundreds of people from every living generation, including the old set, the *"greatest generation,"* as they were called.

There are so many differences in the room; dissecting one or the other's mind randomly would be impossibly challenging, and the law of large numbers was a must for tools to make such broad assumptions. Medical practice, including Psychology, was a practicing art rather than anything so definitive as to be set in stone. If there was any indication of any bias in the room, no one was aware, certainly not Leigh. She was open to hearing and understanding whatever she could glean from the master on stage.

Nothing Dr. Castille would present that evening would be cast as being absolute. Perhaps that was the one reason, in the back of her mind, that Leigh knew she wanted to hear every word he said, to see if she, too, was capable of challenging her perceptions to understand better why people she had known for so long could have done what they did, or in Mathew's case, why he is doing what he is doing now.

The audience sat attentively, notepads and pens in hand, some using tablets or recorders to keep records, and even this practice seemed to be done with a sense of ageism at hand; those who were generally over a certain age relied on written notes, while the younger, the very young in fact, switched on a device which did all the work for them. Understanding societal norms began with understanding who made up what society was: the aged, the less-than-aged, the middle-aged, the younger adults, and finally, the young. It seemed to Leigh, and probably most in the room, that anyone of tender age would be influenced by those who came before them. This, too, was part of the equation and needed to be discussed at some point.

Dr. Castille was apt to walk about the stage, seemingly making eye contact with every corner of the room, even if he could not see clearly past the first several rows before him. He began his dissertation of the evening about the single word that created such havoc but, at the same time, calmed the stormy waters of grammar. *"Let's talk about the word 'the' in all its glory!"* he began.

The smiles and furrowed brows in front of him told him he had hit his mark by announcing the word in question. For those who could not visually make out the man's facial expressions, larger-than-ever monitors hung around the room. *"The word 'the' is perhaps the most important and, at the same time, the least important word of our lives. You may not even realize how often we use it. If you said the words 'avocado' or 'penguin' as often as you say the word 'the', you'd remember it; wouldn't you?*

"In our country, in America, the word is used to set aside whatever it is we're talking about; we say 'the rich,' 'the poor,' 'the Feds,' 'the left,' 'the right,' 'the Republicans,' 'the Democrats,' and you get what I'm saying. We put the 'the' where it belongs so that it quietly, very, very quietly, makes us sound smart. Try it yourselves now. Think about those words I just said without the prefaced word 'the' and see how smart you think you sound." He encouraged.

"Go ahead, turn to the guy or gal next to you and talk about things without using the word 'the' and tell me what or who comes to mind the second you do it." He waited. A few seconds went by as he listened to the louder, increasingly louder hum surrounding him, the sound of the audience lifted into the orbiting air with a thirty-foot ceiling to stop their new-found passion of trying to speak in a new standard way.

"Did you hear anything, or more precisely, not hear something that made you instantly aware of how an entire half of our known world speaks?" He asked. *"In the Asian world, the word 'the' isn't really considered. Why would it be? It's useless, it gets in the way, it's unnecessary, and even crude to some.*

"Here, we, American Westerners, think that the word is king, but in reality, it is just what it is, and it is a word, a tool, and a thing we do because everyone says we should. Not everyone, we see that now, but everyone we know because we are here – right here; where the 'the' is the...well, it's king." Dr. Castille's point had been made. *"I suppose in America, where we don't have a king, the word is more akin to a Kennedy."* He laughed.

He went on to explain that in psychology and the pathology of others, sometimes the *'the'* of the world surrounding those individuals becomes blurred enough to let it slip into oblivion for their mental health, so they aren't forced to be the helpless, or the unfortunate, or the outcast anymore. They are often seen outside of places who would prefer them not to be present.

They are seen or dealt with by those who would just as soon not have to be bothered by their ever-present reminder of what it is like to be less than normal; when in reality those very same people are so close to being one of the ones they ignore or abuse. Something happened to them, and at some point, it overwhelmed their situation.

"No one is born a beggar. No one is born sitting on the side of the street corner, in the alleyway, or up on a storefront stoop with a bent piece of cardboard, hoping someone will show a little mercy." The doctor stated, *"I'm reminded, and greatly so, by our good friend and respected singer and musician Phil Collins, that not every day is a day in paradise when others are forced to live in such a way that their very existence is a menace to others. Each day tests their resilience and resourcefulness, but we don't see that. We see filth. We see dejection; we see a lack of self-dignity and something, some grand something out there gives us the right to cast a shade or shadow onto those who would never want to have ended up where they ended up."* He said.

"The word 'the' is also ignored in a huge part of Western society. Give me your attention, please." He asked. *"When was the last time you went on Amazon*

or inside a bookstore, and you looked up a book's title, adding the word 'The' before typing the book's name? Usually, we don't do that, and they certainly don't shelve those books in strict alphabetical order. Otherwise, the section of books beginning with the letter "T" would be half the store!" The audience joined the doctor in laughter when they understood his meaning completely.

"We exalt the word, only to tear it down, sometimes in the same sentence or action. We go into the store and ask for the book by title, using the word 'the,' but we know it won't be there! We wait for the 'the' to be stripped of its glory, and we get our prize, and we go home, not even thinking about what we did to it or if we even had a part in it because we, you and I don't set the rules, do we? No, we adhere to them. Somewhere along the way, 'they' set the rules; we only live in their world...and did you notice the root word of those two words?"

When the conference ended and the applause ended, Leigh wanted to shake hands again with the speaker to let him know he had driven home a point she had been meditating on for a while. If it weren't for the long line of hundreds of others who had the same idea, she might have stayed long enough to do so, but it was, in an authentic way, the norm or the accepted thing to do, to leave, and think about what was discussed or given in the lecture.

If it meant enough to do so, standing her ground would have taken more time than driving to the convention center in the first place. Her choice to leave was influenced by what she could clearly understand to be a choice made using her psychological pathology, which was swarming with societal norms and mores set and instilled in her psyche many years beforehand, quite possibly in her tender-aged time on the planet. She realized she was overthinking again. She found her truck and drove back to Sarasota, listening to the Bee Gees because she could.

Nineteen

As Leigh drove back to Sarasota from the conference center in Fort Myers, she felt her phone vibrate on the old truck's cushy bench seat beside her. Her fingers drummed against the steering wheel as she drove along the coastal road, the sun casting its last warm glow through the windshield. Her mind was buzzing inside her head with thoughts of what it must have been like fifty or sixty years ago when there were no cell phones to bother anyone or to alert them. "*Let me drive a little, will ya,*" she said to no one.

She wondered to herself, *"Which was it?"* If she picked up the cell and glanced at the screen, would the name that flashed across it be someone she knew or someone else, someone unknown until they weren't? She bartered with herself before choosing to do what was expected of the *"they"* and the *"them"* she had been listening about; she decided to answer the call.

All the while, before turning the thing over to see who it was, she recalled a time her mother told her about when designated non-smoking rooms were set up for workers in offices who didn't smoke; they had the right to clean air, and they demanded smaller rooms to sit in for ten to fifteen minutes at a time to find it, how times change. How norms change; how it all changes.

When she saw the call was a text from her younger sister, Macy, it dawned on her that she subconsciously knew it was not a call, because text sounds are entirely different than ringtones. She knew this, but somehow, one side of her mind hadn't caught up with the side that compartmentalized things of that ilk. She blinked twice to center herself before choosing to read the text. The text read, *"Uncle Ike is gone."* Uncle Ike was a man she had been close to throughout her life, especially as a kid, as he had been their unofficial babysitter for years. Icabod George Hooker had been an enigma of sorts in and around the woods and forests that encompassed what was called *"Frog Level,"* Arkansas.

With Ike and his wife Millie being somewhat related when they married, it was indeed the talk of the town when they set off to make a new life for themselves. They hadn't been raised together, and when he walked into her store to buy bait on a sunny Sunday after church, he had no idea he would fall so entirely in love with a woman who had been fathered by his wayward older half-brother who had returned from the war a little too drunk to care about who it was that he took comfort with. In 1942, Margaret Mellie Pruitt was born in another town some fifty miles from DeQueen, where no one asked too many questions.

When she and Ike fell in love, after discussing their relations, it was decided between the two that, for better or worse, they wouldn't have children. Uncle Ike put himself in the pathway of any child coming into the extended family to make peace with their decision, which seemed fine for everyone. Ike loved children, and children loved his quietude – and his penchant for walking them to the ice cream store on the pretense of buying bread and milk; that was Ike. No one expected him to change; he was the ice cream man for too many years to change.

Leigh was twelve years old before anyone told her that her Uncle had married his half-niece. In that part of the world, and those days in particular, another norm was standard, and another culture existed that would be foreign if not rejected by those living by what was considered commonplace today. Aunt Millie had passed of a brain tumor before Leigh was born, but stories about her flooded her childhood memory. If any thought stuck with her when she read the text, it was that Ike and his lover were together again and in peace.

Texting her sister back when she could, Leigh didn't have to ask if Ike would be buried beside his mother and father in Conway; she knew he and his beloved sweet wife had dual plots purchased in the strangely named city of Toad Suck, which if you threw a stone hard enough, could reach the outskirts of Conway. There were similarities of course; the landscaping, the foliage, the common little houses and cottages that all seemed to look the same from one end of the county to the other, but there enough space between the two areas that Millie felt her point would be made when she spent the money for the plots to forever separate them from the tongues and minds of anyone who said they couldn't or shouldn't be together.

"I'll drive to Conway Thursday; let Mom and Cousin Kate know. I can't believe it's been a year since I've been there to see Kate and them; we spend so much time down in DeQueen we forget half the family lives off I-40." She wrote. The text was longer, but Leigh knew her sister wouldn't scroll through it without reading it. Macy may be wild, but she was at least considerate, perhaps the most family-oriented of all the girls – all the Madsens, for that matter.

Leigh had debated whether or not to invite Mathew to go along with her, but even before she had the chance to do so, he had begged off for the next week or so. Charlie, Dempsey, another few men, and himself had decided to give the Hammons their utmost attention; with Jamee Leard's arrest and subsequent arraignment landing her in jail to await her trial, they had to find a way to keep Amara out of the system at her age; doing their best to find a way to emancipate her so she would be on her own legally, and once on her own, in a place she would both afford to live and be able to live after the fire had done its damage.

Leigh reveled in the fact that Mathew had found purpose so suddenly after nearly a year of being so alone, forging for himself a dark and hollowed life where he could hide and not be expected to participate in anything resembling being responsible. The thought hit her mind like a brick wall; his decisions weren't always logical, but she was thinking from a mindset wrapped in her life experiences.

If Mathew had done anything for her, he would had begun to train Leigh in compassion and empathy. She wondered if he had wondered about having been so influential or if he even knew he had been. The latter was most probable. Mathew James Conner was not one to think too highly of himself; in fact, Leigh had taken note for her mind to know that Mathew was somewhat of a self-loather, something she hoped she could do something about. He deserved to know exactly how much he had to offer himself and others.

Her journey from Sarasota, Florida, to Conway, Arkansas, in the cooler autumn air, was a stark difference in scenery. Leigh found the scenery interesting and refreshing to look at through the windshield as she passed, with the windows rolled down on both sides of the cab. She instantly noticed the vibrant hues of orange, red, purple, and yellow leaves that haplessly painted the sides of the road. She could look down into the valleys to see the same colors cascading over forests and wilderness.

Florida was known as the Sunshine State, but Arkansas brought the rugged nature into her life; the Natural State opened its arms to welcome her and all travelers to its wandering wild landscapes, rivers, and streams. Stopping at a roadside diner before pulling into town, she chatted with locals, including Bob Brake, who had recognized the mint green Ford parked beside his newer model truck.

"You did your grandpa proud with that paint job, Miss Madsen; he would have hung you from the barn's top rafter if he had been alive to see it." The man laughed. *"You know he was a traditional man; he'd be OK with it, I suppose, since you're the one who did it, but he'd have whooped Macy in public and then some if she'd tried to pull that off."* Bob chuckled

For the life of her, Leigh couldn't remember exactly how she and her sisters knew Bob and his family, but it had to do something with Uncle Ike if he was in town to pay his respects. They exchanged a few Southern-style niceties and went their separate ways. Of course, saying goodbye in Arkansas took a little time; by the end of their conversation, she learned much more about the Brake side of the family than she may have ever wanted to know.

When she ordered unsweetened tea with her fried catfish combo, she imagined the world had just spun off its axis for a second. No one in the small joint seemed to be moving; they were seemingly mesmerized by her spoken request. Leigh was quietly and suddenly aware that everyone within hearing distance had stopped what they were doing just long enough to turn and take a look at whoever it was in front of the red tile counter that had asked for unsweetened tea in the South.

"We do have it," the cashier said before turning to one of her co-workers to be sure she hadn't lied to her customer. *"I mean, I think we have it. I'll go back in the back to see if we have any. There's little chance of it being upfront since no one usually asks for it. I've been here a few months now, and I think you're the first to ask for it."* She added, before pivoting to investigate the matter.

As night fell, the temperature dropped, and Leigh realized again that she had stepped into a world where heat and humidity were talked about but not always experienced in the latter part of October. Leigh couldn't resist snapping photos with her phone as she trekked from one point of interest to another; Mathew, she told herself, would love to see the woodsy pics, the rustic farms, quaint town signs, and more.

The colors alone would blow him away. She knew he had lived in Illinois for years, but it had been a minute since he had seen anything as beautiful, and she wanted to share it as soon as possible. When he didn't answer her text, saying how lovely the places were, Leigh's throat suddenly closed with the feeling that perhaps she had taken things too fast; maybe Mathew was using this time of separation to rethink what he had done the night of their first kiss.

One thing Leigh hadn't anticipated but was keen to appreciate was the lack of street traffic, both vehicular and pedestrian; Conway may have a Main Street and a major thoroughfare, but for a woman who lived in the Battery Park area of Manhattan, New York, and now lived in one of the most scenic but hustling places of the Gulf Coast, it was simply heaven on earth to drive through a town at rush hour without having to stop, wait, start up again, move a bit, slow down, stop, and start the process over and over again for God knows how long. That stick on the column thing wasn't her friend when that happened.

She loved the city, both cities; Sarasota, and New York City, for that matter, but there was just something about telling people online that she was headed off to Toad Suck, Arkansas, to say goodbye to a loved one that made her heart melt just a little. She knew she wasn't a hardcore Manhattan financial wizard and wasn't the beachy beach type either. She belonged still to that group of folks who sat out on their porches at dusk to watch the fireflies dance and to listen to the cry of the cicada as time slowly slipped away.

The following morning, the day of Uncle Ike's funeral, Leigh had her first hug from her mother's favorite niece, her other sister by proxy, Kate Hooker Tisdale. Like her middle sister Macy, Kate's reputation had been one of rebellion from an early age. As the story goes, Kate married a Native American man for all of three or four weeks right after graduating from high school at Conway.

Jeremy Lightfoot had played ball for a rival team, and had it been baseball or basketball that he engaged in, no one would have thought a thing of it, but for their Kate, their prom queen and homecoming queen, to have married the other team's leading defensive tackle in the same school year that the Branford Buffalos had taken all chance of Conway from making it to the finals, was not tolerable. It was an annulment no one in town was happier to see come about after Kate had put the man in a choke hold, nearly killing him for what she said he had done to her the night before.

"I hate that we had to see each other under this circumstance, but you know, I don't get myself out to the beach as often as I should," Kate said, reaching for her cousin and landing a hug. *"Girl, I've been so proud of you for so long, with your career up in New York City, then your mama told me how you put the screws to the old goats when they tried to railroad you; I swear, Uncle Ike would have complained about a minute before busting his gut if he knew how you took their money and ran!"* Kate's words meant to mend time between the two women.

Leigh countered, *"I still can't believe you kept your married name after you divorced Rodney Tisdale. My mama took the Hooker name back when she and Daddy split. What's up with that? You don't like being a Hooker? What?"* she giggled. *"It's a proud and lofty name...I'm thinkin' of changing my name from Madsen to Hooker, but I do love Daddy, and I don't think he'd like it if I did that."* She laughed, *"...and you know that's the only reason I keep it."*

Kate caught Leigh up about how she had handled her employer after being snubbed professionally; times allowed such forceful retribution. Kate informed Leigh that women are no longer expected to sit and take it from their employers or male co-workers who think that just because they're talking to a woman, she's to be their whipping child. Kate's story about the photos she had taken and uploaded to the company server seemed to shock and impress Cousin Leigh to the point of them both lifting a glass to celebrate.

"What, you don't drink wine?" asked Kate, not realizing there was any other way to unwind. *"Nope. I've been a milk drinker since I was younger, and when I broke both arms in cheerleading my senior year, you remember what Donny Parron's doctor daddy told me; he said a half-gallon of white Vitamin D milk a day would build up my bones to the point that I could be an Olympic gymnast in a year if I wanted to be. I think I knew the man was kidding himself, but he was authentically authoritative when he said it, so here I am, training for the next games, you know."* She said, clinking her glass to Kate's.

When the subject of men came up, as it usually did among the Hooker women, Leigh had something to add for a change. *"Well now, hold on, little sis, I have to get my bearings here for a minute. You're the last Madsen standing. You've not been out there mixing it up for years, and now you're going to tell me that you have yourself a real live boyfriend? What in the stars is happening here, right here in Conway, Arkansas?"* she asked, realizing that the love of the subject must be taking place under the stars somewhere over the Gulf coast shorelines instead.

"Tell me everything!" Kate smiled. Leigh began to blush, thinking maybe one kiss wasn't much to discuss, and she couldn't call Mathew Conner her boyfriend yet, not if he hadn't even texted her to say the foliage was gorgeous. Still, she was willing to let a little gossip free into the air so that the people she was about to encounter for the first time in years would have a smile on their faces when they came up to give her a hug or two when they saw her in the morning at the graveside.

"Mathew, with one 't,' is a few years older than I am." Her words were delivered with care and ease, not to stir too much judgment from her kin. Traditions run deep in the South; she knew. *"He was, back in his day, the town's star footballer, quarterback, and tight end when he needed to be. He ran faster than the others, so when they needed to make a touchdown, the other guy pitched the ball to Mat so he'd be sure and save the day; as he puts it, he did his part. He's pretty modest, really, and I think he'd fit in with the Brakes and Wrays more than he would the Hookers in some*

ways. He's reticent, keeps to himself, and doesn't tread on anyone's feelings, making him well-liked by most."

Her eyes began to soften as she continued to describe the man she found most interesting; she told her cousin how they had been virtually inseparable for a few days after their first and subsequently only kiss and that he hadn't been inclined to make a more passionate move as of yet, perhaps he was waiting until he could find himself in a better financial footing.

Leigh told Kate that Mat felt that if he could offer more to her, it may make a difference. Still, the thought of trying to become a financial equal to her after they both knew about her settlement didn't make sense. She didn't want to wait that long for their relationship to bloom, and Leigh told Kate much as well; money didn't need to be a factor in their future. It couldn't be. It would undoubtedly be an unrealistic expectation on anyone's part to imagine there needing to be a dollar-for-dollar matching going on before there could be true love.

"The kiss…it happened after dinner one night about a week ago. Mathew was a top chef in Chicago for years, and I wanted to try and impress him with my culinary skills, so I invited him up for some old-fashioned Southwestern-style mac and cheese with Louisiana hot sauce drizzled over the top. I threw in a side salad and those cheesy biscuits they serve at the Red Lobster." She said it, and as she did, she suddenly and unconsciously realized she had said *"The Red Lobster"* instead of *"Red Lobster."* The thought of it hung in her eyes and carried her away momentarily.

Leigh's voice grew softer; her gaze drifted back to the woman sitting beside her on the hotel sofa as if beginning a new distant memory. *"It was magical, Kate. After the many years between working and my life in DeQueen as one of the town's most successful stories of escaping life there, I hadn't been kissed by someone who wanted to kiss me in so long; I had nearly forgotten what to feel when it happened. The whole world stopped, just like it does in the movies. I could have been in Disneyland and not been any happier."* She smiled.

"I recently read about the boy I was supposed to end up with in high school; you remember him: David Tucker. How he'd become a cop in Fayetteville, be married, and they have what, three or four kids now? He's doing exactly what everyone expected him to do, and let me say, if I had married him when we graduated, I'd be sending kids off to high school today and not making the choices or seeing the things I'm seeing. Kate," Leigh said.

"Last month, Mathew and I painted seven apartments for people living in squaller at the projects near our home. We made a difference with just a few hours of our time, and I could and probably would never have done that if I had been on the same track that so many of my classmates followed.

"I remember they liked to say they volunteered, maybe mowing someone's grass now and then, but to go into Johnsonville and try and help the folks who never bought from their stores or whose kids played against them in school; they'd never stoop to helping those people. Leigh expressed her deeper feelings. She

hadn't realized it before, not before that night, just how unempathetic she had been raised.

"I can't, and I won't say I'm better; I would never say that. I will say that being unseen for a change is good. I'm not holing up in a corner; I'm out there but not in the local papers or magazines like before. I'm not on some television show discussing stocks and the Dow Jones. I'm working, but not working for myself. I'm finally giving back, and its ambiguity and anonymity is everything! It's just...perfect." She smiled and hugged Kate again.

Twenty

Jamee Leard's arrest shocked the Hammons community not only for the unbelievable act of arson, which she had committed, but the potentially lethal means of ending her own life and the life of her young daughter as well. Amara hadn't been old enough to leave her mother's house and file for separate housing; her absolute dependence on her mother was the only thing keeping her within the walls of the Hammon housing in the first place.

Amara's lifelong dreams of graduating high school, going to college, and bettering herself were first and foremost on her mind. If her mother, if Jamee Leard, believed her daughter was in some trouble with men, it was only in the worn and obtuse mind of the mother herself. Amara had made herself known, but apparently to hardened ears. Her mother loved her; she knew this to be true. Wouldn't she have wanted all that was possible for her only child? Amara had always hoped this would be the case.

For the scared and often untrusting woman who had authority over her more intellectual and educated daughter, the facts Jamee faced regarding the days ahead must have seemed impossible to comprehend.

On one hand, caring for and loving her only family member was Jamee's only obligation in life. She took the obligation so seriously that it nearly cost her every breath she would ever take again.

Her responsibility was fully encompassing from the moment she gave birth to the day she nearly ended Amara's life, believing she was doing the right thing. Twisted as it may seem to most, Jamee's love for her daughter seared within her to the point that protecting her meant taking all outside influences away from her daughter before she could be subjected to its cruel hand of fate.

Captain Bonet-Thomas spoke with Charlie, Doug Dempsey, Mat, and Creed Stabler of the church on the afternoon they had come to the jail to see what could be done to help the fallen woman. *"It's intriguing really when you think about it,"* Bonet-Thomas said, *"In cases where a less educated person has the authority over someone like Amara, a naturally born American girl who has been raised in the same public eye as anyone else who has been born in this country; whose dreams and ideals are fashioned by what they see on television and what they hear at school, it's no wonder Jamee began to believe she was losing her daughter."*

Bonet-Thomas invited the men to sit in the smaller interrogation room where she had first interviewed Leard weeks before. *"She's awaiting her trial; she was transferred this morning to Lowell Correctional in Ocala; they had a bed available. There's a good jail psychologist there that has a private practice as well. He's agreed to evaluate*

Jamee to get her a lighter or more humane sentencing. We know she'll spend over fifteen or twenty years locked away, but maybe not in some lonely jail cell where she could lose all hope to live.

"Maybe Dr. Brannon can put Jamee into the women's ward at Piney Pointe Hospital rather than having her spend her time in max lock-up where she'll revert to her life experiences from living in Africa." Bonet-Thomas hadn't felt so strongly about helping a known perp in all the years she had been a cop.

"Officer, you're a woman, and you're a woman of color," Charlie said, offering his words to the woman to let her know he was aware of the entire situation. *"You've seen your share of hate in this world. I'm sure you or people you know have been profiled. Even now, after all you've achieved, I bet when you take the uniform off, and no one around you knows or sees who you are, you know more than anyone, except for maybe these two men beside me, Doug and Creed; what it's like to be black in the South. Creed is older than me, and I remember the nonsense; how people were treated even before the riots.*

"Jamee has it ten times harder," Charlie added, *"she's not from here; she's foreign, her ways are foreign, and even her thoughts must be. Can you tell me that she's competent to stand trial? I wish we could afford to get her a good attorney."* He said, knowing the church would not have the funds to make that happen. He also knew he could ask his online audience to chip in if needed; he had quite a substantial following.

The officer smiled, taking a second to hear and accept Charlie Garrett's words for how they were given. *"I'm one hundred percent in agreement with you, Pastor. I can tell you this: Jamee's plight has not gone unnoticed in the media."* She stated. *"Jamee's story was plastered all over the news the night she was arrested, and the next day, after her arraignment and after she and I had talked, my phone would not stop ringing.*

" We had a dozen attorneys from all over the state of Florida volunteering to represent her either because they knew it would help their career, or maybe they had one good artery in their jaded black hearts to see her for what she is: a pathetic woman in great need of true justice and mercy. I don't know," she said.

"I do know this: she will have good counsel soon enough because the judge, in this case, had about eight or nine of those attorneys send him briefs telling him what their plan was for her, and I know they all said they want her to spend time where she'll get the help she needs and be able to be close enough to her only kin who she loved more than life itself; almost literally." Her words struck hard and made their point.

Before the trial, Jamee's fate was sealed; she would sit and wait for the inevitable. While she was meeting with Dr. Brannon, he managed to extract from her the complicated and elementary truth behind her actions the night she set fire to their apartment at the Hammons. It wasn't a story he wasn't familiar with; it was the same sad and helpless story he knew she had experienced for all of her life. Hearing it come from her made it even harder to ignore.

Dr. Brannon wrote in his notes that Jamee Leard was a younger adult, thirty-four years old, and the mother of a girl the about the same age she was when giving birth to her daughter. She, Jamee, was still very foreign to her new country, where she had been given the free rights of every naturally born citizen due to the horrific and terrible life she had been subjected to as a minor, having been literally plucked from and rescued by the Catholic Charities close to two decades before.

Jamee's complex emotional state resulted in the mother clinging tighter than is usually done by those raised under American traditions and cultural mores. She tried to hold onto what she saw slipping away so swiftly; essentially, she believed her daughter was being stripped of her; she had to do something. Her mental capacity differed from those who had been raised in the civility of our nation, and its expectations for its citizenry.

Considering the cultural context of what she had done lent one to consider various social values of filial piety; what must the woman be thinking to have ever conjured such a thought as to raise her hand to harm the way she did; intense emotional fears mixed with obligation, protection, it must have been an overwhelming mental cocktail for Leard.

"What do you think she could have done?" wrote Dr. Brannon in his notebook, asking himself to remember what outcomes could have been more acceptable if his patient could have understood them.

When discussing the matter with Bonet-Thomas, Dr. Brannon mentioned that many people in Leard's predicament would have done the same thing; most of the ones he had dealt with in the past had been of Islamic background, where mercy killings were not only accepted, they were expected if the subject of the act had shamed the family, or had been tainted by someone outside of their faith.

Mores, norms, societal values—none of these made sense to Mathew Conner when he weighed the act Jamee Leard committed against the potential life experiences her daughter would have had if the event had never taken place. It seemed as if Jamee had been struck by an insatiable ennui, such dissatisfaction with life that she had gone too far without realizing her actions were as severe as others perceived them to be.

Now, he surmised, Amara would not only be forced to be emancipated, separated, and cut off from her mother's care but she would also be forced to work, to earn a living, perhaps not be allowed to attend classes and to better herself in ways that, had her mother's mind been more *"American,"* she would have been able to do. If only she had been given the same opportunities as everyone else about attending homecoming, a rite Amara seemed destined to be exclusively excluded from.

Mathew felt his presence with the others in the room was meaningless in some ways. He couldn't do much for Jamee, but the fact that the men had purposely asked him to be present meant they must believe his insight was important. He couldn't bring her any comfort; he couldn't be more of assistance other than just one of the many who felt strongly that life had not treated her with any form of fairness whatsoever. He knew fairness wasn't expected from life, it never is, but somewhere along the line, everyone told everyone else to try and be fair to those they could be fair to; maybe some of it would rub off when they needed it most.

Dr. Brannon's notes were faxed to Bonet-Thomas so she could present them to the attorney once the judge had decided who would represent the demure soul in the future. He had taken the time to write out a more personal note to the police captain, letting her know what he found to be profound in his observations; he wrote, *"As a psychologist, I encourage people to find meaning and grow in challenging situations; but this case is so vastly different from anything I can comprehend professionally. Jamee is deserving of our pity as much as our mercy."* He added.

By fostering an open conversation with the men from The Superior Word church, Captain Bonet-Thomas expressed her love and pride of being counted among them as Christian believers who could and would put Jamee's matter in the hands of a King and Judge would be more merciful than anyone on the bench in their state. It being such a delicate matter to consider, they hoped to collectively stand with their friend, even if she hadn't considered them to be more than just workers and uninterested parties in the past. Change is the only constant in life; these men and Captain Bonet-Thomas had been privileged to know that.

"When we're in that courtroom we see the big brass plaque behind the judge saying 'In God We Trust'; you'd think more people would remember that when they sentence lives like hers to the cells to remain sequestered from the very people who could make a difference in her life and their own. I'm torn when I see that plaque. I wonder if we should bring it to their attention now and again; maybe they'd sit a little straighter in their seats." She told the men.

When the four men left the precinct's interrogation room, Mathew approached Charlie, asking him if he could use his cell long enough to call or text Leigh. *"Hey Charlie, I hate to ask, but I need to use your phone if you don't mind. I want to text Leigh quickly to tell her I'm still alive. I've not had my phone in a few days; she's probably thinking I ran off or something."* Mathew's eyes were doing most of the asking. He said.

He had lost his phone a few days back, he told the pastor, on the beach, trying to save a dog. He didn't know if she was even aware; he hadn't contacted her the entire time she had spent in Arkansas going to and returning from her uncle's funeral. As he told Charlie the events of what happened leading up to the loss of his phone, Charlie couldn't help himself; he asked Mathew if the fact that he'd not seen the man behind the church in the past few days had anything to do with a particular private dinner party he had gotten wind of; the hearsay was pretty cheap in their circles.

"What happened to the dog?" asked Charlie, silently and mentally, counting his own eight dogs in his mind, making sure he had put eyes on each of them

over the past day or so. Mathew stood straighter to look Charlie in the eyes before relaying precisely what had happened; the thought of it churned in his gut again; he hadn't let it bother him until that moment. Charlie reached into his pocket to pull out the new cell phone he'd been gifted anonymously by someone in the church. He had never read the instruction manual, so not all bells and whistles were being used.

"I forget just how tall you are until I'm beside you, brother. If I was honest with myself, I think I'm five-eleven, but you're at least six foot." He told the preacher, who immediately sprung onto his toes to say that he could stand up even taller if he weren't bound to wear his shoes inside the more public buildings. *"They make my feet hurt!"* He told Mat. *"That's what happens when you don't use them; they cramp your style a little...and make you look like everyone else."*

The dog, Mathew explained, after taking the phone and a deep breath, pushing aside the harsh, immediate memories from the event, had been nearly drowned by three boys on vacation on the Gulf coast over fall break. They were northerners whose parents had paid their way to come to the beach to spend four days of unbridged idiocy while doing whatever to whomever they wanted. One of the boys had told the police, after being arrested for their antics, that he believed anything that happened on the beach stayed on the beach. What foolery!

The boys, Mathew said, couldn't have been eighteen; one of them may have been. They flew down from up north, possibly Jersey, and made their way to the beach. Mathew and another man he had been talking to had seen the boys trying to buy liquor at an open beach bar, but they had been turned away. Naturally, they weren't about to give up on finding drinks for themselves or maybe something more substantial than beer, something they could smoke. It was still illegal for them to do, but easier to obtain, Mathew continued.

There were plenty of ways to find alcohol, and the three knew it. Before long, Mathew saw them again, back on the crowded end of the beach, this time higher than they should have been, carrying a medium-sized black wire-haired dog that could have been a Schnauzer mix or something like it. She seemed distressed and tried her best to rid herself of the three, but without success.

One of them had tied a strap around the dog's neck, and when they sat her down, another boy had pulled out a small lighter from his pocket and was attempting to light the dog's fur on fire. This immediately drew Mathew's attention, and he left the company of the man he was with while cautiously approaching the three younger men.

"They had stopped trying to light the dog on fire when they saw me but proceeded to drag her by her legs, and they were bent on doing so. She couldn't use her legs to stay afloat. She was being dragged under as a result, and they kept swimming sort of or running in unison, going further and further out. I panicked a little but kept running.

"I couldn't stand it, but I also knew I couldn't run fast enough to catch up to them; maybe they figured that out too. No one on the beach was doing a damn thing about it. Twenty others must have been

watching, even videoing with their damn phones, but not one of them got up to stop these guys." Mathew's mind raced, his memory growing stronger.

"I didn't think about much; I kicked off my shoes. I knew they'd get in the way, but I didn't take my phone out of my back pocket before running in after them, screaming. Maybe someone on the beach heard me, saw what was going on, and one of them had to have called the cops because, by the time I got to the dog and convinced her that I was going to help her, a few good Samaritans were holding the three until they were taken into custody by the lifeguards long enough to wait on Sarasota cops to show up." He finished.

"You kept the dog?" asked Charlie, still concerned for the animal. *"No. I only kept her for a few minutes on the beach, thinking I'd have a dog for a while until I could find her owner, but someone volunteered to take her to her brother, a vet in Kensington Park. She pulled out her cell and called him right then, and there he agreed to see the dog. I let the woman have her. I didn't even get her name."* He told Charlie, *"But I can tell you this: if those cops hadn't taken those boys in, I would have been sitting next to Captain Bonet-Thomas for another reason today."* Mathew said with purpose.

"You know, T, we hold people to impossible standards; we hold ourselves to those same standards sometimes and don't need to do that. We need to trust God's plan. When you think about it, any problem you have to bring to Him is so tiny by comparison; He created the universe, didn't He?" Charlie asked.

"*Of course, you can use my phone and let Leigh know we're praying for her and her family. She's not told me much about her Uncle Icabod, but if anyone that had to go through life with a name like that, you know he's got some good stories to tell.*" Charlie said, trying to imagine being called Icabod rather than Charlie.

Twenty-One

Her heart skipped inside her chest when she saw Charlie's name flash across the screen of her phone. She imagined for a split second that he was calling her to say Mat had been found behind a bush somewhere beaten and he hadn't long to live. She quickly answered, her voice tinged somewhat with disquieted concern until she heard his voice. *"Mat! I was starting to think you'd hiked to the Himalayas to get away from ever having to speak to me again,"* she teased lightly, trying to hide the nervousness that was creeping up inside of her at the moment. Mathew's laughter caught her right where she wanted to be, between being happy and feeling wanted.

Leigh couldn't believe what he was telling her about the dog, but because he was using Charlie's phone to call her just to let her know he was doing OK, he told her he would fill her in on all the details as soon as she returned. He also thought it might be a good idea for her to get a dog for herself, for protection, but they could also talk about that when she got back.

He wanted her to know he had missed her, that Charlie and the church had prayed for her and her family, and that Hideko had written a small poem encouraging her, and she'd get it when she pulled into her driveway. He wanted to know when he could expect her. She had been gone a few days, and when he had taken off to reset himself over the same few days, time had slipped into oblivion.

The thought of wanting to expect someone suddenly sunk inside him, and he couldn't retract what he had just asked. Knowing that she was expected changed Leigh's perception of what she had thought may or may not have been an actual relationship. Hearing Mathew say he expected to see her meant something more substantial than if he had hoped to see her.

The thought did occur to her that if he had lost the phone on Friday when he said he had saved the dog, and he had presumably gone to church on Sunday because he lived outside of it and he could hear the congregation gathering just outside his door; why had he not asked Charlie to use the phone two days ago, to see how she was doing or to let her know he had lost her phone? She couldn't shake the fact that she was now thinking what she was thinking, and it caused her to breathe a little faster.

"On the dog front," she told him, *"...you don't have to worry about that one."* She laughed, looking over to her right side where a small black and white pitty-mix was gingerly gnawing on a half-eaten rawhide bone she'd found tucked up under her truck's seat. *"While walking out of the Starbucks outside of Toad Suck, I heard a noise coming from inside my truck."* She told him.

"When I opened the passenger side door, I found a puppy with a note neatly pinned to his collar. The note reads, 'You need me, and you know it.' It wasn't signed, but I recognized the handwriting; my sister Macy had managed to tail me from Conway to Toad Suck because she knew I'd stop by Starbucks on my way out of town. She snuck the dog into my truck and took off before she could be stopped."

"I'm not going back to take the dog back; besides, I can only say I know the handwriting. It could be anyone from my family or any one of the three hundred folks who showed up at Uncle Ike's funeral. Let me say that Roscoe is already twenty-something pounds at about two months, so he'll be doing his share of protecting me, I'm sure of that." She said, with one hand on the wheel and the other rubbing the head and the back of the neck of the rowdy little fella next to her.

Hanging up, Leigh knew she and Mathew had crossed another one of those invisible lines that couples create for themselves: the dog line. When a couple commits to having a dog together, they are all but telling the world that they are a couple and that if for no other reason than the complexity of caring for this animal's life, the two will remain together for at least as long as the dog is there to be loved by them both. Leigh sighed a good long sigh before telling herself she had just stepped right over a line she had left drawn in the sand too many years beforehand.

A few hours later, the old mint green Ford pulled into the parking lot outside the Stratford Manor condominiums on Shoreline Drive just after dark. As Leigh opened her door, she presented Mathew with a ball of wigging fur. His eyes lit up, and the genuine smile broadening across his face was contagious. He crouched down a little to take the pup into his arms, allowing Roscoe to lick his weathered face, admiration beaming brightly in his blue eyes. *"He's a keeper!"* he said to Leigh, watching her happiness surge from deep inside her.

Straightening up, he took in Leigh's appearance. It had only been a few days; he hadn't felt this way in so long; he wondered if it would have been prudent to think that way now after such a short time of being whatever they were. They settled into the unit for a few minutes, ensuring the dog had food, water, and a comfortable place to call his own. When it came time to take him for a walk, the two of them walked side by side, almost in unison, their weight causing the pier's boardwalk to creak a little.

Mathew's voice creaked a little as he told Leigh about Jamee Leard, recalling the words of the police captain about what would become of Jamee and how she would spend so many years locked away for her actions. In some ways, he told Leigh, she was trying to be invisible but couldn't have been more noticed if she had tried. Her actions and behavior went so far out of the norms of what the Western world expects that she was deemed heinous when she was doing what she considered to be only virtuous. How could so many differences exist in the space?

"When I lived in merry old England after I graduated college and before I went to New York to work, I couldn't get over the differences between the people of the United Kingdom and ourselves. Keep in

mind that America is a vast place. I think fifty or so United Kingdoms can fit inside our borders. So when I say we have so many differences, I'm saying there were so many things we did in Arkansas that I couldn't do in England or Scotland when I stayed there for a month before coming home.

"The first thing I noticed, because it was just after graduating, and while Arkansas was already heating up to something like ninety degrees in June, is that I was wearing two layers to stay warm over there. I never took off one of them and half the time; I had the hood of my hoodie up if it rained. I don't think I've ever owned an umbrella." She said. Her words created an image in Mat's mind that lent itself to seeing a younger, bouncier, red-blooded American girl taking England by storm; if Macy, from what he knew about her, had accompanied her older sister, it would have taken all of the king's men to wrangle them both.

"The beds were tiny; there was no air conditioning, but we didn't need it then. There were no screens on the windows to be found anywhere in the country, not just in the hotel. There were," she told him, *"folded blankets and sheets on the bed rather than the bed being made as if the maids didn't do that in their country. We were expected to keep the room tidy, while here in the States, as you know, a maid would roll over and die if she left the bed untucked after 10:00 a.m."* she laughed.

"When I went to breakfast, I didn't realize I would have to pay for the second cup of coffee, and the portions they served were so small, I wondered if my breakfast at the poshest posh place I could have found

was one of those Continental breakfasts you hear about over on this side of the pond.

"Let me say that it made me appreciate IHOP; we'll leave it at that. It would have been much more appreciated and affordable, and I would have had a waitstaff member come by and ask me if I needed anything else; that sort of thing doesn't happen when you're in the UK, friend." She said before asking him if he had ever been outside of the United States.

"Does Canada count?" he asked. *"If it does, then yes, I have been. You can go to Detroit and step over the border so you can say you've been to another country, but most of us here in the States, as you said, it's so big, we don't even own passports. I think I read somewhere that only thirty percent of Americans own passports, and most of them are business travelers; we don't, as a nation, go off on vacation outside our borders if we don't need to."* He answered. *"I have been to about twenty or twenty-five states; I'd have to count them up, I guess; same as being in Europe and traveling."*

He said, *"They may have old castles, history, and all that, but we have fifty countries next to each other, with individual personalities, laws, cultures, traits, traditions, you name it, you can't beat the good old United States for traveling and sightseeing; and..."* he added, with a smirk, *"every last hotel in our entire country as far as I know anyway, have screens on their windows, air conditioning, free coffee, and some of those little shampoo bottles that we all steal and say we need more of."* He laughed.

"You wondered why my hair smelled as good as it does, right?" he asked, *"Bonnie Kemp from the church is head of housekeeping at the Sheridan downtown, and she brings me things. She loves me."* He said, laughing but being somewhat serious at the same time. *"I told her once I could use a packet of mayonnaise the next time she goes downstairs to the kitchen area. She told me they only carried Hellmann's, but she would try to sneak a few. I guess she had hoped for Duke's brand, but anything works."* He told her.

Leigh repositioned herself, moving Roscoe to her left side to be closer to Mathew. Reaching up with her free hand, she brushed back a random stray hair from his face to see his eyes more clearly. At her touch, Mathew felt secure again; a warmth spread through him, pushing back a lingering cold of what was once his solitary existence. Leaning into her, they embraced lightly, not allowing complete contact, keeping enough air between them to stare into each other's faces as they made the moment their own.

His heart raced as he looked into her amber eyes, seeing a reflection of his past, his new hope, and something entirely new for him. He could see and understand that someone wanted to be with him, near him for who he was—without strings attached, without something more cynical to push someone else's agenda. This was new to them both, and they hadn't managed to express independently how they handled it. Their silence was enough.

"What made you think we could be us?" she asked, her head resting on his chest, the three of them cuddled up beside a few palms on the edge of Turtle

Beach's central public waterfront. *"You see something in me that I thought I'd never see again."* He answered. *"Thank you. By the way, it feels unbelievable to have someone think good things about me, say good things about me, and to know someone is actually praying for me."*

He said, then quickly reiterating what he meant for her to fully understand, *"I mean, my mother would pray for me, don't get me wrong. I think my grandmother, and maybe a few others, but they more or less do it because of their position in life; they're obligated to do it, no, but they say those stale little prayers that God probably gets tired of hearing because they don't have any real purpose outside of their duty, right?"* he said.

"You actually pray for me; I've heard you. I've also heard others say you do. You don't know that, but Aom, the waitress from the Thai restaurant, told me you prayed for me, too; your secret is out! I know!" he laughed again, thanking her. *"To know someone is asking God to protect me, that goes beyond my imagination."* He hadn't been more serious with anyone about any subject that he could recall.

"I was never protected growing up, not by my parents, my teachers, or even my fiancé's father, who wanted to kill me for doing what I do best: cook. He could have protected that; we could have had something together for the family, but I wasn't family; he made that point clear...and now, looking back, I put myself where I shouldn't have been. I thought money and prestige would equal success; I couldn't have been more wrong." He said.

Mathew's mind drifted before looking again into Leigh's softer gaze, telling her that having someone who cared enough meant more to him than words could express. He held her, not wanting to let her go even long enough to catch another deep breath. He wanted the night to linger on without interruption; this moment, he told himself, was as perfect as any moment he could have ever wished for.

"If you were thinking I would have a lot of words for you, then...well, you've got another thing to think because I don't", she told him, catching him off guard. Mathew froze for a fraction of a second at what he thought he saw flashing in Leigh's eyes just before she fully took him into her arms and kissed him passionately on the mouth. He had expected her to return, but he hadn't expected this sort of welcome when she did.

His arms instantly wrapped around her slender frame, pulling her closer as he deepened their connection. The world and Roscoe were forgotten momentarily as everything else, but they seemed to fade into the distance. When they finally broke apart, he rested his forehead against hers, their breath mingling, paced in unison in the thick, humid night air. He closed his eyes once more, savoring every single second for as long as he could.

"I...I don't know what to say, except this is new territory for me, and I want you to know I want to explore it. I want you to explore it with me." He told her. At that moment, he realized, as she had perhaps realized a few hours beforehand, that his life had taken an unexpected turn, one filled with uncertainty. Still, one filled also with more hope than he had imagined

could ever have happened to him after all he had been through.

"*Let's do this.*" He whispered.

Twenty-Two

Time moved as time moves, and before either of them knew it, they had made plans to shop together for food. He was about to buy groceries for the first time in a long time. He arrived at Walmart and pulled into the store parking lot, picking out a spot where he instinctively knew the truck and its paint job would be unmolested. Mathew parked the old truck close to two shiny, newer model SUVs, thinking about the differences between the years of the vehicles, their purpose when they were made, and how they looked to anyone glancing at them. Almost instantly, the thought occurred to him that he may have been spending so much time with Leigh lately that some of her thinking processes were rubbing off on him.

He caught the subtle differences between the SUV on his left side and the one to his right. Both are dark, tall, rather boxy, and sleek in their own way. If a person didn't recognize the vehicle's make by the little tag on the grill, they could very well mistake a Mercedes for a Chevy; how times had changed, he thought. Their truck had a distinct Ford look, something the manufacturer wasn't about to share with their competition; no one mistook a Ford for a Chevy, not in 1960.

He had to look it up, and he did. Sitting beside the two mammoth brutes of mechanized machinery, Mathew Googled how many 1960 Ford-100 model trucks were made. The answer: hundreds of thousands of half-ton pickup trucks were made that year for Ford in that model. It was the first year for what was called the third generation of the F-100; before that, they referred to it as the F-series; and before that, of course, they were called the Model 50, the Model A, with the first rendition of the thing being called the Model TT back in 1917. *"The things you learn, Roscoe,"* Mathew said, glancing over at the dog who had sat patiently, allowing Mathew to learn a little more than he knew moments before.

"Did you know, Roscoe, that the word 'the' is in front of so many things? No, no, really, it is." He laughed, scratching the pup up and under his collar. *"The F-Series, the Model A, the Model 50, or this or that. They are always prefaced with the word 'the,' Now I sound like Leigh, and I know why she wants to write that book, like her cousin did. She wants to bring more attention to those who don't even know they're being categorized by it; they are the 'the,' and they have no idea."* He spoke under his breath. *"There are too many 'the' people, Roscoe, too many,"* Mat told the dog before reaching down to prepare the dog and walking through the doors together.

"Alright, buddy, let's get you some grub. They can't tell me I can't bring you in with me, not now. I have your little vest on straight with those magical

words of social justice, 'Emotional Support Animal' embroidered right on it." Mathew laughed a little, *"...best money spent! Amazon to the rescue."* His words fell on the dog's caring ears. However, he wasn't sure if Roscoe fully understood everything he and Leigh had gone through to make this moment possible.

As they navigated through the aisles, people took time to smile, wave, and ask if they could pet Roscoe, seeing that his vest didn't say that he was in training or shouldn't be approached. Mathew explained that he was an emotional support dog, and yes, he was in training, but an emotional support dog didn't have to live by the same strict rules about not socializing with others. Roscoe was helping Mathew get back on track to do just that.

"I thought I could just run in and get the food and stuff, maybe take a few minutes. You, sir, are a chick magnet, to say the least; look who you already drew into your little web. You got the best one ever! You'll share, I'm sure. I don't mind either; we'll both be happier with Leigh in our lives and caring for you makes us even more secure in whatever we do." He said.

Mathew knew it wasn't much; it was just a dog, but he felt humbled somehow by the simple joy of providing for someone, another living being. He had thought about finding a way to keep the dog he rescued from the thugs on the beach, but he never got that feeling in his gut that he would do it. This time, he had more than just a feeling about it; he was doing it, and by doing it, he knew he was on the right path to healing for good.

"Let's get you the best stuff they have, pal. Please live a long time, and be healthy the whole time you do it, will ya? Now, don't worry about it; if Leigh doesn't do so, you can sneak over to my side of the table or over to the couch if we eat our dinners there; you can count on me. I'll give you a little off my plate to cut some calories." He told the dog, *"It's always been a good diet plan; why change now?"*

Leigh caught up with the boys in the store, having caught a ride with one of her church friends on their way to the Hammons; it was Saturday again, and that's what most of the married men who attended the small community congregation were. They considered it their *"men only"* time, a place and space where they could talk about life, their wives, family, goals, and such, and in Dempsey's words, *"...get a word in edgewise"*.

Most of the men didn't mind Mathew's company, as he was both practical and had a lifelong history of experiences he would share to fit in and was open to hearing what all manner of advice he could muster from the men, but having Leigh at the projects made things a little restless for most of them; everyone except Charlie. He saw the potential of bringing more women with them when they improved units or sat to talk with people who had been hurt or abused by the more masculine of the sexes.

"There you are! My boys!" Leigh said, giving Mathew the first hug, quickly squatting to get a kiss or two from the ever-growing pup. *"We're in the right place,"* she told them. They scanned the shelves, looking for the right food, knowing it would be more

expensive than the store-brand bags, but every penny was worth it. Roscoe was to be spoiled from the get-go; another Southern thing to say, another Southern thing to do.

"Which would you prefer, Roscoe, for the first official bag since we're doing this as a family? Would you like the chicken and rice or the beef-flavored food?" Leigh asked. When Roscoe nosed the bottom of the bags closest to the floor, he placed his left paw onto the bag directly in front of him. *"Oh, well then, salmon it is,"* Leigh stated, lifting the bag and placing it into the buggy. As she did, she instantly remembered that while living just outside of London, the locals called the thing they used to cart the food around a *"trolley,"* not a cart, not a basket, not a buggy.

"Again, so many differences. Even food! They call a zucchini a courgette. I can't even pronounce it correctly. They call an eggplant an aubergine, and they don't even have mustard greens, I don't think, but they call pop cycles lollies. Seriously, lollies, I'm not lying, but wait, no, I am lying; they call them ice lollies; my bad." She laughed.

Mathew had been in the food industry and was well aware of the names others called squash, melons, and other vegetation. He laughed silently when he remembered the first time someone told him he'd be eating mince and mushrooms, thinking it was something sweet. He hadn't wrapped his head around it before seeing that the dish before him was only ground beef infused with garden mushroom bits and a savory sauce brown gravy that made the whole thing palatable.

"I thought of something I want to run by you, Mathew. I need your opinion on it. Remember, I'm not asking permission; I'm letting you know because I want you to know who I am. I value your opinion, but you have to know I'm not going to do or not do something just because someone disagrees with me. It has to be my idea not to do it if you get what I'm saying." She realized only after the words had left her mouth that she had probably just insulted the man without meaning to do so.

"I get you not asking for permission, but do you at least care if I have a concern or disagree with you?" he asked. *"Would you take what I think or say into consideration, at least? Otherwise, why tell me first that you want my opinion or to know what I think?"* As they walked through the store, the silence between them exploded. Mathew thought of all the times he had made snap decisions without consulting anyone, or if he had, it was only to be polite. He hated that man.

"Can I tell you something before you ask my opinion?" his words barely a whisper. Looking into her eyes, she had already felt remorse for how she framed her question, or was it a statement? She wasn't sure now what or why she had said it. *"I don't want to be the worthless homeless man in your life. I know the value of the word now; 'the.' I see what it means, and it scares me. It scares the hell out of me, Leigh. I'm a 'the' to almost everyone, but I didn't think you thought way about me, too.*

"I don't want to identify as that; I have a place. I have a tiny little corner, but I have a place. It's almost as if the only opinions we share are yours; I don't

know if you take what I say seriously, or if you're patronizing me because I'm something or someone you can count on to be there based on what you have to know now about what you mean to me." He told her, taking a step backward, to distance himself before saying what had to be said.

"That's what it feels like. It feels like I just had a bone thrown to me from off the table, maybe one that would be thrown away, but why not go ahead and give it to Jimmy?" He couldn't look at her while he spoke; after a few seconds, he stopped talking. She felt his words; they numbed her. She hadn't yet learned to curb her abruptness or to soften her approach. Being assertive, even to the point that some would say aggressive, was how she needed to communicate to stay in the game. It cost her more than she could express at that moment.

Pulling out his wallet, he handed her a twenty-dollar bill and told her he wanted, that he needed to contribute to whatever Roscoe needed. As for the rest of the groceries, they were hers to buy for herself, for now, anyway. He needed to get away before he said something he might regret. With that, he turned and left them. Upon realizing the impact of her words, Leigh immediately felt a wave of regret wash over her. She had always been direct, a trait that sometimes came across too bluntly, but she never intended to hurt him.

After leaving the store, he wanted to go back and tell her where he had parked the truck, but to do so would cause him to surrender again, and it couldn't happen. He needed to face this thing that came between them. He couldn't give in and sweep it away as if it wasn't real. They would have their disagreements; this was inevitable. He had walked away; he knew she'd be alright, but the protector in him drove him to walk to the back of the lot where he had parked and to move the Ford much closer to the front where she usually parked so she wouldn't have more to weigh on her mind than what he had just placed.

Her overachieving in virtually every aspect of her life led to many conflicts with coworkers, family members, lovers, and even good friends like Sarina Kelly. Leigh's one overt fault, if she could call it that, was opening her mouth and having the ability to shove her foot so far down it that she could no longer think clearly enough to realize just how much of an ass she was.

Reaching her condo, Leigh carried the bag of dog food and other items through the foyer and to the elevator, where she and Roscoe rode to the eighth floor. Opening the door, she felt an emptiness that could only mean that Mathew had decided to leave, not to stay as they had planned. To her surprise, she found a short handwritten note sitting on the edge of the dining room table, where his plate would ordinarily be. Her brow furrowed as she read his words, concern began to etch on her face.

She understood the situation completely. She had once again managed to alienate someone and isolate herself simultaneously; such a talent, she told herself, one she wished she had never perfected. He told her in a few words that he needed a little time to think and reflect on more than just what she had said. What she had said, he told her, was no more than just a catalyst that sprung another part of his mind, his memory, into gear, causing him to fear and take matters to a place they had no place going.

His words were ominous; he had mentioned that when a man doesn't like being alone, it could very well be that he doesn't like the person he's with; this could be why he enjoyed their time together. She took the pain from him, he told her on more than one occasion; she removed the guilt he brought upon himself for saying things he could never say to another human, but because he was telling them to his reflection, he believed himself.

"Leigh, I will just be a few days; not long. I need it, and I know you wouldn't want me there feeling how I feel right now. You mean too much to me, and I can't let you go. I'm not asking you to stay, but I hope you do. I'll call you. I won't be home or in my place, but I will call you soon. I don't want to be a burden. Love, Mathew". The note was hurriedly written and folded; it was placed where he knew she would find it.

Considering the situation, Leigh allowed her mind to return to what he had told her about the homeless man outside the store the day before: the word. Was he more upset about the word *'the'* or *'homeless'*? She wondered. He wrote he didn't want to be a burden but was anything but. Roscoe stared at her from his new perch on the edge of the couch, inviting her to tell him everything; he was there to support her emotionally, wasn't he? Isn't that what his vest read?

"I'll have to do what he says, Roscoe. I don't have a choice. He's not mine to tie down; I can't claim he is. He's not going to the little store room behind the

church; he's probably walking the beach or taking time with the men over at the projects, if I had to guess; it's Saturday. That makes more sense, I guess." She talked endlessly for another hour to the dog to let him know exactly where she stood on the matter of allowing Mat to have the time he needed, the time he promised to use to bring them closer together.

"He's a little weird that way, Roscoe. Not to be rude or anything, and you don't have to tell him I said this, but the other day, when he suggested we have that 'confession time' when we tell each other things we hate and things we love, I had to stop and ask if what I divulge was going to be stored in his memory banks somewhere only to be used against me in our first huge fight.

Leigh cuddled up next to their dog, and she held him, maybe thinking if she did, Mathew would feel it too; she told the dog, *"You know, I'm giving him ammunition. I told him I hated the word 'derp,' and it's true, I do, but I also hate the word 'bandicoot,' and if I told him that, I think he'd use it – and use it a lot, when I don't want him to."* She confessed before washing her face and thinking of not eating because food didn't mean so much at the moment.

She thought about it; she couldn't not think it through. It was the bane of her life; she was a constant and persistent thinker. Jamee Leard's apartment wasn't finished, but it was enough so that if he wanted to hole up there for a day or more, he could, and no one would try to stop him. It was a perfect place to be if he wanted to be alone while, at the same time, doing what he could be a part of something; such paradox, such

248

contrast. She couldn't stop her mind from racing. Even the candle, with all its minty powers, couldn't help her.

" I just wanted to know what he thought about my idea, Roscoe, about the book I want to write, how I want to live homeless, or what I can do for a few days to see what it's like to live that way. In England, again with the whole difference thing, to keep that vibe going..." she told the dog

"They call it living rough. They say the people are homeless, but they say 'living rough' rather than living on the street. I think it's because they're out under the stars and in the elements, but not necessarily on the street itself." She rubbed the dog's neck, shoulders, and back, assuring his undivided attention.

"I heard a folk singer from Edinburgh talking about his experiences while I was there. He told the audience in the little theatre we were gathered in to hear him sing and tell his testimony that he lived rough. It was the first time I had ever heard the term. It fascinated me; everyone else fixed their eyes on the man, but here I was, trying to figure out precisely what that word meant.

"He went on to say that he lived openly, outside, and sometimes he found himself under the streets, in cutaways or what I think he called vaults; something unique to that area since Scotland is way older than America; we don't have the same structures lurking about like they do." The dog's attention span had changed somewhat; he sighed and closed his eyes.

"Roscoe, listen to me. I'm talking to you." She scolded. *"The singer said he lived rough and that he did so intentionally. He would bounce from shelter to shelter but got kicked out of them all because of his tendency for violence; he had a penchant for getting into fights over alcohol or maybe drugs he wanted to score. I can't remember. He said he had outstayed his welcome everywhere and with everyone. He said he had become a burden! There it is! He thought of himself as being a burden; is that what Mat thinks?"* she gasped, *"God, I hope not."*

She asked the dog another rhetorical question before retreating to her bedroom, rolling over on her bed, and allowing herself to cry. She took a few deep breaths, letting her chest inflate and deflate purposely while her eyes searched the ceiling for hope and understanding. Inwardly, she hated the moment she had created but knew this wasn't the first time she had painted herself into a corner she couldn't step out of alone.

"You're nearly forty, Leigh!" she said out loud and to the heavy air around her. *"You'd think you could figure out how to stop being so stupid!"* Mathew wasn't anything like the others; he wasn't. He may have had similar experiences, but there was something deeper inside of him that never let him go through with some of the things he told her he thought about; he wasn't suicidal. He loved life.

"Roscoe, he cries, and I love that. Most men don't want to show their emotions. They're afraid to be genuine; they've been told that real men don't cry – but they do, Roscoe! They do cry." At that moment,

Leigh understood so much more about him than perhaps she had allowed her heart to explore or accept. She knew something else, too: that real women cry when they can't say how sorry they are for being insensitive.

Twenty-Three

Charlie Garrett was a very young man, not even a teenager when he had fallen head over heels for the most beautiful creature in the world. At least, he thought she was, and her name was Hideko. What a name, he told himself. He repeated it often, saying it slowly, allowing each syllable to fall from his tongue and catch on his lips when he whispered it.

A soft smile spread across Charlie's face at the mention of his wife's name, Hideko. *"Depending on how it's used, her name could mean 'excellence,' 'beauty,' or even 'child'; she can be all these things simultaneously."* He told Leigh. *"You wanted to know more about how you're feeling right now, and I think maybe my wife could be the better of us to tell you, but she's out with two of the dogs now; she took them to the vet for shots and a good look-see. One of the dogs is getting older and will require more attention soon; it happens, you know. We get old."* His smile broadened as he said it.

Charlie explained how he knew they would be together when he first saw his future wife. He didn't say they would be married; he was a kid. He didn't think that way, but he knew he would always be with her, and she would always be with him. He had never really thought about a girl like that before. She wasn't what he would consider pretty; no, she was out of this world amazing! She was such a sight.

If he had thought about it longer, he told her, he could start comparing her beauty to the heavenly realm and all the things God has in store for us later: the colors, the smells, the sights – He dropped Hideko right in front of Charlie to prove there were much better things to come in the future.

"One of the things that drew me into this unending love affair that I have with my wife is that she was already working at her tender age for her family store here in town, and in the back, she was the one helping to prepare the food that was cooked and packaged, then sold to the workers down the street for their lunches and breaks. It was long before there were those food trucks. She and her family had a food store!

"I was a kid and thought I knew everything. My mom knows I knew everything; she always reminded me, saying, 'Charlie, you think you know everything, don't you?' I'll shoot off my mouth again and say, 'Yeah, I do.' She tried to pound me when I did it. It's good that I ran pretty fast back then. I've always been barefoot; in fact, I know for a fact that I was born that way. I think the only time she ever caught me was when I was wearing shoes! I may have tripped over the rubber soles or something. I guess I didn't know everything, huh?" he laughed.

Charlie leaned back in his chair at the front of the church where he was preparing Sunday's message; he knew Leigh's heart was heavy, so he took a few minutes to comfort her, letting her know that even the best of relationships have their rough spots; best to sail through them together, he told her, rather than allowing each other to be alone too long. *"Give him a little space for now, and I'll keep an eye on him to be sure he doesn't forget to find his way back. You're one of the best things to ever happen to him; I'll tell him I think so. He thinks I know everything, too."* Charlie giggled.

Leigh wanted to know more about Charlie's love and his reason for smiling, as he told her and his congregation on several occasions. *"I used to go to her family store every day after I saw her there and realized she was in the backroom stocking or making stuff I thought I might want to try. I had no money, and her dad didn't like me hanging around if I wasn't buying something. He was strict with her, her mother, her siblings, the store, and everything else. He epitomizes the typical Japanese man who owns what he owns, and you won't have a part of it."* He told her.

"I used to go to the store just to see if I could catch a glimpse of her. I swear, she was the most beautiful girl with her long, long, black straight hair and those eyes; so soft, so forgiving, even at her young age, she had a peace about her that made me think of angels flying all around the room if I saw her from the door of the store since her old man wouldn't let me inside if I didn't have money to spend.

254

"She had this something about her, this way, I guess Leigh. Kind, patient, and graceful, the way she would glide across the floor. I don't think she walks much; she glides," he said, standing and making his best impression of the woman he holds every night when he rests. *"She let me have some food when her dad wasn't looking. She'd tell me with her expression to meet her in the back of the store. She'd pretend to take the trash out and then hand me something; I didn't even know half the time what it was, but she made it, so it was bound to be good."*

His praise wouldn't stop. He told Leigh how they began a secret relationship that lasted several years and how they finally got old enough to be seen together. However, they had been together for a more extended period, wholly hidden and unseen; it was their way of surviving the harshness that would have been shown to them if anyone knew. Who needed to know? He asked her. It was their choice to be together; they were the only ones who needed to know, and since they knew, that was enough.

"We've been married almost forty years, not quite, but if you knew how old I am, you'd know we've been together a lot longer than forty years." He told her. *"She's never made a bad meal, not once, but if she had, I would never have said so. She puts her heart into feeding me. I'm her everything, and she's mine. I think we could save a lot of money on valentines because we know that, but I'm going to always bring her one. I can't help myself."* He told her.

"She has fed me when I'm sick, when she's sick, or when she's too tired to do it. She's been a great mother to our two kids, kids we adopted from two

very different parts of the world. She's been the best mother, wife, and daughter – so if you hear what I'm saying, you'll hear I've decided to love her. I made a choice. She made a choice." He told her.

As Charlie explained, love wasn't something that falls from the skies; it isn't something dainty, frilly, silly, or slight. Love is stronger and more durable than anything else there is to know or have in one's life; love, after all, is said and done and is stronger and more important than hope and faith; the Bible said so, and that was good enough for Charlie. He hoped it was good enough for Leigh as well.

He looked over at Leigh, her eyes clearing; the redness from her crying had nearly ended. *"We've had our ups and downs, Hideko and I. Every couple does, but our love stays strong. Even when she wanted to throw a few mangos at my head, which she's done a few times, she loves me, so she doesn't aim that well when she does it. She allows me to get away and think about whatever I did because we both know it was my fault. She's perfect; it couldn't be her; I know this."*

Their conversation continued with Leigh asking questions, somewhat knowing the answers. She wasn't some young thing who hadn't experienced life. She was hardened in some ways, jaded against becoming too committed with someone who hadn't run in the same circles that she had; she was quite aware, and told herself, that Mathew James Conner was something completely foreign in that he wasn't born into a Christian family; he hadn't been raised in the South, and he wasn't someone who had much experience getting down and dirty. The man hadn't even heard of noodling until she explained how she got the scar on her inner elbow from grabbing a long-tailed Oklahoma muddy-bottom catfish her senior year of high school.

"He said, 'They may as well give it to Jimmy.' I know he's called Mathew by most, and his middle name is James, but I'd never heard him refer to himself before using the name Jimmy. Do you know what he meant by that, Charlie?" she asked.

After thinking about his answer, her pastor decided to play it as safe as he could; yes, he knew who Jimmy was, but if Mathew hadn't told her yet about his past and how he had needed to change his name to protect himself from those who were hell-bent on harming him, then it wasn't Charlie's place to do so. He gave her that fatherly look he had garnered over the years for when he needed people to understand his words meant what they were intended to mean.

"I'll let him tell you, Leigh. He's opened up a little about it to Doug Dempsey and me; maybe Creed knows the whole story, too. If and when he's ready, he'll fill you in on it, but suffice it to say he left that man, Jimmy, back in Chicago over a year ago, coming on two years soon. When he arrived, he wanted to know what he could do to hide from anyone and everyone he walked away from. They could have been a problem for him.

"He left Jimmy and found Mathew; he started over. He didn't do anything illegal, let your mind rest there, but he had to shed who he was so he could become who he is, and that's a story he needs to tell you, not me." He said. *"Besides, you wanted to hear all about love today. So let me get back on track and tell*

you more about my sweetheart." He said this just as he looked up from their conversation to see his bride of so very long coming through the door with two of his herd. Excusing himself with another smile, Leigh knew her time with Hideko's protector, lover, and husband was over.

Thanking them both, she took a freshly baked doughnut to go, letting Hideko know she was not only a great cook but the reason she had come to see Charlie in the first place. Charlie, like Leigh, was the articulate one. He was outgoing, extroverted, seen and heard. She needed to have her compass realigned; knowing that iron sharpens iron, she looked back at the two love birds who, through their actions, proved that love never dies and it never really rests; it just takes a break to breathe.

Twenty-Four

The urge to find Mathew and check on him was more vital, stronger perhaps than she had imagined it ever would be. He's a big boy, she told herself. He chose to be on his own; he wanted this time; she wanted to respect his thoughts now and his decision; she owed him that much after what she had done. She tried to force herself to think about the moment they reconnected, the moment she could compare or contrast what she had witnessed between the Garretts, who must have only been separated a few hours.

Promising herself that he would call her, as he said he could, she dug her heels in, the heels of her heart and mind, to let herself know that she would not try to find him. She would not try to make amends; she would not make a fool of herself again, but the wait took all of her immediate energy. She had been too engrossed with her new project, the book, to be as attentive as she knew now that she needed to be.

"I'll focus on the book again since it's the thing I thought was so important in the first place. This will give me time to relax, meditate, study the subject matter, and get all I need to prepare myself for writing up the outline and then filling in the gaps with

facts, fluff, stuff, and more facts." Her one-sided conversation lent herself the freedom she needed to find a way to center her energy to create organically from the inside out. She knew the book would help fund the resort, so the book must come first.

It wasn't a surprise to her that no matter how hard she concentrated on the details of her new book, the more she thought of him; he was more or less the reason she felt inspired to write about those who have been both known and unknown; and why they would choose one particular status over the other. She decided to use a subject by another name and to give him all of Mat's personal traits so she could write ambiguously and not constantly find herself being distracted by her anxiety or fear for his well-being.

Leigh pondered her plan to rent an Airbnb and live 'rough' for a few days, maybe two or three, to truly get the gist and understand what her book would bring to light. Tapping the tips of her polished nails over the surface of her desk, she allowed her thoughts to recall numerous times she had taken risks in her life and the outcomes. She wanted her readers to be aware of their surroundings and to notice the people who were often sharing air space with them, but then again, who was to say, she reasoned, that those reading her work wouldn't themselves be the very homeless, the unhomed? The thought of it stuck hard in the back of her mind.

She admired those who, through sheer determination, had made their way to the top of their professional careers. Until recently, she had very little personal empathy or compassion for those who struggled every single moment to make it to the next without collapsing under the extreme pressure of being without anyone other than themselves.

She leaned back in her chair, rocking, thinking. She crossed her arms over her chest and gave a quick huff. Despite her confidence in the plan, she couldn't shake the tinge she felt every time her mind's eye reminded her of what the Scottish singer had said: that he had learned to only half-sleep to be sure he'd wake up the next day.

Why had she purposely questioned him on the point? Was it so hard for her to relate? She knew the answer; she had never been involved enough to do something. That needed to change; it had to change, and this book was another way for her to show him and herself that she was, in fact, changing. She was in love with, or well on her way to being in love with, someone who had been to the top and had fallen from grace and society's view. She was in love with a man who was determined to become a new creature; he was well on his way to doing just that.

She had to figure it out if it took every brain cell she could muster. Her defense mechanism was thinking and working things out cognitively in her mind; if she could keep her mind separated from her heart long enough, she could pull it all together and make it work. Still, she couldn't stop thinking that she and he had already built a strong foundation for themselves; why had she been so harsh? She knew thinking was overrated, yet it prevented her from making mistakes most of the time. Her mind had been her best asset too often, and she couldn't let it fail her now.

As Charlie put it, being alone was a choice. He left his other life behind, and in doing so, for whatever reasons it caused him to be in the circumstance, it wasn't permanent. She knew that. Others may not be willing to make the necessary changes, but she could see that Mat wasn't anyone; he was Mat. That was the awareness she was trying to conjure for herself first and then for her readers.

After considering her options and searching through websites to find the right spot, Leigh considered her potential challenges. *"I can't tell the owners of the Airbnb I'm going to sleep in their backyard and only use their shower after I pretend to walk to the YMCA to take one; that would surely set off alarm bells. I also can't sleep outside by myself, which wouldn't be good – even I wouldn't give myself the green light if I had sense enough to ask.*

"I think what I'll do," she told Roscoe, *"...is to find a spot in a lower economically affluent place, one that has some noise, industry, stores, and foot traffic, and that way, I can be close enough to a shower or a toilet if I needed to find one....I'll rent the place for a day or two, maybe take you with me, and see what I can see. If there's a backyard with a privacy fence, I can make believe it's not really there and try to place myself in the would-be shoes of someone living rough somewhere around there."*

She explained to the dog that he'd need to be ready to pounce if anyone came through the locked gated fence or wasn't welcomed into their space while she was working; she knew he understood. He had that contented look on his face, the one he had when he wanted to eat, sleep, play, or go for a ride. The dog was many things, but he hadn't yet mastered the art of expression. *"Give it time, boy, you'll figure it out. You bite the bad guy, and I'll write about him…"* she told him, *"either way, he'll feel the pressure."*

After going over the details again in her head, because it seemed so ridiculous when she said it aloud, she decided to run the idea by the only other mind she respected. Leigh respected Sarina's opinion enough to seek it out whenever she felt she hadn't quite thrown all the balls into the basket. Pacing back and forth from her kitchen to the open living space lined with wall-to-wall, ceiling-to-floor length windows, Leigh kept the cell held close enough to speak, though, through speakers, she could hear her best friend chide her, chipping away at every move she made plans to make.

"You know Leigh," Sarina began, slightly veering her voice into mother mode, *"it might be a real eye-opening experience for you, but in more ways than one."* She told her best friend of over three decades. *"Living without comforts, you've done that. We've done it a hundred times when we went camping; we can live without our cells and our deodorant, but taking the year, the times, the differences between when we were ten and however old we are now God, don't tell me, I don't want to know…it may not be the best choice to go this alone without taking Mathew with you for protection. I know you have the dog, but he's a puppy."* She told her.

"You should get his thoughts on it, and you should take him with you because, if nothing else, if what you've told me, he's been there, and he's done that so that he can show you the ropes. You wouldn't

go rock climbing without my son, would you?" she asked, knowing her middle-school-aged boy Rory had landed the top spot for the region in the up-and-coming sport.

"Rory knows rocks, I'm just sayin', and Mathew knows the streets. You go to the mechanic to fix your car —I mean, you don't. You get a book out and read the instructions, but everyone else I know goes to the mechanic to fix their car, and they don't go sleepin' out in the backyard of an empty house where everyone knows it empty, to begin with, and then someone sees you through their blinds and calls the cops on you." She laughed and took another sip of whatever box wine she poured herself.

"You might do that, but we don't. We, you know; those with brains. We don't do that because we know it could get us killed. You can stick your arm down the throat of a big ol' fat catfish, bring it up out of its hole, and skin it for dinner, but you've never been alone in the dark in a place where you don't belong. At the parks, they have rangers to watch over us; it may have been different for our folks, but we had rangers, and now they have required lights, licenses, and all sorts of things to safeguard people who choose to give up their beds for the full experience." Sarina hadn't stopped long enough to breathe but had taken a sip or two more in between thoughts.

Leigh's only argument that made sense to her good friend was that the research of it all would bring about a book wrought with anticipated expectancy. If Leigh was good at anything, Sarina knew; it was getting people to see whatever she wanted them to see, and they weren't allowed to look away until she made it possible for them to do so.

"This book is everything right now; I can study what Mathew went through. I don't have to ask him all the details; I can observe and learn from those who are going through it now, who have been through it, and what people who don't understand say about people who can't live among the masses who do most everything to satisfy someone other than themselves." She lamented.

"We girls don't dress and put on makeup for the boys, you know, we never have. Girls dress up and get all pretty for other girls; we're trying to impress them so we can either be one of them, outshine one, or both simultaneously. It's the same with this book, Sarina." She admitted, before admitting also, that she and Sarina still called themselves girls rather than women. She noticed it a few years back but was unwilling to do anything.

"I'm writing it; I'm studying the concepts of loneliness, homelessness, and being vastly independent so I can better comprehend Mathew; he's deeper than that massive body of water I'm staring at right now, and from this high up, it seems like my emotions are a lot more like those waves crashing than I care to concede." Her analogy stung both herself and her friend.

"You know what, girl," Sarina stated, *"...you'll never be homeless. You'll never understand it completely, no matter what you do or where you spend the night; you will never be without a place to stay. If you lost all your money and couldn't pay for*

gas to come home, I'd send it to you through good ol' Western Union.

"You'd be under my tin roof, and if not mine, you'd stay with Kate, Tanya, Robin, Jeannie, even Macy if you had to, but you will never, not one day in the next fifty or sixty years, will you be alone if you don't want to be. That's where you need to start with your project. Mathew wanted to be alone; he thought being with you could cause a burden. He's serious about being with you and wanting you to want him to be with you. Start there." She said, and with that, it all clicked.

As she was about to ask Sarina for her sister-in-law's recipe for creamed corn pudding, her phone's call waiting feature buzzed to alert her that she had an incoming call. The unfamiliar number had a Florida area code but was not one she recognized. Almost in passing, Sarina mentioned that it had been a couple or three days since the incident at the store, and maybe the caller was Mathew; she could at least check to see.

"Hello," Leigh answered, after figuring out how to accept the one call without inadvertently disconnecting the first. *"Leigh?"* the voice said, relatively quiet, rather still, *"It's me, it's Mat. Did I catch you at a good time?"* he asked. She had checked her phone every few minutes for the past three days, hoping to see where he'd put in a call to her, maybe a text. There couldn't be a wrong time; anytime was a good time as far as she was concerned.

She hadn't thought he would use a different number, but now it made sense that he would. His old number had a Chicago exchange; the new number, the new man, the new Mathew had finally rid himself of the last piece of whoever this Jimmy guy was, and things could start from where they were; she answered him, letting him know she needed to let her friend go but that she would be right back.

"If I hang up on you, I'm not hanging up on you. I can spin gold out of straw, but I can't figure out how to drop one call and keep the other. Don't go anywhere; I'll call back if I lose you." She assured him. When she returned, her first words to him needed to be as warm as she wanted them. She wanted them to ask for forgiveness, hug the man, and wrap him so tightly that he would never wonder about her intentions again. She prayed before she hit the green button to return to him.

His voice filled the room, piquing Roscoe's ears. The little dog gave out a quick yelp of approval and recognition. His voice was lower, she thought, maybe even a little raspy. Had his voice always been this way? Perhaps she hadn't heard it as much as she had felt it before. She closed her eyes to imagine him standing in the room with her. Her first words to him proved to be everything she had hoped; she assured him she had not meant to hurt or cause him to think less of himself; she was wrong, she told him, and she wanted to apologize.

Maybe it was the time of day, the time when the sun sets out over the horizon. Something about that time made her feel more confident about speaking her heart. Settling into the corner of her couch, Leigh opened her eyes once more to see the sky vividly painted with strokes so broad, so open, so welcoming in their hues of purple, then pink, caressing what was left of the yellows and orange rays sinking lower into the water. The ocean was too deep to be any color than all of them mixed, a metaphor she believed for the emotions she had put them both through recently.

Twenty-Five

Mathew shifted his weight nervously from one foot to the other. He ran his hand through a three-day beard, thinking it had been a while since he had counted as much gray in it, but at nearly fifty years of age, he should have expected what he found in the morning mirror's reflection. If it wasn't his heart pounding, making it impossible for him to hear her voice, it was his voice, making it impossible for him to breathe. He waited at least ten seconds to catch his breath before speaking to her again.

"If I told you I wanted to spend the evening with you and Roscoe, would you open your door?" he asked her. Somehow, between the first step he took to walk away from her and the last one he managed to take, which led him to the hallway of a place he knew she could see him if she was apt to look at the tablet on the wall, he had fallen deeper in love with the woman.

When the door flung open, she saw him, the man she had been missing, the man she had wanted to share every word and thought with; three days had been longer for the two of them than any period had been before they had kissed; what was time? Had they known each other long enough, she wondered if she could say it; was the word 'love' supposed to be reserved for some milestone, an anniversary, or another meaningful event? Was she overthinking it again? This was at least the concept she believed in before she found herself blurting the words and unable to catch them and hold them for another time.

"I love you, Mat. I don't care if I'm not supposed to or if there hasn't been enough time yet. I don't care if anyone thinks it's stupid to fall in love with someone you've just met, but it is what it is, and you have to ...you have to....Mat, I love you, OK? I am so sorry for what I said to you, and I'm...I love you." She said it. It was there.

Without hesitating, Mat stepped forward, out of the hallway, and over the threshold to take her into his arms. He breathed again, something he hadn't entirely done in over three days; he clung to her form, tangling both of his hands through her hair as he gripped her, pulling her as close as he could. The warmth of her body seeped into his. It had been too long since he'd allowed himself the security and the freedom to love. A jolt of electricity ran through them both; it was unmistakably genuine.

He held her tightly, savoring the sensation, listening to her heartbeat, counting her pulse against his. When she pulled away, she looked at him, her amber-colored eyes finding his stare long enough to show him how much he truly meant to her and that she never wanted to endure such pain again. He kissed her again, with his eyes closed to see them in his mind's eye: the man, the woman, the two of them together.

"Thank you," he told her, *"...you made me understand a few things that I had literally thrown away, hoping or at least thinking I would never have again. I didn't want to feel it. Love hurts too much; it always has. I couldn't see it happening again; I couldn't see me going through it again, but then I hurt worse when I thought I'd never be with you. I made a choice, which I think you may agree with, seeing how you're still holding onto me. I want to spend the evening with you and Roscoe, but I never want the evening to stop."* He said.

"The sun can come up, the sun can go down, that's OK, but I don't want what we have to stop, and that means from this moment right here, right now, we keep it, and we hold it, and we know it, and we....we love it. We make it whatever it's supposed to be. I had about a million things to tell you, but I didn't want one of them to be told. I know I have to give you answers, but the questions hurt; they hurt, and I have to face that." His voice filled instantly with sincerity, and she knew he was giving her the most significant thing he could: trust.

Once inside and the door closed, he asked her again if they could be together until time ran out. *"I...I don't know if this is a proposal, I don't know if it's what I hope it is, but it's what's coming out of my mouth right now, and if it sounds like something out of a Hallmark movie, it could be that I've binged about forty of them over the past few days; and they all end the same."* He laughed, holding her, moving her hips before lifting her into his arms, encouraging her to wrap herself around him.

"Can we do this whole together thing, because I think I'm on a roll here? I could bottle this and sell it, make a million, and maybe pay someone to do a movie about us...what do you think?" he asked, hoping she wouldn't say no. He told her he would hold her until she said yes, and if she did say no, she could count on never breathing correctly again.

He must have been smiling for the both of them because his smile had been taken over by hers; she didn't ask permission, and he didn't stop her. They kissed for several moments before he carried her into the bedroom to lay her down as softly as he possibly could. *"I was going to bring you flowers, but now that I think about it, they may have ended up scratching you; good move on my part; there you go, Mat, thinking...thinking."* He snickered under his breath, his mouth returning to her neck.

They lie on the bed quietly, giving themselves a little time to think about what could or would happen in the next few moments. Leigh was quiet, hoping to stop her mind from running marathons, looping, looping, creating new thoughts like some Gatlin gun exploding in her head. One memory stood out from the others: the night she invited him to help her cook – she had hoped it would one day turn into a date and then another, and maybe they'd start something that couldn't be ignored.

"There was this one time," she whispered to him, *"...this one time when I was standing by the window, and it was just about sunset; a time I love, a magical moment of spellbinding imagery and eternal enchantment. I watched through the blinds because I*

had pulled them to the top. I had the full scope of the moment before me – it was as if I was the only one the spectacle really cared about. It was for me, and only me.

"I watched the pinks and purples of the horizon droop into the vibrant splashing colors of the brightest tangerine you've ever seen – and just as the greys began to make their shady ways across the boundaries of the skies, inching their way toward the sinking, burning orb, my phone rang – distracting me from the most beautiful thing I have ever experienced." She told him, *"and when I next lifted my eyes, having opened the door, it was there; the ending of the thing, it was, without question, the most beautiful thing I could ever imagine in my life....you."*

As she looked at him, looking into and through him, he began to cry. Tears filled his eyes, somewhat distorting her form and keeping him from fully seeing her how he wanted to. A heavy weight had been taken from him, lifted off his back, his chest, and his heart. Her words were a balm to his soul; peace replaced anxiety; it washed over him and filled him. Pulling her close again, holding her, he began telling her more about his life and asking her to try and accept rather than to understand.

"What we did before we met is what we did before we met." She told him. *"Who you are is who you are choosing to be. I don't know that I would have given Jimmy O'Conner a single thought, but this man, Mathew James Conner, now, that's a man I'll fight for; he's a man I can truly trust and believe in. I do want to hear more about what happened to you. I*

promise you that no matter what words come out of your mouth about it, about your past, I will love you."

Then, as if she were switching gears to lighten the moment, she told him, *"If you had daughters, you could pinky-swear with me, but you find yourself in one of those awkward and unfortunate predicaments in that a man cannot on his own steam do a pinky-swear. He must have at least one daughter to do so; if he is without daughters, he can for a moment, and a moment only, consider his dog to be a stand-in for said absent daughter, and by this and this only, he may accept the fate of what could happen to him should he ever break the pinky-swear."* She said, giving him a half-cocked tilt of her head. *"Do you agree to these terms, sir?"* she asked. *"I do,"* he answered.

Calling Roscoe to the side of the bed and encouraging the dog to join them, the two lovers wrapped the pinky finger of their right hands together. They swore to one another that upon the fate of fates and worse, they would remain faithful, loyal, and above all, honest with each other, accepting one another for who they were. If nothing else, they would always have the setting sun to remind them of their promise.

"It's moments like this," she told him, *"that I wish I had invested in those crazy lights that you can clap on and off...it would be so cool to do that right now, don't you agree?"* She said that with such a deadpan effect, they were both sent into a roar and laughed about it.

Twenty-Six

An even calmness lulled over the empty beaches; its soundlessness broken only by the calling of a few gulls who hadn't had their morning fill. January inched its way into their new beginning, with the passing of their first Halloween, Thanksgiving, and even their first Christmas season being anything but what would be considered traditional. The air above and around them snapped with a coolness they enjoyed. It wasn't quite sweater season in sunny Florida. A suitable hoodie wouldn't be out of the question if worn over loose-fitting draw-string shorts. Footwear, as Charlie was apt to tell anyone, was optional.

Neither Mathew nor Leigh had attempted to leave their home over any of the holidays, as the tranquility of what they had become and the silence of the season promised to keep them bound in solidarity. The two had melded into one, saying *"we"* and *"us"* more often in conversations, even going so far as to use permanent words such as marriage; calling each other their significant other rather than fiancé was another choice that both had to get used to doing.

Over the next few weeks, Mathew took his promise to Leigh very seriously, pouring over job listings and skill sets he could learn to contribute to their newfound family. His past as a top chef still created a duality of good and evil when he scoured the internet for positions he felt qualified for. Everything LinkedIn or other job boards offered regarding someone needing someone of his level of expertise wanted their new chef to relocate back to Chicago or perhaps down to Miami. Still, both options were out of the question. If he were going to cook again and be paid for it, he would not be able to work for anyone else, and he knew it. The search drug on, but he was adamant about what he knew to be true.

Because of this, more than one of her friends and most of her family with whom she had shared intel regarding Mat seemed to think he had the better end of the straw. They claimed he could work if he wanted to, but why do it, they said, if she was willing to keep him and let him freeload? The word offended and offended to the point of her absence over Thanksgiving and Christmas dinners back in DeQueen.

"Mathew, have you ever thought of opening your own catering business?" she asked. *"It would be a way to keep yourself busy and earn what you have been used to earning; either you make it, or you don't, but money isn't the key here; we both know that. If you struck out and went down swingin', you've been a success! I'd be willing to front the capital you need, and you don't have to pay it back since we're together. Just do your best – if you want to; it's just a question, not something I'm sayin' you have to do."* She said.

"That's the way I look at it anyway," she told him, *"...and if you make it, and make it how you want to make it, you would be the one to decide if you wanted the publicity or if keeping it quiet and on the down-low would be a better plan."* She asked him with a question in her voice, giving him the out he may need to say no, but she also felt that she had held open a door he was poking at and maybe wanted to walk through.

She continued, *"You can make it yours in every way: big, little, whatever you want to serve and whomever you want. If you have a restaurant, you must accept whoever walks through the door, but if you're catering, you can always tell someone you're booked! Think of it as your hidey-hole, and if you want to work, you work, but if you don't, you don't. Take the jobs you want, and turn the others down politely."*

He paused, wiping his hands on his apron, and answered her almost before she had finished her sentence. *"I guess I could; it wouldn't be breaking my promise to you if I gave it my best shot and tried. I don't have to earn a million dollars or anything like that; if I break even, stay afloat, and keep busy while doing what I love, it can't hurt to try."* He said, *"Leigh, it's a wonderful idea."* The thought of it started his mind up in ways he had been hoping to use; he had a thought, she had the plan, and they had a good thing.

Before their minds set on planning for the new business, Leigh wanted to share her progress on the latest book with him. *"My cousin told me I could use her as soon as the book is finished. She'll read it, give me a blurb to put on the back cover, and have one or two of her producer and director friends do the same; they'll also write up reviews on Amazon.*

"That helps with the sales, of course, but because the book is nothing like the genre I've written under, it's almost like starting completely over again. I'm a novice in some ways, but experienced enough in the means and methods that I know I can write, create, produce, and publish the thing independently; I don't need a publishing house to change my words to suit their agenda."

Mathew sat beside her; he was all ears. Nothing could have entertained him more that evening than waiting for their meal to slowly cook on the top stove, simmering to perfection, and listening to Leigh tell what she believed she knew about a life he had lived firsthand. To his surprise, however, Leigh had begun her book with another sect of individuals who were purposely avoided or intentionally ignored by others, a distinction without a difference.

She started her brief, which she told him would be anything but brief in its rendering. She mentioned the tragic reality that some underpaid employees of nursing homes have been quoted when interviewed anonymously that they've become jaded and even desensitized to their duties, even going so far as saying they've ended up resenting the people they are charged with caring for due to their jobs being so demanding on them without being matched in their compensation.

"It boiled down to money, Mat. In more than most of the cases that ended up in court for neglect, even homicide, if you can believe it, the workers claimed that they were taxed mentally and challenged physically. Still, when they opened their paychecks, they weren't given anywhere near what they needed

for the work they put forth. Now, keep in mind, they aren't licensed caregivers; they're not even certified in most cases, but you and I, we won't go up to the Cannon Falls Home or to Summer Pointe to change diapers, empty bedpans, keep people upright who can't seem to hold themselves in place.

"We're not going to do that sort of hard work for minimum wage; asking someone to do it who may or is probably less educated than a skilled job would require is a recipe for disaster." She said, shaking her head at the thought of what must be going on just a mile up the road from where they sat, and if at Cannon Falls, it may very well be happening all over the United States and, of course, wherever the elderly are taken all over the globe.

Leigh expressed sorrow when she told him the statistics that all but gutted her emotionally when she read them. The people representing those numbers, she knew, were once vibrant members of their societies, left to spend their twilight years alone, in solitude. It was heartbreaking. She told him to remember that almost everyone has someone to call family. Still, some of the patients who were interviewed claimed they would have been a burden to their loved ones, choosing to live alone and hoping to see their family but not calling them or writing to them to do so because, after a particular time, it just didn't feel like anything they tried would work. Their helplessness equated to guilt; they were unwilling to put their sons, daughters, or grandchildren through the shame. Turning to him, she whispered, *"Burden, I never want to hear that word again. It cuts too deeply."*

Some of the more vocal residents, she told him, had reported being kicked by staff workers; others had said they ran into the wall, not being strong enough to report their abuse to the administrators. It wasn't as bad if an older resident had a family member or two or someone who came to visit regularly, but the stragglers, as they were referred to, people lie at the mercy of whatever shift manager was willing to listen, and being paid a few dollars over the bare minimum wasn't a guarantee of being recorded or even heard. What would be told would soon be forgotten, even after a pattern of mishaps seemed to happen repeatedly.

Mat leaned forward, resting on his elbows, about to stand up and check his dinner to see how it was coming along. *"You're raising awareness of all of these facts. You said you couldn't remember exactly when you told me, but you said that only three or four books were ever written that bring light to the fact that our American elderly are facing this kind of neglect.*

To show her he had been listening, he reiterated her own words to her, *"You're talking about loneliness now, but I'm saying the worst of it is the fact that your research has brought up cases where people right here in Sarasota have been beaten, bruised, pushed over when they can't set themselves in a seated position; you said that the one young man was charged with manslaughter after leaving an eighty-eight-year-old great grandmother in the tub with the hot water beating on her for over an hour. Who does that?"* He asked.

"Right, I mean, it wasn't his great-grandmother; she was African American, and he was a white kid from just over the way there; he knew their family well enough. They played baseball and other sports together. He was on the varsity team and played catcher, I think. He had a full ride to U of Miami for it but threw it away when he couldn't put his job first for a few hours a day."

Leigh brought up that after investigating the case, the Sergeant interviewed at least a half-dozen teams that had scouted the young man. He was on his way. The jury had to decide if what he did was intentional and if a hate crime had been committed. Mathew could tell she was going over the more delicate points in her mind, trying to hold back details that could cause them to skip their dinner to discuss what was weighing on her; he shook his head in agreement with her, compassionately absorbing the story as it unfolded.

"The kid admitted he was live Facetiming with his girlfriend when it happened. He wasn't trying to hurt anyone, but to leave a helpless old woman in the tub, turn the hot water on, and not remember to come back is outrageously neglectful. He got the max, I'm told, but I don't want to use his name or hers, for that matter. I want people to know this sort of thing happens," she told him.

"One of the biggest challenges I'm facing is if I write the book as a fiction piece, say a novel, I can say more, be more explicit, and tell more of the real story than I could if it were non-fiction. When it's non-

fiction, it has to be strictly fundamentally on point with every detail in its place; otherwise, you face a mountain of trouble when such-and-such's family decides to sue you for liability." Her explanation made sense; he hadn't thought of that before.

Serving her dinner, he told her he would have to think about whether or not he wanted to hire people if doing so meant having to vet them to the point of knowing every little thing they did or were capable of doing. *"Think about it: if I hire someone and they go inside someone's house and spill hot food all over one of the guests, I'd be the one to be liable, and that would end me."* He told her. It's a new world; everyone sues everyone, whether warranted or not.

She comforted him by saying that in the days they were living now, having something more aligned with a small kitchen where orders are placed, and the parties either pick it up or call a company like Grub Hub to deliver it made more economical and insurable sense. It would take very little to start up, she told him, with the most significant costs being advertising, and again, she told him, that would be up to him. They could post, or they could plaster. It made no difference to her. She promised this would be his baby, but she would be around to relish in his success.

"Oh…I see what you did there, Leigh-Leigh," as he is apt to call her, *"You're giving me a way out so I don't have to be responsible, and yes, thank you, I appreciate that. Nothing would please me more than to be able to cook for people, to do the best that I can do, and know that the people, those nameless and faceless wonderful people who would then enjoy*

whatever it is that I concocted, would be pleased enough with my creations to not only give me good reviews on Yelp, but they would come to me, and pick up the food or as you say, have it taken to them. Win-win!" He kissed her forehead and took her hand to lead them in saying grace.

He lifted his head and squeezed her hand. *"I hope you like what I made you tonight. It's an older recipe from one of my notes back when I took notes. I'd eat somewhere and take notes about what I saw and what I smelled. If they let me go back into the kitchen, I talked to people, the people who prepped, the people who cooked. Sometimes, I asked; other times, I pretended to go to the bathroom and just took right or left to hang out with the chefs.*

"This one is a dish from Iceland, of all places. Anyway, it's a variation of the real thing because I'm not using aged goat; this is a lamb and potato soup called Kjotsupa. I used what I could find, and tomorrow, if you don't mind, I'd like to take a trip to the Mediterranean store on Delta Bay Avenue and that little Cuban store Dempsey told us about last weekend."

He asked her if her book would become a fiction novel; he told her he hoped it did. That way, as she put it, she could tell the truth, and no one could accuse her of anything. Leigh agreed with him, appreciating his perspective and letting him know that his opinion mattered to her. When she said it, she looked into his eyes; he knew she wanted him to hear what she had to say.

"*The beauty of novel writing over nonfiction is so vast; we create worlds and people that reflect our thoughts and truths without worrying about the constraints of reality.*" She told him before asking him if he was ready to dive headfirst into this new adventure, letting him know she couldn't do it alone and that he was the only one she would ever want to share the experience with.

Twenty-Seven

Fire Chief Douglas Dempsey took a long sip of his mug of steaming hot coffee, savoring the bitterness that seemed to mirror the countless days and nights he and his good friend and professional colleague Police Commissioner Peter Stefka had managed to survive over the past thirty-some-odd years. In that time, the two men had seen most of everything there was to see, one inviting the other to a scene to take in the raw and gritty details that were being exhibited so openly public after a fire or a gruesome homicide.

Their friendship had started the same way it presented itself in the present, with both men respecting the other for who and what he had become. As a young man, Doug Dempsey, a strong educated black youth from the urban streets, stood toe-to-toe with the recent Russian immigrant who hadn't yet passed every test to become a firefighter in Sarasota, Florida. There were only a few slots available to be filled at the firehouse. When Stefka's application was rejected, it was Dempsey who, through a bit of encouragement from his mother, had poked his nose into the office of the hiring manager for the City of Sarasota to garner an application for his rival to put in an attempt at becoming a police officer if he couldn't be on the truck or engine.

In those days, a high school diploma was the only requirement to apply for either position, but due to the sheer number of men signing up to fight fires, Stefka's lack of community experience led him to find a one-way ticket to the front door. When he applied and was subsequently accepted through another door, the one leading to the Sarasota Police Department, both men had forged a friendship over the common decency of one and the dogged determination of the other.

"Can't believe it's been three decades since we started drinking ourselves into the grounds." Dempsey laughed before feeling obligated to bring Stefka into the woeful pun he had just created. *"Grounds...get it? We're...at the coffee house. Never mind, we've been coming here a long time, friend, and let me say before anyone else has the guts to do it, sir, you have yourself one helluva beard goin'. It's not as impressive, of course, as my own. You can accept the truth, but it is quite the manly man's display."* And with that, Dempsey raised his mug in celebratory cheer.

Peter Stefka lowered himself at the waist to give a bow before applauding his friend for the joke and thanking him for his compliment. *"If you are not a sight for sore eyes, sir, I'd say it pains me to look at you."* Was Stefka's quick retort. After a few more garish banters between the two men, one or the other began their daily conversation exactly where they had left it the day before.

The only day the two men missed their daily meeting at precisely the same time in the early mornings, at exactly 6:30 a.m., was when they met for their weekly coffee at church on Superior Avenue at around 8:30 every Sunday morning. Saturdays were, from time to time, up for grabs in terms of timing, but if one wasn't able to make it, the other was to keep their table free of any would-be squatters who may try to weasel their way into the joint if they thought the opportunity could arise.

"You know what I find particularly odd about what you and I were discussing yesterday is not that Jefferson Davis could have, and might even have had Lincoln killed, but that every school house Marm since that day has been telling kids that John Wilks Booth danced his way through security, up into the box seats where you know there had to be at a couple of armed men; the war was going on! He could not have been in that place without security.

"I'm sayin' that every American student aged somewhere between nine and eleven years old has been lied to, and you and I may be the only people on God's green earth willing to track down the name or names of the real killers." Dempsey stated, before adding that Davis, being the then President of the Confederacy, would never have done the deed himself; he had it done. One of the guards did it; this was his theory, but he needed records, police, employment, and military records to prove his point was plausible." Dempsey stated with the confidence of a bull.

"She's dead, you know." Stefka droned before taking another sip from his cup. *"She's dead; the woman to spread the lies in the first place. Whatever*

schoolhouse it was, she did it. She told the lie; she told it over and over again, and pretty soon, everyone just started to believe her. After she retired, no one was willing to go against her words or her reputation. We don't have to worry about that happening in today's schools." He paused for dramatic effect.

"Today, no one respects the teachers, and everything they say to anyone is torn apart for any reason. It amazes me that my daughter has stuck around for as long as she has at Dale Randell Elementary. She's 25, and she's been there a few years, I guess. What she puts up with from her administration floors me!" Stefka said, balling a clenched fist and setting it down hard on their little table.

"It's no wonder some public teachers go to the private schools now or opt out of going into the classrooms. With the way these kids scream like they're being killed, or some are saying their teachers touched them when they didn't, it's incredible we have a school system in this nation; any school system.

"I think it's this way across the world except maybe in Mongolia or someplace where they behead someone for manipulating a kid," Dempsey said, shaking his head. Turning to his friend, he very seriously asked if it worked in the reverse. *"Could a kid be held accountable for lying about an adult? What would that do to our Department of Education, I wonder."*

The two old friends sat quietly, drinking and thinking, a familiar silence lingering between them. Their timing had become a science, nearly an art. Doug watched the people pass by, seeing in them the faces he'd sworn to protect, but at the same time, wondering if Peter was thinking about arresting any of them. He couldn't help but wonder just how many lives the two of them had come in contact with, how they had met up with and introduced themselves to the same people for entirely different reasons.

"You know, Pete, I remember when we were both rookies at our jobs. We used to dream about making it to where we are right now. You said you'd buy a boat, and we'd sail around Florida just because we could." He reminisced. *"Do you still wanna do that?"* he asked. The Police Commissioner reminded him that the plans he made for the boat were for after they had both retired, not when they were top dogs and had as much responsibility as they both had.

"Chief and Commissioner, here we are. Just keeping the peace and puttin' out fires." Doug crowed. *"Who would have thought we'd make it this far in the first place?"* he asked. *"Your wife. She knew we'd be someone someday."* Stefka mentioned. *"Your wife Carianne told my first wife Leisa Warner Stefka, who, by the way, has remarried and is now, I kid you not, Leisa Leister, that we would be at the top, and not only that, she said we'd make the men and women below us better and stronger than any other two leaders in the history of Sarasota."* Pete gestured, tipping an imaginary hat to his friend. *"My Carianne said all that?"* he asked, *"Well, bless her heart*

Taking another drink, Doug waved the waitress over to ask if he could get his cup topped off anytime soon; when assured he could, he continued to talk about differences he'd endured over the past few years, some of which seemed to cause political and personal discomfort. *"We can't say what we want to say now, and we have to hire people we don't think we should hire."* He said, *"I'm not being mean when I say this, OK, I know we have to be all-inclusive and tolerant of everyone these days, but there are too many factors, too many mental factors in our jobs that require men and women to buck it up and not become too emotional in the middle of an arrest or when dealing with a potential waste hazard.*

"You know, we're called into duty to do so much more than just handling burning buildings; we put our lives, both of us and our people, we put or lives on the line every day for people who, through our great Constitution with its significant rights and amendments, are protected from us showing the slightest bit of bias; but damn it Pete, sometimes a man has to stomp his foot down and say no when the world is screaming yes at him at the top of its lungs.

I'm talking about a guy we hired last month or so. The problem is that I won't tell you his name, but I'm sure you can figure it out. He comes from a broken home; who doesn't these days?" Doug asked, *"...but his mother is a lesbian, and his father is calling himself a transgender, but if you look at the guy, he looks like any other guy. He's not wearing heels, dressing up, or doing anything to creep anyone out, but the problem is someone telling me he's not going on an assignment if someone with that lifestyle is involved. I can't have that in my squad!*

"He's saying he's 'triggered,' and if I hear that word again, I'm gonna put my own finger on a trigger; then you and me, we'll be talking again, but for a whole other reason!" Doug stated, somewhat calmly looking to his right and left to see if anyone had heard his rant. Dempsey wasn't a bigot; he had his fair share of being discriminated against, but he wasn't saying the man couldn't do his job because of some bias; he was saying he couldn't do his job because he lacked the withal it took to do it. He was claiming an exemption for reasons not covered in the job description.

Times had changed; that fact could not be challenged. It wasn't he thought, only the younger set who had to deal with all the gender bias; he was thinking of someone closer to his own age, at least not too far from it, who had been subjected to that and other mitigating factors in his early life that formed a few formidable hurdles to overcome on a personal level. To Dempsey, if a man had a little age under him, he could handle most situations.

Peter Stefka thought about it for a while before he added a tidbit of gossip to the morning conversation, which he decided to ask his old friend about; since they both knew the subject: Mathew Conner, the chef from the church, that Peter mentioned lived outside in the storage closet, thinking perhaps the Chief wasn't aware. *"You and I, we're supposed to bring that sort of thing to the attention of the authorities, but we haven't yet because it's our preacher who's allowing the man to squat there; it's not safe, and it's not legal either. I can think of at least six codes that aren't being met for residence zoning.*

"Talk about a betrayal of betrayals. The mom, Conner's mom, left her husband for a woman and her husband. Think about that for a minute. She's not leaving him for one, but two, and one of them is another woman. Talk about sideways betrayal; he said he was raised in Springfield, and there's no way the schoolhouse, the church, the library, and every other body in the city wasn't busting to talk about it. It's big, but not that big; no wonder he left and went to college in Kansas City."

Stefka continued, but in another vein, "Did you know, Doug, there's a law coming up through the House with a lot of steam here in Florida? It could potentially swing the custody and final decree pendulum the other way. It's putting the onus on the one that leaves if they turn gay or decide to become the gender they weren't assigned at birth. It would fall under the same category as lying to your spouse or deceiving them, causing them to breach their marital vows. Charlie might agree with the bill; I'll tell him about it on Saturday when we see him."

Dempsey wanted to know if the woman had ever apologized to Conner, his brothers, or his dad or if they had an open thing that, for whatever reason, didn't include the father. "I mean, thinking about it, and yes, now I am indeed thinking about it, that could explain a few things about Conner; he's not altogether there now, is he? He has a good heart and head on his shoulders; I can say that he works hard, and the man can make a mean Gnocchi di Patate." Dempsey said before admitting his wife had taught him how to say it.

"He's with Leigh Madsen now, and he has been for a while, yet still sleeps outside of the church now and again, not in his bed. Charlie tells me they're fine, and Hideko tells Carianne they'll probably marry soon. I don't even want to pretend I understand that one. I'll say that times are what they are, not what they were. Maybe our parents did crazy things like that, but I don't remember it if they did....and no one did that sort of thing in Russia." Peter stated as his friend nodded; the two waved to the same man crossing the parking lot simultaneously before asking the other if they recalled who he was.

Twenty-Eight

The hour-long trip to Ft. Meyer had been less remarkable and more meaningful for Leigh, who had determined to end the suffering of at least one underprivileged person if it was the last thing she ever did. Jamee Leard's trial was approaching too quickly for those who had hung their hopes for Jamee's defense. Having appointed a fine Floridian lawyer for her, Judge Trudy Hofstede found herself at the center of attention with nearly every media outlet with an angle on the case. The venue change had been her idea as well.

Some held the position that Jamee wasn't really an American and that she could be sent back to her native country of Chad in Africa to be tried; while others knew her to be a naturalized citizen, but one they felt had been at a stark disadvantage from the beginning; even before she had attempted to burn her apartment down with herself and her daughter in it. The judge wasn't about to let on that her feelings in the case could be manipulated or compromised; her choice for Jamee's counsel came with the understanding that whoever was chosen must be competent, empathetic, and genuinely willing to make a difference in the woman's case.

He or she would need to provide valuable insight to the jury concerning Jamee's past, present, and, of course, future. Dr. Castille would provide her psychological profile, as he had volunteered to administer the Myers Briggs assessment free of charge; it was the best way to prove the woman inside the body of Jamee Leard was less likely to kill and more likely to protect.

"If you like," Dr. Castille said, *"I can contact Jamee's attorney directly to explain the process and my interest in the case. I can offer my services as an expert witness, not just administer the test; this way, the test and the testimony will go hand in hand, and the jury will better understand what I am trying to say. It wouldn't be a bad idea to subject every jury member to a lighter version of the test, so they, too, understand the importance of its outcome and the gravity of the situation at hand."*

Dr. Castille sat back in his chair after switching on the speaker of the office phone so that he and his guests could hear the entire conversation between the newly appointed attorney, the judge, and the psychologist. Leigh had been asked to accompany Jamee and Captain Bonet-Thomas, giving the tiny inmate strong shoulders to lean upon when needed. As unorthodox as it seemed, having Leigh Madsen in the room made more sense to everyone; she had been the first to gain the trust of Ms. Leard long before the others, and she was a steady figure when called upon to recall events where Jamee's behavior had been anything but dangerous. When the judge announced she had the inmate's counsel with her in her chambers, those on the other side of the conversation breathed a collective sigh of relief.

"I can provide a comprehensive psychological evaluation for you, counselor," Dr. Castille said before asking the attorney's name. *"I'm sorry, I'm Anita Moynihan; I should have introduced myself earlier,"* came the answer to a vividly surprised audience of four who had not realized the chosen counsel for Leard had been a woman and a woman, who had apparently been born and perhaps raised in New England, her accent giving her away.

Her name, Anita Moynihan, had a familiar ring; Leigh couldn't put a pin in it but knew she had heard the name somewhere in her past. *"I'm sorry, Ms. Moynihan, I hadn't been told who had been given the case. As of this morning, I believed they were still on the fence between John Crowe and Victor Steinman. I was trying to make my mind up as to which man could be more sympathetic; I guess I don't have to worry about that now.*

Emilio Castille then welcomed the counselor to Florida, offering her anything she needed if he were able to provide it for her. When Moynihan mentioned she had lived near Jacksonville and had for nearly two decades, she also mentioned she liked splitting her time between northern Florida and New York City when she could. She told him and those in his office that most of her cases were either pro bono or close to it. Having benefited from years of settling class action cases, Anita found her days free to pick and choose who she could defend.

"That's where I've heard her name before," Leigh whispered across the desk to both the doctor and the Captain; *"She's won every case out there for breast cancer, lung disease, anything really that has been in the news because some drug or some vaccination caused thousands to become ill; some have even died.*

"She's won them all! You've seen her; she wears those power skirt-suits with large lapels, she's about four foot ten and wears six-inch heels to bring her up so you can see her speaking at a podium. You know who she is," she told Captain Bonet-Thomas, gesturing with her hand just about how tall the lawyer maybe if she stood straight enough for the cameras.

With a nod of understanding and smiles to match, the officer and physician were happy to know they had a ringer in Jamee's corner; everyone was pulling for her, that's for sure. With everyone wanting the same result, the focus on a robust defense strategy began to take shape as their conversations continued. Dr. Castille leaned back again, taking out a pen and pad of paper to take as many detailed notes as possible, unwilling to miss a word. This case could be one of the highlights of his medical career.

"Tell me about the test, Dr. Castille. Have you performed it yet? Have you given Jamee the test, and if you have, sir, what are the results?" asked Judge Hofstede before asking if, in his opinion, Jamee Leard was sane enough to contribute to her defense. Before explaining the test, Castille wanted to lay the groundwork for them all, making sure they understood its place and how it could or would be used to give Leard the best chance of helping herself should she be called a witness.

"*The Myers Briggs Type Indicator is what it's called; it can provide valuable insights into a person's true personality, but it's important to remember that it is not a diagnostic tool, nor should it be used as the sole basis for any legal defense. It's one component; it merely offers a framework from where to begin our studies of her behavior.*

" It can say what she is likely to do or most likely to feel, but it isn't absolute, and it isn't perfected." He added, "*Now, having said that, I can tell you that Jamee Leard, no doubt due to her extreme treatment over her entire life, is categorized in the subcategory of what is known as an 'ISFJ' or an introversion, sensing, feeling, judgment type. However, the word 'judgment' may not be what you think it is.*" He stated with confidence before explaining.

"*The judgment part of the test evaluation will play its role when a person has to make a decision. They weigh out the decision by considering the pros and the cons, but the way she approaches those pros and cons may not be the same way you or I would do because we have a more traditional foresight and insight. She hasn't been privileged to have either of these as a guide to be consistent enough to do the same things repeatedly; she may fluctuate between what we would say is normal and what seems right or best for her.*"

In explaining the ISFJ type, Dr. Castille needed to clarify that the test considers answers to over 400 questions, many of which are purposely very close to being the same question but asked from another point

298

of view. It is designed to see if a person will consistently answer the same way, and if they do, they are more likely to adhere to the parameters of what Myers and Briggs consider to be their nearly etched-in-stone decisions; in other words, what constitutes an "*E*" for Extrovert, and an "*I*" for an introvert. Since she was a sensor rather than intuitive by nature, she had the "*S*" in her results.

"The 'F' in her test results indicated that she was a feeler, not a thinker. She is emotional, quite emotional at times, in fact, and this could have led to her deciding to end her life and her daughter's life to come to the result she had determined through the 'J' part of the equation, the judgment factor. The judgment factor allowed her to weigh out both results that could happen or would most likely happen should she zig or zag.

"If she had been an ESFJ, with the component of being able to speak out, we might have had a completely different rendering of the entire event. She may have picked up the phone to call someone to go over her plans, but the introvert in her stopped her from doing so; she couldn't bring herself to be rejected after she had given grave thought and determination to the matter." He explained.

He further explained that those people in the world who fall under the subcategory of being ISFJ have the nickname, given by the test's creators, as being called *"The Protector."* It made sense. They rightfully and naturally defend that which they own or believe they own. What is theirs is theirs. Hoarders often have the ISFJ personality trait type, and they can control what they collect.

"They are usually considered warm, responsible, reserved, and reasonable. Some of their strengths include being compassionate to a fault, loyal to anyone showing loyalty to them, and they are, as I said before, overly protective, to the point of death." He reiterated. *"It's in their makeup. It's not something she just thought about doing on a whim. She put her life into it as well as considering the life of her only child."*

After several seconds of silence on both ends, a voice from the other side of the line came through clearly; it was that of Judge Hofstede, asking what some of the weaknesses would be if the test showed strengths; it should also show a negative side. She wanted to know if these were equally demonstrative in the inmate. The answer to her question hung heavily inside the mind and mouth of the psychologist who, again, stated that by no means is the test absolute, or to be given so much weight, that it would be the only factor to determine the woman's fate.

"Jamee and those with the ISFJ mind are often hard on themselves regarding change. Throw in that she was born May 1, which makes her a Taurus, another sign of stubborn-mindedness. They can be unmoving and hard to convince, and because of this, they are perhaps the ones we often call loners; they don't confront anyone for any reason so that they don't have to face change or the challenge to change.

"The ISFJ doesn't like abstract ideas either; they are, again, as we would say, black and white in their decision-making. It isn't as harsh as being digital, off or on, but it's close to that. She doesn't see

shades regarding what is right and what is wrong. This is why once she has determined that what she did was right, there would be very little chance of making her understand that even if it goes against our societal rules, it remains the right thing to do in her mind."

Castille had hoped he wouldn't offend Jamee, who had been seated less than ten feet from him during the exchanges. She had been in America long enough to understand English well enough to know exactly what was being said about her. She wanted to help herself and contribute generously to her defense. Still, as the doctor had already stated, she believed her actions were warranted and necessary.

After the call ended, and the Captain had taken Jamee back to the patrol car to be transported back to Ocala, Leigh and the doctor spoke openly about the conference he had hosted in the fall, as well as the results of her own Myers Brigg test; one she had taken many years before as a prerequisite measure of being hired with the finance firm. *"They only wanted ENTJs, if you can believe it."* She told Emilio Castille. *"Only those of us who stood out from all the others no matter how big or how boisterous the crowd."*

Dr. Castille's eyes lit up at the thought of being with Leigh, knowing he had scored a very close personality trait to hers. *"ESTJ,"* he said, *"I sense things where you know them. You have more confidence in your decision-making than I do; at least, that's what the test reveals. I guess it would make us pretty good partners in some ways."* He said, leaning forward and resting his elbows on his desk.

"My wife, God bless her, is an INTJ, again, like you, only she doesn't tell me what she's going to do; she just does it, and I have to figure it out with that big S in the middle of my personality. We're all in trouble if I don't sense it before she does it." He laughed. Castille had administered the test a few thousand times over his career and was never truly surprised when the results were read. *"You have the same trait type as Whoopi Goldberg, Candice Bergman, and Margaret Thatcher if that tells you anything about yourself."*

Not wanting to beat a dead horse, he assumed that anyone with the personality trait of ENTJ, whose more excellent nickname was *"The Commander,"* would know that those following that path would be precisely where Leigh was today, making sure the little guy, or in this case, the little lady, was being given every chance possible; she was, as all ENTJs, a formidable mind of practical thinking, dogmatic decision making skills, and the sense to know when to retreat; but most ENTJs would never consider a retreat to be an option; not before digging in and powering through with the hard-headedness of a bull.

"Couple that with the fact, Dr. Castille, that I was born a stinging Scorpion, and you've got yourself a force to be reckoned with." She said, *"It's probably why I outlasted and outwitted the boys in the firm. I saw the out and took it; I didn't retreat; I used their own game and beat the hell out of them."* As she left his office, she shook the man's hand; staring into his eyes, she said, *"Thank you. I know you know; I mean that."*

Twenty-Nine

Mathew sat his cup down on the edge of the coffee table, trying not to let it fall off the corner; catching it just in time, he laughed. The look Leigh shot over her reading glasses calmed the man and simultaneously sent him into a heady spiral. Thinking about what he was about to say, he quickly substituted his words with a glance to match his partner's. The two could speak for hours without saying anything, which pleased them both.

"There it is again," he said, pointing to a strangely melodic sound coming from either beneath them from an apartment on the seventh floor or perhaps immolating from another unit on the same floor as they were on: the eighth. If it was coming from the eighth floor, the man felt he would have known something about the curious music that seemed to randomly sprout out of nowhere, lifting his spirits and creating such hope in his mind; it was striking. It was beautiful.

"I don't think it's a recording; it sounds like one person on a saxophone or a clarinet, but with the tones I hear, I think the lip action for that sort of sound could only be a tenor. It has to be a tenor sax; the clarinet

couldn't go that low and carry its voice this far." He imagined, closing his eyes to hear the melody weave in and out of his ears. *"I think what I love about it is the randomness, if I had to be honest. It's either a kid who has to practice, so he grabs the horn whenever he's in the mood to do it, or someone who has their CD on loop and hits the button whenever they need to push over the edge of the universe. God, I love it."* He paused.

"If I die and go to heaven right now, I want someone to teach me how to play the saxophone when I get there." He smiled before admitting his lips could never quite make the embouchure like they should back in middle school when he first tried out for band; he couldn't pull it off. Demonstrating his inability to do so only led to another round of kissing, which could have been Mat's calculated plan all along.

Leaning against him, Leigh snuggled her man and dog: two arms, two chests, perfection. *"Is that why you chose guitar?"* she asked, *"You didn't need to pucker with that one. However, it would be best to toughen up your fingers; make them calloused enough to do your bidding. That would've taken much time and patience; you must be commended."* In a not-so-subtle way, she hinted that if he wanted to pick up the Aria guitar she had brought with her from DeQueen, she wouldn't stop him.

"I still can't believe Collin Raye is your cousin." He stated, reaching across her and trying to stretch his fingers far enough to get the neck of the instrument she wished to hear him play. *"Collin is a Wray, spelled W-R-A-Y, and a Brake I believe. All the DNA in that part of the country runs similar, if you must know."* Her

words made him snort a little under his breath. *"True, we're all related, sort of like the Royals.*

"Collin is my relation on my mom's side of the family, but he's related to her mother and her father in one way or another. The Hookers, Brakes, Stringfellows, Elliotts, Locks, and Wrays are all mixed in there together. My mother is a Hooker, and her half-sister is a Stringfellow, but don't get me started on the family tree." She said, *"It has a few branches that stick out further on one side than the other, and they all sort of twist back where they came from."*

He plucked a few notes, tuned the top keys before playing, and asked her what her favorites would be so he could be sure and store the answers in his brain for the future. He wasn't surprised when she mentioned that anything bluesy or jazz could make her stop whatever she was doing to sit and enjoy the moment. With his cue, he began slowly as she explained herself. Her words quieted so she wouldn't disrupt this groove; she said, *"I think what I like about jazz, and I guess the blues too, is the improvisation of it – the way you're doing right now, just playing.*

"The musician chooses the tune, whether or not it's anyone else, and just goes with it. It's like life. We start one way; we add a note here or there. We decide we like it and keep playing that one, maybe branch out and find a new chord. Before long, we're playing the entire set how we want to until we're forced to play it the way someone says it has to be played. But then, sometimes, like now, we stop what they think is right and turn it around. We play us again, find it, find that chord we loved, and build on it, bringing in the notes and the sounds we believe best suit us."

He smiled at her thought. He wanted to believe her. He tried to pick his chord and make it stick. *"We start with the same basic tune, but it's unique because our tempos are different; not everything is the same, but it's close enough that we recognize when someone else is feeling what we're feeling. I can hear it in your words, the way you move. I can see it. I can know you and say you are the same being I am – but you know, you're different too. I think that's what jazz does for me."*

When she finished, he continued to play, and she continued to listen. His music drowned out the sounds of the harmonious saxophone from wherever it was. Before the evening had closed, they had enjoyed listening to various playlists stored in the memory of their devices: Ella Fitzgerald, Miles Davis, Billie Holliday, and, of course, Louie Armstrong.

"Something about that man speaks to me," she told him. *"If you don't know his story, you have to read it. He was raised at the turn of the 20th century and told he could do anything. He was strong and ambitious, and being raised in the Bayou of Louisiana, you know he had to have seen more than his share of racism, bigotry, hate, and worse, but it didn't stop him.*

"He played, and he listened; when he got the chance to play, he did, never stopping to think that where he was going could be off limits because it wasn't for him the way it was for others. He believed in himself and in his ability to play. He forced himself to be seen at a time when so many people in his

community were anything but – he made his dreams come true."

When they had retired for the evening, having walked Roscoe around the beachfront so his growing fan club could also see him, mostly women who couldn't resist giving the canine a rub and a few kisses, the two lovers strolled past a temporary marquee that had been set up just outside the entrance of the condo's front drive. On it read, *"Valentine's Day Supper for all, no admission, bring your love, bring yourself, but be prepared to hear the Word and know what true Love is all about."*

The sign was a blatant attempt by a local church to bring in the masses on a day that was typically reserved for couples; because the church and so many others knew that the same day meant for most to be one of togetherness and love, could also bring about sadness and empty feelings for those who didn't have someone to share it with.

Love, as the sign read, wasn't about two people holding on to one another; it was so much deeper than that. Someone, probably a pastor much like Charlie, was putting feelers out and getting the word out to as many as they could before the big day.

"Valentine's Day, huh? I guess it's next week, isn't it?" Mathew asked. *"I guess I need to think about more than just music to impress you. I need to ask all the probing questions like, what kind of flowers do you like the best, and do you prefer milk chocolate over dark chocolate."* Before she could answer, she gave him that look again, the one that let him know he should already be fully aware of the answers to both of those

questions, seeing how he had been gifting her more often than anyone she had ever been involved with.

"You're sure you're not just fishing to see if I'll ask you what kind of flowers you like because from where I'm standing, the dozens of roses and tiger lilies that have flooded the apartment should give you a hint that you've been spot on since last Thanksgiving. I have never given you flowers; men like flowers, right? She questioned. Mathew nods to let her know she may need to ask him again if he prefers one over the other. Either that, or she could pay more attention to him when they happen to be in or around the floral shop the following week.

"You don't have to ask about the chocolate, sir. I don't believe they've ever gotten around to making a bad batch anywhere; just as long as it is chocolate, I'm good...but that does exclude the white stuff, that's not chocolate; we both know that." He squeezed her tightly and kissed her to show he agreed; he knew the flowers had hit their mark occasionally.

"Leigh, before you ask, I made reservations for us at the Thai restaurant; you and me, of course, but I can almost guarantee we'll see a few others. I was asked last year if I wanted to get on the list for the five or six special dates that they make their exceptional dishes. I said yes, but before I knew it, I also volunteered to cook – at least for Valentine's.

"That was before we got together, but I can't...I can't say no now. You'll not be alone, I promise. I'll get a word over to Charlie and Hideko. I know Doug and Carianne will be there, but I'm not sure about Creed and his wife; she's so quiet you don't even know she's

in the room." He told her. He knew there would be many members of their community and congregation; the place was a magnet for loyal customers nearby, and Alessio and Elena were bound to make another appearance as well.

Leigh's heart swelled with pride when she realized she was walking beside someone who had the opportunity to be served but had chosen to do the serving. She knew he wouldn't be paid for his contribution; he had volunteered. His heart was more significant, she knew, than most. Here he was, what some in her family had dubbed *"her project"* or *"her misfit,"* the one she was keeping or propping up so he could siphon what he could from her and her bank account. Here he was, she told herself, not only being willing to give back, but with his talents in the kitchen, his gift was more valuable than most could comprehend.

She hated her family and some of her friends for their empty, thoughtless words. They hadn't met Mat; they hadn't given him a chance before jumping to the one conclusion people typically jumped to: he didn't work for a living. He hadn't had a steady income for over a year; he must be a deadbeat. They couldn't see what she saw in him. They couldn't possibly know, she told herself. They couldn't begin to see it.

"It would cost that family literally thousands of dollars to pay a top chef to come in to make what I believe you will make for those lucky enough to have made the reservation list year after year. I know Charlie makes it an annual thing; I can only imagine fifty or sixty others doing so as well. You're making the

best foods, the most exotic, most exquisitely flavorful foods ever, and not charging them a penny.

"You have to know that brings me joy, Mat. You must know there is no gift you could give me to match it. You're the gift. I've said it a thousand times to myself and others, but I'm saying it right now: you are my true gift and my forever Valentine. I am so...I am so happy right now." She smiled at him, asking him to tell her about his prepared menu. How could he resist?

When the day came and the evening approached, her imagination had danced its way into reality. The restaurant shimmied and buzzed with the electric energy of everyone's anticipated hopes of what would be served. Each course consisted of a symphony of spices, filling the air with hints of garlic, onion, cumin, chili, and tangy lemongrass. They knew the presentation would be everything—his masterpiece. Each dish was worth the wait, and each bite was savored and explored.

Behind the scenes, Mathew Conner worked hard to prepare each entrée perfectly. His crafted noodles were perfectly al dente and coated in a rich, tangy citrus sauce, making their taste buds sing. Fresh prawns, crunchy peanuts, crisp sprouts, and more, topped with slices of egg, sizzled over an open flame in the center of the room.

When Mathew entered, he did so with muted style, carrying a large, heavy black slate slab topped with lean beef, lamb, and pork, ready for the heated grills. He smiled and welcomed everyone to the main course, assuring them they would not leave hungry or disappointed, not if he could help it. Theirs was to be a convivial affair indeed.

Carianne, a little tipsy from a glass or two of sweet red wine, raised her hand in celebration, tipping the goblet just a little toward the kitchen to make a quick impromptu toast; *"To our chef! May he forever be filled with imagination, brilliance, and his keen senses; this dinner is always to be remembered. Happy Valentine's everyone!"* she cried a little louder than the music that seemed to cascade from out of nowhere lightly. The tinkling of the chimes and sweet, lackadaisical flutes invited the couples to relax, recline, and remember their reasons for loving each other.

Thirty

Her mother's voice thundered as it came across the speaker of Leigh's phone early on a Thursday a few weeks into spring. Her words were not necessarily chosen, but they were overly upsetting, and she seemed to criticize and scold. Leigh had never cherished this behavior about the woman, not when she was younger and certainly not now, not at her age.

If she didn't know better, Leigh told herself she was on the verge of becoming a one-parent child, not an orphan, as both her mother and father were still living. Still, she was very close, in fact, to tapping the red circle on the phone and never picking it back up again if she knew her mother was on the other side of the call.

Cathy Jo Hooker couldn't have been madder than an old wet hen on Sunday as she tried to bring a little sense to what her youngest Jewel had told her; that her oldest, Leigh Avery Madsen, had gotten married! Not only had she gotten married, but she had married that no-good, vagabond! A man Leigh thought hung the moon, her mother said; a man who didn't work, wouldn't work, and no doubt had every intention of taking every last hard-earned dollar her firstborn had ever earned or been awarded by the settlement she garnered from the firm. Cathy Jo didn't know how much it was, but she knew her daughter could afford to lose a man if she tried hard enough. Maybe she could give him a payoff of some sort, some hush money to go away.

"Mama..." Leigh began, huffing quietly under her breath, holding the phone out from her head to give her ears a rest. *"Mama...no, Cathy Jo, are you listenin' to me? You better damn well sit yourself down and pay attention right now because if you don't, you'll never hear another word out of my mouth, and that includes when we get on the other side, do you hear me?"* she asked, impatiently waiting for an answer.

"I won't listen to a word coming out of your mouth regarding how a woman ought to love a man. You've been married three times and lost more boyfriends over the past two decades than I can shake a stick at. With you...shush!" Leigh scolded back, not giving the woman a chance to rebut.

"You'd better stuff it, or I'll start swearing, and I ain't supposed to do that! I'll hang up this...Mama, listen, it's about." She paused, *"...OK, here it is, I'm hanging up!"* Her words caught hard up under her mother's heart, and against her better wishes, the mother acquiesced to allow her daughter to speak.

Leigh took a deep breath, bracing herself for the rest of the conversation because she knew at that point she held the scepter; she was Queen now. Pacing the room, the hardwood floor cool beneath her bare feet. Launching into her explanation of what she felt and knew about Mat to be accurate, she began, *"Mama, you remember when you told me that there were no perfect men left, that your grandpa had been the last, and he died before you were ten years old? Remember that? You mentioned a few things about him that made me think that maybe he wasn't perfect either; no one is.*

"Mat Conner means the world to me. He's kindhearted, caring, thoughtful, and believe it or not, no matter what you say about him, he's a hard worker. He's a very hard worker. He isn't paid a penny for it, no, you're right, he's not being paid, but he's out there week after week helping men from the church build furniture, cabinets, railings, walls, even room renovations for the people in the Hammons housing project. He feeds them; he nurtures them. He teaches them how to play guitar.

"He has shown me time and time again that being raised under the worst conditions means he has to climb higher, move faster, work harder, and have more on the line to make it to the top. You can Google him, Mama, you can Google him if you want to, but I don't think I like you doing that either because once you find out who he is or who he was, you'll have something else so negative to say about him.

I'm 39 years old, Mama; I'm not your kid anymore, and no, you're not gonna tell me who I can or who I can't live with, love, or marry; do you understand me?" she asked; her words beginning to crack under her emotions. *"My happiness doesn't depend on you; not you, Macy, Jewel, and anyone in our family – not anyone I know except myself and my husband. He is not just my friend Mama; he is my husband.*

"If you don't like it, I'm not here to make you like it. I'm just telling you now, and I guess I should have said something before, but I don't have to ask your permission to marry Mat or anyone else. I don't. I won't ask your permission for anything, not ever again. If you so much as spit, and I think you did it out of your nasty spite for whatever you think of Mat, I'll never speak to you again....never!"

The silence on both ends of the conversation could be heard clear across the many miles that separated the two; several minutes of it, several clinging minutes of pause, when she said something, she all but whispered. *"Leigh, I can't lie to you, girl; I won't,"* her mother said. *I can't, and I won't change my mind about that man overnight, and you can't expect me to either".*

"He's just not going to crawl up into our family like he did and be accepted; there's not enough time that's gone by to give him more than that, but if you think you're sticking to it, I can't change your mind now. You've gone and done it, Macy told me. I guess you said something to Sarina Kelly. She told Jewel, but I think she thought we knew. We didn't know!" Her mother's voice began to rise again.

Leigh stopped the conversation before it went down the same road it usually traveled when they had more than a few exchanges; they would never be on equal footing. She could have reminded Cathy Jo that she hadn't graduated high school or attended college. She could have forced her to recall that she had filed for bankruptcy twice and had once been fired for embezzlement. Leigh refused to be mean; it wasn't in her.

They were never going to see eye to eye. *"I don't expect you to change your mind or to accept Mat overnight, but you will respect my decision. You will respect my choice. You will respect me. If you can't...if you can't do that, there is no reason to call me again."*

With that, Leigh waited, allowing her mother time to think, to say something that may somehow resemble her understanding, or maybe even to retreat. Still, when it was clear that her mother would not utter even a word that made good sense, Leigh Avery Conner terminated the call.

Her husband had been showering on the other side of the unit. Upon hearing Leigh's muffled sobs coming from the dining room, Mathew's heart clenched. He approached her cautiously, pulling his robe around him and tying it tightly so he could hold her close as quickly as possible. Unsure of comforting her without intruding on her privacy, he slowly took the phone from her shaking hands.

His movements were slow and deliberate. He wrapped his broad, strong arms around her. He could feel her begin to collapse beneath his grip, and he moved her carefully to the couch, where they could sit in silence. He rocked her gently, shushing and cooing a little, telling her everything would be all right.

"What happened?" he asked softly, his voice laced with concern for her well-being. *"Tell me everything; don't let anything slip by; I need to know. I want to know."* He told her. *"Your mother, right? She*

didn't know we were married; I take it. I guess I thought you told them." He said. Unlike his wife, Mathew, or even when he was going by his birth name of James Matthew O'Conner, he wasn't particularly close to anyone in his family. For reasons he kept firmly to himself and out of the media, Jimmy O'Conner had been touted as a man of men, on his own, able to achieve and conquer any feat on his own.

The cold, hard facts surrounding his upbringing were left for gossip rags and those who had systematically lost their fascination with the man they had watched on television and followed on social media for over a decade. Seeing him fall from the pedestal most believed he had positioned himself upon was pleasing to some to get behind; most of the stories about him were false, grossly overstated, and exaggerated, but no one would stop that train once it gained momentum. It brought his countless once-devoted followers a perverted sense of accomplishment to see him wallow in defeat, or worse, in fear of being tracked down and got to what they assumed was his fitting end.

When he testified in open court about what he knew about the Aiello family and their connections to organized criminal activities, he knew the weight of the situation would be placed on him to bear. If he hadn't testified, he would have been indicted with them, perhaps serving in the kitchen on Rikers Island for the next several decades.

"We can't change the past, but we can control our future." He told her. *"I might be a loner by nature; I know I am. I may stay out at night and sleep somewhere for a night or two, and I know you'll be*

concerned, but I also know it's for the best." He told her. "Some of those Hallmark movies made less sense than the others. Most of them had families that all stuck together, did things together, and hoped the best for each other, but that's now our reality, sweetheart.

"I leave to reset – and it didn't start with you. It started when I was in my teens. I'd see what I saw, and I couldn't make it make sense, but I could leave it, so I left it. It all collects in on me and pushes at me. I know I have you to talk to now, but even then, sometimes, I'll never be that guy who will ever be completely settled. I can't be.

"You bring out the dog in the wolf, but I'm still a dog in some ways. I hope that's not going to be too tough to live with." He asked if she had purposely not told her family or anyone about their secret elopement because of something he needed to change or be aware of, something that upset her about who or what he was. He begged her to be honest.

"I told Sarina; I told my best friend. I didn't post it because I didn't want to invite their smack talk; you must have overheard her. You had to have heard what she was saying, Mat. She's heartless and as cold...well, she's cold, and she's not the one I'd ever take advice from now; I probably shouldn't ever have taken advice from her. She got all the intelligence she's ever mustered from reading the back of the cereal boxes, and even those couldn't hold her attention if they used big words." Leigh vented.

She looked at her husband, her eyes red-rimmed and filled with sadness. *"Mama,"* she began, her voice breaking, before her words tumbled out effortlessly and fluidly, shoring up your true feelings about her past and now, her future. *"Mama doesn't own me, Mat. No one owns me or has the right to manipulate me into doing and saying what she wants from me; it's always been about her, no matter what I achieved.*

"I have always fallen short of what she told people I had become. Enough so, in some cases, that I appeared to be the liar and not her when I didn't roll up in a new Mercedes to their little family gatherings after I had spent such a long time away from everyone while living abroad or in New York.

"I didn't have a car then. I couldn't drive one overseas and never needed one in New York. My first and last car was the V.W. Bugs I used to buy and fix up in DeQueen. She knew that. I'd buy one, put a few hundred into them, drive them out to Dallas or Austin, and sell them for seven or eight times what I had in them." She laughed a little at the thought of it, remembering the years she told people who wanted to know that she sold bugs, not drugs. It made her feel good again to laugh.

"When I told Sarina about us getting married on Valentine's night, it was at least a week later. I wasn't being mean by not telling the others. I guess I didn't think about it. It was our night, our wedding. I was too happy when you suggested it, really surprised when Charlie produced the license you had bought and brought with you to the restaurant." She continued, *"I know you had to pull a string or two to get Mason Theiss to let you take the thing without me signing for it at the clerk's office, so yeah, I never told you, but kudos to you, friend."* She laughed again,

allowing him to snuggle into her even more, brushing Roscoe to the floor for a better position.

"That's what matters. Getting married after dinner on a whim, with dozens of excited and eager friends parading out onto the beach to see the two of us hitched by a barefoot preacher man with one hand holding his bible and the other holding his wife's hand; that's the way everyone should be married!" she sobbed, allowing her tears to warm her, allowing her voice to become still. *"I love you, Mat Conner."* She told him. *"I love you, and I love your dog, our dog. I love our dog."* She sighed, taking him into both hands and releasing her breath.

Mathew listened to her; he listened to every word she said. As she shared her excitement and sorrow over breaking family ties and the genuine prospect of it being more permanent than he could imagine, he gave her a genuine smile. His heart was swelling; pride, joy, love, hope, everything—every emotion balled up into one lump just under his ribs, promising to explode. He cleared his throat, trying to keep his own emotions in check.

"Just remember, no matter what they do, say, or anything –we promised each other even before we were married that our lives were ours. I speak from personal and first-hand experience when I say I need help and have it in you." He told her, squeezing her just enough to emphasize that he would never let her go, not for anything or anyone. They were stuck together, come hell or high water, as he knew her grandpa would have told him.

"We don't have to forget what they say to us when they say mean things, but we will need to find a way to forgive them. It's not for them," he told her. *"Forgiveness is never for them but for us. We can't have that bottled up inside of us. We have a greater reason, a greater purpose."* He grinned, knowing his words were comforting her. He meant every one of them.

Thirty-One

Dr. Emilio Castille's mind nearly exploded as his eyes skimmed the long email he received from Leigh Conner, asking him to consider becoming a partner in her future adventures involving starting up a place for women and children to feel safe enough to go to and be trained in the daily activities of life that sometimes cause anxiety and fear. He followed Leigh's social media, Instagram, and LinkedIn pages; he knew she was making plans for what she called *"the resort,"* but he had no idea she had put so much stock into it that it was becoming a reality was genuinely starting to happen.

"What a wonderful initiative!" he exclaimed to his secretary, begging her to get Leigh on the phone as quickly as she could; he had to take the call coming into his cell, but he wanted to speak with Leigh the second he was free. The idea of providing free counseling, education, and support for the women and children of cities in and around the county was just such a fantastic cause; of course, he would do whatever he could to be both helpful and, if he could, be involved.

"Leigh!" Dr. Castille said into his office phone a few minutes after reading the woman's email. *"Hot off the press is right!"* He agreed with what she said. *"Are you sure you can do all this without my help? I can pull a few strings if you need the financing."* His generosity didn't go unnoticed, and she promised he would be the first to know if she could not make ends meet.

"What we need, and I've been thinking about this for a long time, is to have the counseling performed by students in the programs to become future psychologists; this way, they get the needed experience, and the folks get good help without paying anything. They'll have to sign a waiver knowing that the counselors are not yet medical professionals, but that shouldn't be a problem," she explained, *"It will also be in the guidelines when they come in,* and in the booklets, we pass out."

To start such a venture, they both understood they'd need to establish a non-profit organization first, which would require registering with the appropriate state and federal agencies. To be considered a charitable organization worthy of the 501 c 3 status, in the first place, more than sixty percent of what is pledged in donations must be designated for the cause to stay afloat; if not, it wasn't a viable charity. More than sixty percent of anything in the resort would return to it; that was not a problem.

When no one was around, she wondered privately if she had suffered a little from what she had been reading in Dr. Emilio's book about becoming an effective leader. Did she create or suffer from outcome bias? Was she afraid that she would be a success and that her success could stop her from pursuing other goals she may have set for herself?

It bothered Leigh to think that anything she had poured her entire self into could end abruptly through any unforeseen outcomes; even something as unpredictable as the next hurricane could wipe away all she had worked so hard to achieve. She worried less when she remembered that insurance was not only a necessary device; it wasn't a necessary evil; it was the right choice to make to protect her and everything else.

The idea of making a place for the women of Sarasota who needed help was great; they all believed in it, but it could take longer than she had wanted to wait. However, she understood that the plans of any good enterprise often take a while to get underway. Securing the funds through grants if she could get them, donations, of course, and her investments were part of the overall plan. She had even worked out a sort of side plan where some of the profits from Mathew's catering business could help pay for the things that would coincide with his talents, and if he became incorporated, he could be a partner as well. Win-win. They were both too excited for words.

"Right now, we're just talking. We're spit-ballin' and getting it all lined up, but I wanted to add you to the infancy stages so you're in the know, looped in, so you'll be informed every step of the way. Dr. Castille, I want you to know that we're using both of your books as readers in the office. Still, we'll work a deal out with you and the printer to get your first book, 'The Leader in You,' into the hands of everyone who steps through that door and will commit to being

a part of the growth; this is organic. It's not just our resort; we want women to come in, become involved, and get excited to make changes in their lives and their friends, families, and neighborhoods.

"We want women to have the skills to push through the hard times, save, lean on each other, work through the heartaches, and find reason and purpose for themselves and their kids. So many of these women were left by their boyfriends, fathers, and husbands.

"I know there are many men out there, too, who will want a place to go, and maybe we can branch out and create something like the one they have in Indianapolis: a place called 'Fathers and Families'; her good friend and accountant Gordon Flick had worked at the charity for years. This is sort of like that but for women. Once locked down and running, we can branch out to other cities, expand it to include men and recruit others to start their resorts.

Dr. Castille mentioned that some best practices came to light when hospitals and prisons became publicly owned and operated. He talked about how they looked around and noticed that people were people, not numbers, to be crunched for profit. The resort, he felt, needed to happen; he'd help Leigh find the best sponsorships, even the best suitable location for the first resort, keeping in mind the required size she would need for growth. *"This thing will take off, I'm sure of it. It'll grow exponentially, and before you know it, you'll need to buy temporary buildings and bring in more psych students to schedule more meetings."* He said, barely able to contain his excitement.

"*Recruiting the qualified therapists, social workers, educators, and trainers shouldn't be a problem if you're willing to take those willing to be a part of it, those whose lives will be enhanced by gaining the experience. I'll talk to the schools to see if we can give extra credit to those students who want to go on rotations for eight or sixteen weeks.*"

Emilio's face lit up again when he heard himself and the resort's creator making plans. "*Leigh, this is going to be epic!*" he cried. "*I know it won't be easy, but the impact you could make with a place like this will be immeasurable. If you ever need anything for it—advice, guidance, books, you name it—I'll find it!*" he told her.

Mathew joined Leigh at their favorite corner café, his eyes lighting up as she spoke about her plans; they had already taken over her life, it seemed, but he wasn't complaining. "*They let Roscoe come into the place; that's why I love them. I don't even have to bring his little vest, but I did anyway in case that one wayward soul needed to tell us how to live our lives.*" Mat teased.

"*I can't help but feel a sense of pride when I think of you, woman.*" He told her. "*You mentioned Dr. Castille wanting to be involved, but none of this would have occurred if you hadn't had that pulling, that tugging at your heart when you first found out about Jamee Leard before she was arrested. I think she impacted your decision to start this thing.*" He said, sharing a nod with Leigh while a mutual friend passed them both, taking his seat a few tables over, probably waiting for his wife to join them.

"Do you think we can talk Hank and Miranda Runser to join us too; she's a hell of a wedding organizer and techy up the Wah-zoo! She can make things happen if it's got anything to do with computers." Leigh mentioned, looking at Hank to notice he was glancing at his watch. *"I bet Miranda gets off work about now; it's close to four o'clock; she'll eat something fast with Hank and go over to the chapel to get a bit more bang for the buck tonight."* Leigh laughed.

"We're in the wrong business, Mat, we are. Miranda makes bank on the chapel rental. She's ordained, so she marries people and plans their bouquet ceremonies to fit their budgets and their personalities, all within reasonable rates. She can use and reuse the decorations, and since they're just renting, no one has to buy anything." Leigh explained.

"She marries at least three or four couples a day! I asked her what she gets for a wedding, and she told me they start around eighty dollars for the ones that host four to ten people, a few flowers, and maybe a book for memories, and it goes up from there. She makes six to seven hundred at larger weddings; she has dresses for the women in various sizes and, of course, tuxedoes for the men.

"She told me she's a lot like more Raising Cane's and not KFC in that she is constrained with her choices; you get the blue, the pink, the teal, or the maroon dresses, and if you're a guy, you get the black, grey, or white tux, but of course, you can bring your waistbands, ties, socks, and hats if you want them." Leigh giggled a little when she told him, thinking about what they would have picked out if they had known

about Miranda's corner on the marriage market; they didn't know!

"We got off pretty lucky, I guess," Mat whispered to keep his words out of hearing of Hank Runser; *"Charlie only charged us a dinner, and there were no shoes or socks to be seen!"* Mathew took a bite of his sandwich, encouraging Leigh to tell him more about the resort and what she had made happen in the few hours they had been apart.

"Maybe," he told her, with his checks puffed out, full of the club sandwich he had just chewed, *"I can start with the basics when I teach guitar; nothing fancy. I'll only do a five-week thing to get the classes situated; after the first two or three classes take off, I'll better understand what I need to do with them."* He smiled, promising with hand gestures not to continue talking until he could do so with more civility.

"Me? I think you're onto something. Start low and sell high; work your way up to it. Listen to me, I just slid right into that stock market thing, didn't I? Maybe I'll hang back on teaching anyone anything about trading and focus on 'this is a checkbook' or 'this is your phone app that used to be a checkbook,' which is more like it." She laughed.

"I'm probably the last person on Earth to teach simplified finance, but I'll give it a go. I think the women we will encounter will be living check to check if even that. They'll need to learn about hacks to save money and time. I have a few of those tricks and tips I can teach." She told him, trying not to beat herself up for all her memories of bouncing checks back in DeQueen before she learned how the whole *you-have-*

328

to-have-money-in-the-bank-for-the-checks-to-clear thing worked.

They both thought, *"This is it."* This is happening; it's shaping up and will be the most exciting but challenging time for both of them. Starting something from nothing is always tricky, time-consuming, expensive, and challenging on many levels. If it takes off, they must maintain it; if it doesn't take off, they must live with their defeat and all the time, effort, money, and energy they poured into it.

"It's going to be tough; I know it will be." She started, her lips tightening slightly. *"The biggest challenge I can think of right now is finding the correct location. Dr. Castille mentioned today that as I think the thing will grow and probably grow pretty quickly, we may need a place that can be expanded or maybe rent or buy a place that's already capable of housing all the things we need. It's a tricky thing!*

"On the one hand, I want to get a 10,000-square-foot space and fill it up slowly. On the other hand, it may be more prudent to start small and move when we feel the growing pains." She thought about it briefly and asked him what he could add. She hated how her family hadn't given him the time of day when they talked about him to her. He wasn't some crazed freeloader; she knew him to have a very keen sense of fiscal responsibility, and he'd been through at least three different start-up businesses before the trial that ended his incredibly bright career. She let him talk, she listened, and she hoped to learn.

"People, of course, will want to see it happen; they'll want it to be successful. Maintaining it after it opens is the hard part; at least, that's my two cents on it." He told her. *"You have to be there rain or shine unless you hire others to be so. If you say it's going to be open certain hours and certain days, you'll have to be sure it is and that the staff is kept up; we can't have a lot of kids in the place unattended if their moms are in counseling, or if they're in classes learning to cook or play guitar.*

" We'll have time to think it out, to think it all out, but I like how this is going now; just rolling it around and talking it out. I like the energy. I can see it; colors and shapes are starting to make sense. You'll be a success, babe, an important and intricate part of this community." His voice softened when he finished, *"It's a risk; it always is, but I bet you'll make it worth it."* He said with just enough pride to make her sit up a little taller than she was.

"I know it's worth it. Mental health care is too important; it's just as important if not more important than physical health. We have gyms on every corner charging less than a few cups of coffee to join each month, but the doctors and clinics won't even set an appointment for someone like Jamee or any of the other women I think will be first in line to see if we're for real." Leigh's determination began to show through; that Commander in her, the ENTJ personality, she couldn't hold back once it found its footing.

"We are going to do this. We'll have to start your catering business first so you can incorporate and use that entity to join this one, making it even more secure for future stock options. When people think good food, they'll think of you and know you're all about good and complete health; your brand is just as important as mine, Guapo." Her words tickled his tongue as she kissed him. *"Guapo, now, is it...well, thank you, I'll take that. It's been a while since anyone told me I was handsome in any language."*

As their conversation shifted to lighter topics, Mathew was drawn to Leigh's sporadic and random laughing; she couldn't stop. Every breath took on a new life of its own throughout dinner. It was infectious; he couldn't help but smile every time he heard her. When she wasn't paying as much attention as she had at the beginning of their date, he noticed she had turned from him, even flushing a little.

"What is it," he asked her, thinking she might have thought of something she had forgotten about her plans. *"I want to kiss you."* She told him directly. *"I don't know, I just want to be a distraction for you, taking you away from whatever you're thinking long enough to give up thinking altogether. It's just me, I guess, but I love your face. When I kissed you, I realized how much I truly love brushing up against it, your beard, and, of course, your mouth."* She whispered.

After all they had been through together, he felt time owed him something for keeping him from her for as long as it did. *"So, what did you have in mind for this distraction you speak of?"* his eyes roamed from the top of her forehead, skimming her face and lower still. His actions were deliberate, personal, and playful. *"We need to pay the cashier and maybe take the dog back to the condo for a while; he seems tired. I think, yes...yes, I think he needs to take a nap."* Again, he smiled, treasuring her laughing more than she would ever know.

Thirty-Two

The city's heartbeat pulsed, rising and falling with every easy breeze creeping across the bay and into the open windows of the homes lining Turtle Beach. Leigh's gaze drifted to her collection of antique model cars, her thoughts churning about whether or not she would be considered normal by the standards of the normal; probably not, but what exactly is normal anyway? She asked herself. When the phone rang, her curiosity set off a little red flag; Mathew was on one of his several days-out binges when he left but, of course, promised to return.

Could he need her help? Was it the police or some other authority calling her because they'd found his wayward phone on the side of the road and hers was the only number registered? She laughed when she thought about the truth behind her exaggerated thought. Reaching past the dog, she dropped the cell again, something she did regularly whenever she tried to stretch her body that far to grab it. Roscoe's girth had more than doubled when he'd been with her; she thanked her stars quietly that hers hadn't done the same.

"*Hello,*" she quietly inquired, seeing the "*private number*" message dance across her phone's screen. She heard it before she realized who it was; that familiar voice of her past flooded through her like she had been suddenly and magically transported through space and time to West Siloam Springs, Oklahoma. It was a small but rugged outdoorsy town with a reputation so friendly that it was rumored that Chick-fil-A had been training their staff in the secret hollows of the place.

"*How's my favorite Grand-niece?*" Asked her mother's aunt, Sharon. Her velvet voice was enhanced by the woman's Southern charm, an accent so thick and smooth, creamy melted butter became envious when she spoke. Leigh knew precisely what was happening; she hadn't reached her age and been in as many tight spots as she had been and been able to wiggle out of them, not to know what she was about to get into with one of Oklahoma's most treasured gems. It was her alright, the belle of every ball that could call itself a ball: *Miss Sharon Taye Barger.*

"*Oh, you naughty woman, you, Aunt Sharon. You're not calling me because you love, miss, and want me to come by and have a bite to eat. You're callin' me because my mama told her your other favorite Great-niece, Amy Ann, that I'm not speaking to her anymore, and you're wantin' in on the thick of that piece of meaty gossip. You can't fool me.*" She teased the former beauty pageant queen of several surrounding counties, who, at nearly ninety years old, had the hearing of a coon dog and the wit of a biting cobra if she needed to use it.

"Your mama ain't worth a dern plug nickel to me, never has been, but I was just too happy to hear that you slammed that phone down on her and told her where she could take a piss!" the old woman sneered.

"Tell me you done give her up for good; tell me you have. Tell me you won't step foot in Conway anymore; you keep coming this way and settle in with me if you want," Sharon begged. Leigh shook her head, blushed under her collar, and knew if she looked in the mirror just then, she'd find her face five shades brighter than it had been a minute before she answered the phone.

"First of all, Aunt Sharon, we can't slam a phone down these days. Not one of us, not even you, has a wired landline with a receiver; don't you play with me? I know your brothers' kids, and they bought you the best iPhone ever made, so go off and tell me what you need from me today; I dare you to say it." Leigh loved it when she could get a rise out of her Aunty; it never took too much to get the job done. *"Go on now, I'll pour myself a big tall glass of chocolate milk if you please, Ma'am, and you just tell me what's on your mind this fine Friday afternoon."*

When Sharon Barger mentioned that the only thing worse than having to listen to good family gossip was knowing that she wasn't the one being talked about, Leigh had to laugh. *"Your mama, that sweet, no-good, spendthrift of a woman, never let your daddy keep a dime in his pocket. She'd go digging for it, and when he finally cut her loose, I think he owed every bank and every department store in the county. They both filed for bankruptcy about a year after marriage, and she had to do it again five or six years later. She's been pretending men are made of silver since she landed on the planet."*

When Leigh brought up the subject of her recent marriage to Mathew, her Aunt only scolded her for not bringing him to *"Ol' Icabod's"* funeral. *"I didn't know him; he's on your daddy's side. You know I dated a Hooker or two; you can't avoid it in this part of the world. I could have gone to the funeral, and I would have found someone to drive me to see you if I knew you were there. At least we did Facetime; I got to see you."* Sharon continued.

"Your sister told me about your man and his past, but you know Macy and your sister Jewel are entirely different souls. Jewel told me how he was arrested and put on trial for murder and money laundering, but Jewel doesn't see how the world works. She says words she should not say these days before she gets her facts straight. It's like the girl never heard of Google. Macy told me Mat's mom did an excellent job with him, but she had issues with her husband and them not seeing eye-to-eye all the time.

"Macy also told me about Mat running off to China to teach English and how he almost got himself hung or beaten or something worse just because he spat on the ground like a lot of men do over on this side of the world. Is that true?" she asked, not believing it until she heard the details from as close to the horse's mouth as possible. Not being able to imagine the hate and pain a soul would endure in a country full of people who didn't look, think, talk, or act like the ones a body is used to being around.

"Not exactly. Not everything you hear from Jewel, Mama, or Macy will be true. You can take a nugget here and there, squish them all together, and find something that resembles the basics, but nothing any one of them has to say about me will be correct, and you did the right thing by calling me and asking. That means a lot to me, Aunt Sharon, more than you know." Leigh said.

She began by explaining that Mathew wasn't called Mathew in his youth. He was born in Springfield, Missouri, and considers himself Southern even though they had gone over the boundaries of the Mason-Dixon line at least a half dozen times. In his defense, Mathew held to the general concepts of political soundness that most people in the South, particularly in the red states of Oklahoma, Texas, Arkansas, and Missouri, held to. He was a registered Independent like Leigh was, but he, like Leigh, clung to their opinions, only sharing them when the time was right to do so.

Leigh further explained that being born James Matthew O'Conner was normal enough, and as the eldest son of four boys, he fits the stereotypical cliches you'd find written about first-born sons; so if her aunt wanted to do a deep dive into philosophy or more modern studies of human behavior; Sharon could do well by comparing what she read about the often gender-oriented psychology behind the medical journals that described the typical American male aged fifty or thereabout; he was going to turn the big 5-0 at the end of August; wasn't he?

"His mother left his father but couldn't take Mat when she did. She didn't take any of the boys; she gave the younger ones, the twins, to her mother, and his

dad tried his best to raise Mat and Mitchell. Money, time, lack of it anyway, and work seemed to keep him out of the house, which allowed booze, drugs, girls, and nonsense into the house while his dad was gone.

"Mat was a full-blown alcoholic by his senior year, and he dropped out of high school but got his G.E.D. He moved to Taiwan, but I can see why Jewel would say China; it's very different. Laws, people, and culture are miles and miles apart when it comes to being compared to one another; it's like saying Okies are Texans! You don't need or want to do that, but OK, he was there to teach, but he decided to drink and party instead. That doesn't bode so well in that part of the world, so yes, he was arrested and detained." Leigh mentioned.

"He still has four hard, long scars on his back, hip, and lower part of his thigh, where he was caned over twenty times. It wasn't good, and he considered suicide more than once." She told her aunt. She also told her he wasn't like that anymore; he wasn't anything like any of it, not now. The man she married was giving, thankful, helping, and he would do anything for others before putting himself first.

He had his moments, times like what he was going through at that very moment, when he needed what he called a reset: time to think, meditate, and return to what he knew would be the right path. "I'm his compass; he tells me that. I hope I always point him in the best direction; that can be a lot of pressure if I let it be." She said.

Leigh explained how Mat's mother put her house up for a second mortgage to get the money to pay his captures and the government for the money he owed them. She had him found, taken away from where he was being kept, and driven to the airport by a private American company man her brother knew from college. He was rescued, almost plucked out of their hands, when the men holding him decided to ask for more money for his safe release.

When he returned to the States, Mat bounced from friend to friend, home to home, and from church family to others, just trying to stay dry and out of the elements. After a while, he learned to manage on the streets without actually being on the streets. His rise to fame as one of the nation's top chefs began at a corner bar tucked away under the shadow of a brothel on one side and a known mafia hangout on the other.

"Mat made Italian food better than the Italians did; they liked him and wanted him to work for them full time, that is, both the brothel and the mobsters. After years of living and working around them, he almost married one of their kin. Still, when it came down to it, after being given the breaks no one ever gets and rising to the top like no one ever manages to do, they shot him down faster than a flaming kite on a windless day!"

Leigh told Aunt Sharon about the RICO arrests made in tandem all over the City of Chicago about three years ago; the *Chicagoland Cakewalk* was what it was called. Leigh asked if she remembered hearing about it or watching it on the news. *"CNN was all over the stories from every angle. Some of the anchors pitied the gangsters, saying they owned the area and shouldn't be subjected to the mainstream laws that govern everyone else, but for the most part, the law was king, and Mat had to decide if he was going to obey it or be swallowed up by it. He chose the former, and he testified."* She said.

"He was given complete immunity for his testimony but wasn't put into any witness protection program; it's not like what you see on television. They don't have that kind of money to invest in keeping people hidden; the hidden cost an arm and leg to keep that way. At least he didn't have a wife and family talking to people, telling them where or who they really were; can you imagine how hard it would be in the age of instant communication?

"I guess I'm saying I'm happy he never had to do all that, but he changed his name a little. He didn't change it completely. Instead of being James Matthew, with two T's, O'Conner, he's Mathew, with one T, James Conner. He told me if anyone asks, he's still Irish enough to kick their ass." She laughed. She believed him. Mathew wasn't some waif or dandelion; if he were a flower, he'd be one of those sunflower stalks that take root and take over. They shine, but they're not supposed to be anything other than what they are.

If it had been her, Leigh mentioned, she would have changed her name to something so different that no one would think they could find her, but Mat told her once that the truth has the opposite effect; no one would suspect him of having chosen a name so close to his actual name. They're looking for Rogers, Williams,

Larrys, or Toms. He's hiding in plain sight, seen but not seen. Not seen, but there he is.

Sharon sighed a little and leaned back again in her chair, as she had found herself involuntarily sitting up straighter and straighter as Leigh carried on about her man. *"He seems like a good one if you ask me."* She said before adding, *"But you can't ask me; I never got married, did I?"*

" I never found a boy good enough to suit me; one wasn't enough to keep my attention long. I liked to travel, and if any of them boys would have told me to stay home and make babies, they'd had a foot up their backside quicker than you can spit seeds; tellin' you that right now." The feisty woman pledged.

"I'll go ahead and tell you something, Aunt Sharon, only because Jewel or Macy or even your own people on your side of the family may get around to telling you, and I don't want you to hear it second or thirdhand, but I got a dog. That's right; as the gossip goes around those parts, I got myself a dog. Someone, one of the Hookers, I think, but it could have been Brian Brake, now that I think about it, put a dang puppy in my truck when I was in Toad Suck! I knew I should have locked them doors!" Her accent seemed to sweep in to take hold of her when she got a little riled.

"I think I understand why someone would drop him off the way they did; I'm mostly a loner, and they didn't want me goin' through life without a good friend. I kept him, but I feel so guilty about it 'cause I know your neighbor, Michael Whitfield, does the dog thing. He's got the market on it in those parts.

"You said he owns a place next to yours and comes down from Stillwater now and again; he raises English Bulldogs; if you see Michael again, and you start flapping your jaws about me like I know you will, you tell him I'm sorry about saving myself five or six thousand dollars; I feel just terrible about it." She snickered, trying not to sound too broken up.

Sharon Barger nearly shot her soda through her nose, trying to hold back the roar she held too tightly within herself; she hadn't had the pleasure of giving her favorite gypsy neighbor her two cents about how he and his hobby had ended up making West Siloam Springs the loudest, most howling little city in the Southwest. *"There's more Whitfield puppies in this city than Carter has little pills."* She told Leigh, *"...and every last one of them as cute as bugs ear."*

Thirty-Three

Mathew met Leigh at their scheduled time, a place he had chosen to bring her to, a place he felt she would appreciate and understand its meaning. He had decided to use the days they were absent from one another to finally get ahold of some of the estranged emotions that had held him captive for so long. *"What do you think?"* He asked his wife, sitting on the back of an elephant the size of a giant Mack truck.

The refuse in Bay County had become the go-to spot for retired circus animals whose parents, grandparents, or other relatives may have ventured to live before them; some in Sarasota, as they both knew and others at the Claymont Elephant Haven, just three days' walk from where he had started. The time, he said, was used to think, really think, and patch up any doubts he may have had lingering in his head about their future and the plans to start the catering business and, subsequently, the women's resort. *"I thought I'd rent this gal for an hour or so; we can be at her mercy, letting her roam around and deciding where she'll take us."* He said.

"I'll need a hand to get up there, you know. Can I use the truck? I parked it pretty close," Leigh asked, pointing to her Ford. *"I can climb up onto the top if she gets close enough, but I swear, if you drop me when I grab your hand, you're gonna need more than a few day's head start to get away!"* she warned, looking around to see how Mat had managed to mount the mammoth. He told Leigh that Pixie was an African elephant even though her ears weren't as large as they could be for that particular species. He also told her that he and the sweet pachyderm shared a birth year; They were turning fifty very soon.

From up on top of Pixie, the world seemed impossibly untouchable; the smell of the animal kept them from noticing anything else they may encounter, and Pixie's long, deliberate, slow moves helped Leigh stay balanced throughout their ride. *"I won't even ask you how you knew about this place; you have some of the best-kept secrets, and I don't ever want you to tell me. I want to keep being surprised; you tickle me pink."* She told him.

His time spent in meditation and reflection showed that it had done the man well. He could feel a renewed sense of purpose boiling inside him, coursing through every one of his veins; it took the weariness out of him. He told himself that he had never felt better, not once in his life. This was it, he told her; this moment is the best he's ever lived.

He was ready to take on whatever life had in store for him – it was just a matter of time. *"Time, that's what I wanted to talk to you about. I'll let Pixie listen in; she's got those big ears; she'll keep a secret, but she'll likely never forget what I have to say."* Mat Conner was also known to bring up old cliches and even a bad joke now and again; his pun about the elephant's memory and ears was just him getting started.

They discussed his plans to open the catering business, but he wanted it to be more than just a catering business. They both knew that part of the money he made through the profits of his work would go to the resort, but he wanted more. He understood the accretion his contribution would bring to the whole enterprise, but he also wanted it to mean something personal. He tried to use his influence for good and bring attention to the lesser-seen and lesser-loved animals of the world, not just the humans Leigh and he had been trying to get more awareness of.

"I ran into Paul Tarion down here yesterday, here in Panama City, the actor. He and his wife summer down this way and are getting the place ready for the upcoming season; who knew people did that?" he asked, but took it back as soon as he'd said it, *"Of course, people do that, it's Florida's Gulf coast! Hundreds of homes sit empty around these parts for sometimes eight or nine months out of the year."* He lamented.

"Stray cats and dogs are going up and under porches to give birth. We need to help the locals find ways to spay the strays and keep the streets free of feral animals if we can." His words were delivered with passion and compassion, pleasing his wife thoroughly. *"I'm not that concerned about the elephants or the monkeys they have in the buildings just south of here; they have grants to feed them and keep them healthy."*

It was the dogs Mat was worried about, even more so than the cats, but he did want to seem at least unbiased.

"Interesting guy, that Paul Tarion," he told her, rubbing his newly bearded jaw. *"We talked about many things, things that most people try to steer away from, but when he realized who I was, he admitted to me that he had believed some of the hype they wrote about me, and if he weren't sitting down talking to me right then, he would have gone on believing it. I asked him because I thought, why not? He's a man of the world. I asked him who the unseen were. Who did he believe was unnoticed, ignored, or set aside? You might be surprised at his answer."* Mat offered.

"Go on, tell me what he said. I want to hear his opinion. I wouldn't say I liked his character much in the film he made about ten years ago, the one about John Gotti and the Gambino crime family; it didn't ring true to me." She had studied the family too long and followed them when they made real-time news.

"Tarion makes a good-looking Paul Castellano, but he wasn't as savvy or as smooth. He had a little Buster Keaton in his act; it didn't go over as well as if someone else had been cast." She didn't let it bother her; a character is just that. Paul Tarion paid his dues; he also paid his taxes. He had an opinion that was just as valid as anyone else's.

"I told him we're pretty passionate about the venture. When I told him, we were digging deep inside our hearts to find ways to bring awareness to those who won't help their cause or maybe who can't find

346

the energy left to make things happen. Tarion tells him that the worker bees on the sets are the most ignored.

"Production people; makeup artists, wardrobe, even script runners; those who work tirelessly behind the scenes on the sets are often overlooked and underappreciated. They're underpaid and overworked. He did agree, though, that they had to hustle. They were counted on, not ignored, but if being unnoticed was the criteria, that was his input.

"So, I asked him again, are there people not noticed and overlooked in the business who are trying not to be seen? For that, he had another opinion. He said sure, some were very happy being paid a little and being able to do things that others couldn't do, go places others couldn't go, see famous people all day, work within the industry, and not need to be at the top or even close to it as long as they had a steady gig.

"He also said that some moonlight; some are even caterers. He told me he'd be my first customer and knew anything I made would be outstanding; he'd been in my restaurant a few times in Chicago. It was during the Gambino film; I had a few actual 'family' members there nightly. The Paul Tarions of the world, they're given a pass. They can do what they do, but don't let them ask for tips of the trade to make them look better on film than the real bosses...that won't do." He smiled broadly, showing off every tooth in his head.

"Hey Leigh!" he said, almost as an afterthought, *"Why can't you see a pterodactyl going to the bathroom?"* the question surprised her, coming out of left field as it did; she nearly lost her balance atop Ol'

Pixie. *"Oh...geez! I don't know, tell me."* She said. He answered, *"Because their 'p' is silent."* She groaned, and he laughed. Pixie walked along the wooded path as if nothing had changed; nothing had been good or bad; it was just life as she knew it.

"Leigh," He asked, making a move to stand up on the elephant's back. *"...do you wanna try and stand back here and ride Pixie like they ride the trains down in Mexico? Hunkered down and surf the air."* He asked her, laughing. *"My brain thinks that's a fun idea, but my stomach just told me it might be the last thing I ever did in an upright position."* She told him.

The stroll they took was meaningful, quiet, and unique. For a few minutes, they were silent, just taking in the glorious afternoon weather and sending out good vibes to one another, having been apart for nearly a week. *"Doug Dempsey called me this week. You had just left, and he wanted to run something by you to equivocate somewhat before he committed to it on paper,"* Leigh mentioned.

"I'll let you hear the voicemail; you'll love his Willy Wonka impersonation; he must have had a few of those delicious chocolate margaritas he and Pete are planning to bring in as a suggestion to your place if you ever get around to catering drinks. He was going on about the factory, this and that, and how he could give tours to the kids when they got old enough to be taught the rights and wrongs of being responsible drinkers." She told him.

"He said when he was a kid, and he's about ten or twelve years older than you; maybe you'll remember this. He said that cops and firefighters

would come into the elementary schools and do live demonstrations of how to be safe on the streets. Do you remember that happening in your school?" she asked; she tried to think about what sort of thing happened in DeQueen and wondered if it was a beach-related thing and if living the salt life was different in some way than living the cowboy way.

"I think I remember something called D.A.R.E., and they had cool cars, but I don't ever recall anyone pulling out a bent spoon and heating it to show how liquified coke can cause brain damage." She explained, her eyes meeting Mat's with a hint of concern for her excellent friend Dempsey and his trip down memory lane.

"That's another avenue we can stop and think about, Leigh. The lost art of teaching kids what's truly good and bad. You're right," Mat said, then added, *"Doug is right. I do remember D.A.R.E. and their cars; they had dogs, too, and would take them to the schools to show the kids why they shouldn't hide drugs in their lockers. Dogs. In a word, dogs."* He said.

"Doug asked me to run a few questions by you because he has to write them down for the bankers and the investors regarding you and what you are able and willing to contribute to the resort. He knows you're doing the catering business, but we're married, and the resort will be in my name, so it will also be in yours.

"He wanted to know if you had owned the restaurants up in Chicago, saying that if you had been, there could be some lingering debt. I told him you hadn't mentioned owning anything but were

promised ownership once you proved yourself.” She mentioned, *“…if you ask me, you got arrested just in time. If you had been deeper in the mix, you might could still be in the pokey and not here on top of this massive, grey, bumpy grass eater.”* She opened her eyes widely and pretended to steer Pixie using imaginary reins.

“Might could?” He questioned her, making fun of her Southern ways. *“I’m tellin’ you, Mister, you are just not Southern, no matter how much you may think you are. If you could be, you would be, but you ain’t, so you need to wake up and smell the elephant you’re sittin’ on because she might decide to dump both of us if we make her giggle.”* Leigh teased.

“This view, though.” He said quietly, again, rubbing his chin to see if she had picked up on his new beard, the goatee style he had chosen to start the new look. Had she noticed, he wondered. *“You don’t think I’m going to fawn over you, do you?”* she asked, reaching over to get a better position, leaning against him as best she could under the crowded circumstances.

“The view? Yes, the view. I see a man with wisdom, grace, and style.” She told him. *“I see a man with just enough grizzle in his appearance to make an unwavering statement; the statement is that he’s ready. He’s there. He’s present. He’s powerful enough to command the world’s largest mammal so that he and his wife are gliding through life on the tip-top of the world!”* she said, and that’s what I see; that’s my view.”

"What are you calling the center?" He asked her. *"You've never said what you think it should be called. You've used words like resort, training center, and workshop, but they must be named before incorporating them. Have you thought of the name yet?"* He questioned and gave her that open-eyed stare as if to fake surprise.

"You know what I'm calling it; you gave me the idea when you said it was for those of us who are in need, those who are empty, those who hurt, who are forgotten, and just for us. It will be called 'Us,' and if someone wants to think it means something, it can, and if someone wants to make up another name for it, they can, but I think when we say it, it puts everything in perspective. There are so many 'the' people who need to be loved, and they need to be loved by us."

Leigh smiled when she said it; he smiled back at her, showing his agreement with his eyes. Pixie turned around and returned to the barn, hoping someone remembered to refresh her feed bucket.

The

Mention:

As I mentioned in my disclaimer, Charlie Garrett and his wife Hideko are real people who live in Sarasota, Florida, too. Charlie is the Superior Word church pastor, located at 6512 Superior Ave. You can find them on YouTube and Facebook, too. You can do yourself a big favor and visit the church to sit in with the small congregation and listen to Charlie teach and preach; he does both.

Hideko will be there, too! She stays pretty close to Charlie most of the time, and they have a pack of dogs about the same size. He has Dachshunds, Chihuahuas, and mixed-breed dogs. You'll probably hear them before you see them. Don't forget to look down to see if Charlie is wearing his shoes. I think he only does that on special occasions! You can just about always talk him into going to the Thai restaurant around the corner from the church; it really exists, too! (Don't look for Sunil or his family; they're not real.)

Charlie and Hideko Garrett with Tosha

Author's Notes:

Jude Leigh Stringfellow is a Scottish-American author who, for years, has written whatever she wished and in whatever genre she wanted to write. Jude is a native-born Oklahoman whose father, Reuben Wayne Stringfellow, was born in Frog Level, Arkansas, between the cities of Horatio and DeQueen. She spent many meaningful summer vacations in the natural hills and creek beds of the area, running around with every Hooker in the county! She also ran around with the other Stringfellow, Brakes, Wrays, and anyone else who came to those overstuffed family reunions.

Jude raised three wonderful children, including her son, Reuben, who is about to retire from the Army, and daughters Laura and Caity. Reuben and his wife Josie have two children. Caity, a writer in her own right and an online gamer, is married to Brandon, and they also have two children. Laura is a writer, steamer, cosplayer, and voice actor. Jude spends as much time as she can with her family, and she loves traveling – usually to Scotland if she has the chance and she loves to cook, hike, play at her guitar since she can't play it – and, of course, she writes.

"The" is Jude's 15th book, and she hopes there will be many more. Charlie Garrett is Jude's actual pastor! She watches him weekly at http://www.superiorword.org and attends his Thursday Bible Studies.

www.ingramcontent.com/pod-product-compliance
Lightning Source LLC
Chambersburg PA
CBHW031440160726
47994CB00005B/1806